KU-121-102

CATALOGUED LIBRARY

C/177412
F(IR)
6206
Donation

To John

This book is published with the assistance of The Arts Council / An Chomhairle Ealaíon.

Acknowledgements

My grateful thanks for their help, support and encouragement to my mother, my children and to, Christine. Thanks also to all at Attic Press and to Mary Rose Callaghan, 'my writing Group', Michael Hodson, Jonathan Williams and Deans Grange Library.
Dublin, 1991.

JOAN O'NEILL was born and raised in Dublin. She now lives in Bray, County Wicklow, has five children and has been writing fiction for several years. She is the author of bestselling novel *Daisy Chain War* published by Attic Press in 1990.

Though the mills of God grind slowly, they grind exceeding small.

Though with patience He stands waiting, with exactness grinds He all.

Longfellow

Chapter 1

The chapel was full. Flickering candles cast a shimmery haze over the flowers on the altar. As the organ played softly, the bishop came forward to meet the little procession of six postulants, dressed as brides in white satin, with lace veils covering their faces, waiting to be received. A hush fell as the first postulant, Hannah Dempsey, moved forward to receive her blessed habit and veil. Her family watched eagerly from the side altar as she knelt before the bishop and took the folded habit.

'What do you seek, my daughter?' The bishop looked kindly at Hannah, the steel-rimmed frames of his glasses glinting in the sunlight.

A hush fell as Hannah gave her response. 'The grace of God and the habit of holy religion,' her voice rang out clearly.

Reverend Mother standing in the wings of the sacristy breathed a sigh of relief. Though she never showed it Hannah was her favourite postulant, with a keen desire to serve God, a true sense of obedience, and good health to carry out her duties.

'Do you desire to serve God in obedience to the rules of the Sisters of Good Counsel?'

'I do.'

'From now on you will renounce your baptismal name, Hannah Dempsey. You will be known as Sister Marie Claire, your name in religion.'

The bishop prayed in Latin, his voice rising and falling, while one of the priests turned the gilt-edged pages of his enormous missal. When he finished Hannah rose and withdrew, carrying her habit in her outstretched hands. The next white-robed postulant took her place and the bishop repeated the sermon. When it was over, the six brides rose in unison from the foot of the altar and genuflected, before walking down the centre aisle, heads bowed, to take their places among the rest of the novices in the community. The organ flooded the chapel with the 'Magnificat' and the voices in the choir began softly, 'My soul doth magnify the Lord and my spirit hath rejoiced in God, my Saviour. For he that is mighty has done great things to me, and holy is his name.'

The evening sun slanted across Hannah, lighting up her hazel eyes. Her veil, almost concealing her long fiery hair, cast a lacy shadow across her beautiful face. As the chapel bell chimed she prayed for the grace to fulfil her duties to God, and to her sisters in religion, for the will to accept the discipline of unquestioning obedience. That she would recognise her faults and correct them, and continue her life under the strict rule of the order, enforced by her novice mistress, Mother Clement. From now on everything she did in her life would be a total commitment to God.

The voices of the choir rose to a crescendo, and the whole congregation stood up as the bishop left the altar, escorted by his entourage of five priests, to prepare for mass. The nuns silently watched from their pews, giving no sign of the hustle and bustle of the previous days of preparation, when the postulants were drilled in the procedure of the ceremony.

The novices, in the meantime, were escorted to the sacristy. There they quickly removed their bridal gowns, and a nun helped each of them to dress in the heavy black serge habit they had made during postulancy. Sr De Santus, her old friend, helped Hannah. Then the young novice gazed down at herself, straightening the pleats that fell in graceful folds around her tiny waist. She moved forward slowly, the weight of the garment dragging her down. A white veil was placed on her head, covering her luxuriant hair.

Returning to the chapel as the organ burst into Bach's triumphant music, the new novices resumed their places before the altar. The bishop waited, face glistening from the oppressiveness of a packed chapel, incense, the heavy scent of flowers, and strong afternoon sunlight that filtered through the stain-glass windows. The mass was rich in music and blessings for the young women who were dedicating their loves to god.

As they filed out of the chapel to the joyous singing of the choir, Hannah felt like a little girl whose wish had been granted. At last she was about to embark upon the life she had chosen for herself so long ago. A life that freed her from all earthly duties so that she might strive for perfection, in her devotion to prayer and in her service to others.

Her mother was waiting for her with outstretched arms when she emerged from the chapel. She gazed at Hannah's hauntingly pale face. 'You look so tall and graceful in your habit,' she said, her eyes filling with tears. She embraced her carefully, as if she were a fragile piece of rare china that might break.

Hannah hugged her and went to her father who stood back among the crowd. She put her arms around him and held him tightly, aware of his distaste for any outward show of affection.

'Everything went well,' he said, fumbling for his cigarettes, while her six-year-old brother David grabbed her, wanting her all to himself.

'You've got so thin, Hannah. Are you sick?'

'No,' she laughed. 'It's this long black habit. It makes me look thinner, that's all. Did you enjoy the ceremony, darling?'

David wrinkled his nose. 'It was too long, and it nearly made me cry.'

'It was a beautiful ceremony.' Hannah hunkered down beside him, and putting her arms around him, held him close to her.

'It means you won't ever be coming home. That's what everyone says. Is that true?' His lips trembled as he looked at her. 'I like your veil.'

'Oh, you are a sweetie pie. Now listen, ever is a long time. We never know what might happen in the future. Anyway you'll come to see me often. Won't you?'

David looked up at his father. 'Every week, won't we, Daddy?'

'It's a bit far for a weekly visit. But you'll see plenty of Hannah. I promise. So will I.' He smiled at her, holding her elbow while she straightened herself up.

'It'll take you a while to get used to that ridiculous ....'

'Now Daddy, you promised ...'

'Yes I did. Sorry.' He looked tense again, and her mother, conscious of the little time they had together, pulled her away and linking her arms through hers, walked her along the convent path, away from her father and David.

'Are you happy, Hannah? I don't have to ask. I can see it in your eyes.'

'Yes, I'm happy. It's a strange feeling really. I don't feel hemmed in by the order, or the rule, as I imagined I would. I feel a kind of freedom. From now on whatever I do I know it will be God's will.'

She caught her mother's eye. In that instant she saw her mirror-image reflect the pride and joy, pain and sorrow, that had brought them both to this moment. For an instant her composure slipped as she struggled to keep the tears from her eyes.

'I never thought I'd see this day,' her mother said.' It takes me back to that other beginning when we came back to Ireland, and I wondered had we made the right decision. Everything seemed so different to what we expected. Do you remember Hannah?'

'I remember.'

* * * * * *

Hannah well remembered that journey home from England when she was eleven years old. The sluggish traffic through Birmingham in their hired Morris Minor. Cars hooting, engines revving, their little car speeding up, then slowing disappointingly as it choked in the commuter traffic. Out in the open countryside with nothing but miles and miles of fields and rollings hills, Hannah's eyelids drooped before she lay along the back seat. Her view of the fields was replaced by gathering clouds huddled together, then separating. She shaped faces and made patterns out of them before they faded into blackness.

When she woke up she saw the dark sea, and the lights from the huge white ship reflected in its depths. While they queued up she imagined the ship was a whale waiting to suck the passengers into its jaws and swallow them up before they reached Ireland.

There was a rush of wind and the smell of salty sea as they embarked. In the freezing cold her father's voice sounded excited. 'Everything will turn out alright now. Better than alright. You'll see,' he said to her mother.

'I'm just happy to be going home,' her mother said, oblivious to the cold sea and the jostling crowds.

She secured Hannah tightly to her and sank her into the red leather seats in the lounge of the 'Cambria'. Her mother was already making lists and plans, and telling her father about them. He seemed to listen intently, but his eyes were fixed longingly on the crowded bar. More people gathered and finally he was surrounded. Someone put a pint of beer in his hand. He looked important as he chatted and smiled easily. Suddenly Hannah could not see him anymore. He was screened by people as he edged away from them. She wondered if he'd done this to avoid her mother's disapproving glances.

People craved her father's attention. He was at ease with everyone and could talk about anything. He could make things and fix things. Hannah loved watching him working and continually asked him questions. He'd laugh and say, 'Here comes Questions again,' but no matter how busy he was, he always had time to answer her, even if he had to stop and think first.

He explained other things to her. He told her about his responsibility as foreman in the local factory, in the new town they were going to live in, in County Cork.

'They're a fine bunch of lads. Not a bad apple in the barrel. I was lucky to get this job. You'll be reared in Ireland and get the best education in the country.'

'You'll have those men eating out of your hand,' her mother said.

Hannah was disappointed when she saw Strand Bay for the first time. Sitting on the top flight of stone steps of her new home, while the removal men lifted and dragged heavy furniture up to their flat, she hugged her coat around her knees, and searched in vain for the strand. The changing patterns of the sea that stretched before her fascinated her. Her skin crawled as she watched the gulls bobbing about, imagining their yellow eyes watching dead men afloat. The movement and excitement the huge ship generated, when it docked in front of her house, almost allayed her disappointment at not having a sandy beach to dig in, with her new bucket and spade. When she discovered she could not bathe in the sea, or lean over the restraining wall, in case she fell in, her disappointment gave way to disinterest.

Her new house was another disappointment. One of a row of tall, dull brick houses, it stood full face to the tide, dignified in its impoverishment, while patiently waiting for the seal of condemnation from the council. Her bedroom was cold. The rain beat rhythmically on the parapet and leaked down the wall, streaking it in long, rusty drips. Hannah wondered if the hypnotic spell of the sea could make her wish for a big house in the country come true. A house with a garden to play in, perhaps a summerhouse in the centre of its huge lawns, which she could use as a doll's house. She could invite her new friend Nancy, from down the road.

Fat drops of rain fell in slow motion, and the steps around her darkened to a duller grey just as her mother poked her head out of the upstairs window.

'Hannah.' Her voice was shrill in the wind and Hannah knew not to delay.

'Coming.' She ran into the dark hall, along the passage, taking the stairs two at a time, barely leaving the imprint of her shoe on the ridged rubber edges.

'Hurry before you catch it from your Ma.' Mrs Murphy from the first flat was leaning against the jamb of her kitchen door, waiting to see her get into trouble.

Hannah rushed past her but then skidded on the highly polished surface. Cringing and crimson, she stammered 'S... sorry Mrs Murphy.'

She hurried on. If only she was not too polite to say 'drop dead' to her or 'kiss your arse you old cow,' like Tim Ryan from upstairs did. Hannah hated her! Mrs Murphy rejoiced in people's desperation and polished her landing floor purposely so that people who were in a hurry would break their necks on it. She was an enormous woman with a back like a wall, and thick pale legs, with hollows at the backs of her knees that fascinated Hannah.

The smell of fried rashers and sausages greeted Hannah as she entered the living-room. Her mother was setting the table.

'A few more minutes and you'd have been soaked,' she said, eyeing her childish gawkiness.

'I was waiting for Daddy. His boat is late.' Hannah took Scratchy the kitten up in her arms.

'They're doing overtime tonight. Put that cat down and go and wash your hands.'

Mary Dempsey's voice was gentler when they were alone. Her cross voice was only to impress Mrs Murphy, who talked endlessly about discipline and the strictness that must be exercised when rearing children. A strictness Hannah's mother did not possess except on rare occasions when outside influences intruded, like her father's drinking. Hannah noticed these things because she was growing up.

There was a knock on the door. It was Mrs Murphy and Hannah's mother went out to talk to her on the landing, in the semi-darkness. Hannah stood still behind the door wishing the violin music on the radio didn't squeak so much, making it difficult for her to hear the conversation.

'I can't bear the thoughts of it again. The labour pains. When I was having Hannah they dragged on and on for hours. I thought she'd never be born.'

'I'm sure you're dreading it. All that poking and pulling. I couldn't bear it. Why do you think I've only the one?'

Hannah's mother laughed a little. 'It's early days yet, Mrs Murphy. You might have a string of them.'

'Not on your sweet life. This is no place to rear children. Sure the whole place is condemned. The stairs are falling to bits. Look, dry rot in the bannisters.'

Hannah heard the squeak and pull of the stairs as Mrs Murphy shook them, to emphasise her point.

'You must have been off your head to get pregnant before you had settled down,' Mrs Murphy said.

'I suppose I was. But it wasn't really planned. Of course as soon as I realised I was pregnant, I told Tom we were going back to Ireland. I wasn't going to rear a family in that pagan country.'

'Well at least something good came of it. If you were living here from the start I doubt you'd ever have a family.' Mrs Murphy laughed loudly and

Hannah heard her mother's instant hurt in her quick retaliatory 'What do you mean?

'I heard Tom this very minute below in the pub from my sitting-room window. There's no mistaking his laugh. Sure he's rarely home. That's what I came to tell you. He's down the road in Mooney's if you want him in a hurry.'

Hannah really disliked Mrs Murphy. It sounded to her as if Mrs Murphy was trying to cause a row between herself and her mother. Worse still, she might be trying to cause trouble between her mother and father. She wished her mother would not talk to her. If she called her she might come in and close the door, before something awful happened. Her mother would kill her for listening. Supposing she fell and cried. That would send her mother running. What she could not understand was why her mother pretended to be friendly with Mrs Murphy when she disliked her so much. She could not stand her. Hannah heard her say that to her father.

'That's kind of you,' her mother's voice was flat, as if Mrs Murphy's words had beaten her. 'Tom works so hard he has to relax sometimes.'

'What about my poor husband, melted in the heat from standing over that bloody furnace all day, or racing up and down them ladders. Tom Dempsey keeps them on their toes, I can tell you that.'

'That's what he's paid for,' Hannah's mother said sharply. 'I have to go. I was just about to feed Hannah.'

'Sure Hannah's a big girl now. Can't she feed herself. Come down for a drink later when the house is quiet.'

Hannah could not hear her mother's mumbled response. All she was certain of was that her mother would not go.

She often thought back to that conversation, her mother's face full of anguish when she finally got away from Mrs Murphy and shut the door. Her movements were slower too as she heated up their meal. Her face was damp, and her rosy cheeks had faded to the colour of putty.

'Mrs Murphy is a nosey parker.' Hannah hoped her mother would concur.

'I told you before to stop listening at doors. "Eavesdroppers never hear any good of themselves." That's a saying worth remembering.'

'Did you hate it when I was born?' Hannah asked, a slight tremor in her voice.

'Of course not. Oh, God, I didn't mean it like that,' her mother said in a tired voice. 'What I meant was that it took a long time. I suppose I was afraid something might be wrong with you. That's all.'

'Why does it hurt?'

'Because babies have only a little space to get through. You are delaying things, Miss, with all your questions.'

'You promised you'd tell me the facts of life before someone else does.'

'And I will. Tomorrow when you come home from school.'

'Nancy said she'd tell me only I'd run home and tell you what she said.'

'It's not up to Nancy to tell you any such thing. That one is a bit of a know-all if you ask me. It's my job to tell you and I'll do it in my own sweet time. I'm tired now. Let's eat. It's going cold.'

Her mother blessed herself and bowed her head. 'Bless us Oh Lord, and these ... Come on Hannah, say your grace without mumbling.'

They ate in silence for a while. Then her mother said, 'It won't be long until the baby comes. You'll have to give me a hand with him. Or her.' She cut and buttered Hannah's bread.

Hannah nodded, her mouth too full to talk. She had no idea what caused her mother to grow babies, apart from the fact that her Daddy had something to do with it. There was a vague idea in her head that someday she would wear posh clothes and high heels and get invitations to parties. Then she would get married and have a baby too. Nancy hinted as much in a whisper to her at one of their 'secret group meetings'. All she was sure of was that since her mother got fat, an awful weight seemed to focus and settle in around her swollen tummy. Her slow, tired movements made her fumbling and cheerless. Hannah, worried by these changes, folded herself into her small quiet existence, and buried her emotions in her own childish events and daydreams.

After the meal she did her homework by the fire, while her mother's hands worked nimbly, weaving a darning needle in and out of a sock for the umpteenth time.

'Are you nearly finished?' she asked.

'What?'

'Don't say what. Say pardon.'

'Pardon?'

'Finish your homework and get ready for bed, like a good girl.'

Sometimes when Mary reminisced, Hannah let vague thoughts circle in her head about people and places. How they came to be what they were. She liked to look through the black imitation leather album with the frayed corners, straining to recall the faces from long ago. Weather-beaten faces of farmers with beaked noses and toothless grins. The careworn faces of the women. She would wonder what part they had played in her life, if any? Her mother could not even, remember who some of them were.

She stared at the fire until the flames became the red-coated cavalry of the British empire, under her gaze. Her dull living-room changed into a gilded ballroom where they waited for beautiful ladies to arrive in cloud carriages, drawn by seahorses, through miles and miles of air, to dance with their knights in shining armour. In Hannah's ballroom.

'Hannah, it's bed time. Go and brush your teeth, like a good girl.'

She swished the water over her hands and face in the old wood-panelled bathroom, off their pokey kitchen, hoping she'd escape to bed before her mother said the rosary. If only her Daddy would come home soon. It was Friday night and when he left the small brown envelope unopened on the mantelpiece, her mother stopped complaining. Secret smiles passed between them. Sometimes they laughed together and everything was alright for days.

'Did you wash behind your ears?'

'Yes.' Hannah lied and ran into her bedroom.

When they unpacked, she heard her mother tell Mrs Murphy that their stay would be temporary.

Gazing at the lawnmower among their belongings Mrs Murphy said, 'Are ye going to mow the carpets? You'll have to take your turn at washing down the stairs, mind.'

'Of course.' Hannah's mother replied.

Her Daddy came home before Hannah fell asleep. 'How's my girl?' He gave her a hug and slipped her a bar of chocolate.

'Don't tell your mother I gave you that. She'd kill me for rotting your teeth.'

'Will you be staying in tonight, Daddy?' Hannah asked.

'I have to visit Billy Mooney. All those kids and he on the flat of his back in hospital in Cork. No insurance. He's only temporary and they're living from hand to mouth.'

'Everything in County Cork seems to be temporary,' Hannah said sulkily.

'What do you mean?'

'Nothing.'

'You're a strange little one. Now go to sleep. I won't be late. Honest.'

He put his arms around her and she leaned her weight against him for an instant. He kissed the top of her head and was gone. Hannah knew that when he said 'honest' it meant the opposite, and that there would be trouble between her parents, because he would not come home for hours.

The wind howled as Hannah closed her eyes. She could hear the fog horn whine in the distance. She imagined that the little houses in outlying areas would cling together while the wind tore into them, rattling shaky windowpanes, as it reached fever pitch. She would not let herself sleep until the storm died down, and she had heard the click of her parents' bedroom door, and knew that her father was safely home.

Chapter 2

The reception for the new novices was held in the nuns' refectory to accommodate their parents and families, the bishop and other church dignitaries. The novices were allowed to eat with their families for the last time at the sumptuous table, set with crystal glass and delicate china, and lined with vases of summer flowers. Reverend Mother, the novice mistress, Mother Clement, and other members of the community moved among the guests, stretching out long sleeves to clasp hands in welcome. Nuns appeared from nowhere, greeting guests with the pressing of cheeks and smiles of genuine pleasure.

Nervously Hannah sought out her father's eyes for comfort. He looked away. She knew he would never understand how she became part of this life, among these strange creatures, with their cultivated anonymity.

'What a wonderful day to witness the gifts of the Lord,' Reverend Mother gushed.

'It's the happiest day of my life, Mother Albert,' Mary Dempsey beamed at Reverend Mother, and

Hannah concentrated on the life-size painting of the crucified Christ on the opposite wall.

Nuns with pinned back veils served, while Reverend Mother directed her conversation to her guests, explaining 'the Rule' and 'the Great Silence.'

Hannah stole her father a guarded look and saw the invisible hurdles he encountered each time Reverend Mother spoke. Her mother's voice fell to a whisper as she said to the elderly woman beside her, 'I'm so proud of her.' Her eyes were full of tears. Tense and quiet, Hannah sat listening to the bishop extol the virtues of prayer and vows, and the value of striving for perfection in a life dedicated to the glory of God.

Finally it was all over. Hannah could hardly look at the tear-filled eyes of her parents as they kissed her goodbye.

David began to cry before she had time to hug him.

'We'll be down to see Hannah often,' her mother consoled him.

'How often?' he insisted.

'As often as possible, darling. Now come on, we've a long journey ahead of us.'

David clung to Hannah, his damp cheek pressed against hers.

'Promise me we'll see you soon.' His eyes, big with tears, gazed into hers for reassurance.

Hannah looked at her mother and said, 'I promise.' She hugged him, reluctant to let him go.

As soon as the heavy oak doors swung behind them and the latch clinked into place, Hannah went to begin her new life in the Novitiate. It was a building adjoining the convent, occupied only by novices and their spiritual directors. Mother Clement was waiting to sweep her through a dark corridor, past the sacristy, through the dimly-lit cloister. The setting sun beamed bars of light here and there on the highly polished wooden stairs that led to her cell. A tiny room at the end of a long corridor, it was furnished with a bed, a wardrobe and a wash-stand which supported a large china basin and jug.

'Your home for the next couple of years.' Mother Clement allowed herself a smile that hinted at cheerfulness, then said, 'It's sparse but you have everything you need.'

'Luxury,' Hannah said, remembering the dormitory she'd shared with ten other postulants for the last nine months.

Mother Clement left, the swish of her veil the only sound she made as she silently closed the door.

Hannah unfolded the long serge habit and hung it up in the tiny closet. A wave of loneliness for her postulant friends who had left towards the end, several at the very last minute, swept over her. She began filling the shelves with her belongings, sent over from the convent. Lying in the hard, narrow bed she suddenly felt drained from the exhausting day, and the emotional parting with her parents. Her mother's joy, her father's silence. Her own fear that he might break down. His bewilderment as he whispered, 'Is there anything you need?' while feeling the humiliation of being rendered powerless to give, by virtue of her vows and the life she had chosen.

Finally Hannah fell into an exhausted sleep. She was awakened by a loud knock on her door.

'Benedicamus Domino.' The voice proceeded down the corridor, the repetitive words growing fainter.

The weight of the black serge habit dragged her down, with its endless folds and pleats, and voluptuous sleeves. Awkwardly she tied her little white cap under her chin, then secured her white veil in place with pins. The habit enclosed her even more than the convent. In the corridor she joined her sisters as they hurried, veils rustling, to the chapel. Hannah took her place in the row of novices' pews, the familiar smell of beeswax, flowers and palpable holiness making her feel at home.

The chapel was silent. No distractions were allowed to intrude on the sacrifice of the mass. During meditation Hannah contemplated on her nine months' training as a postulant. She had learned to abandon self, had been tutored in discipline.

'You must die to the world in order to live in Christ,' Mother Clement had repeated over and over. She remembered her initial distress and loneliness, when studying scripture, or spiritual reading, in learning charity and consideration for her sisters, in meditation of God's will, and in expressing human love for her community.

The more she learned to become detached from the world, the more she had thought of her parents quarrelling over her decision to become a nun. Her father's protests to her mother, 'She's too young,' and her mother's response, 'It's a direct calling from God that cannot be ignored.'

'She's turning her back on a life she hasn't even begun to live. How can anyone make a decision like that at the age of seventeen? 'God damn it, Mary, she's rejecting everything that's good and wholesome. She's giving up her freedom.'

'She's doing a wonderful thing. It's not for us mortals to question the ways of the Lord.' Her mother had gone to the sink and clattered dishes, indicating that the argument was over. But her father would not let it go. 'She's not mature enough. She hasn't had a taste of what she's giving up yet,' he reasoned, pale and tense.

'She's sensible enough. She grew up quickly, remember.' She'd shot him a deliberate look, intimating that he was the reason.

Fine needles of rain fell as the choir sang the *Te Deum Laudamus* and Hannah watched the grey sky through the narrow chapel windows. Now at last she could pray without feeling the pain of her parents' agony.

After mass she lined up with six other novices, awkward young girls in identical black habits, clothes specially chosen to suppress personality. Mother Clement eyed each girl critically before listing out her name.

'Clare Meeney
Jean Thornton
Sarah Farrell
Patricia Kelly
Hannah Dempsey
Mary Murphy
This is the order you will walk in wherever you go.'

'Yes, Mother,' they answered in unison.

'Remember,' she added, her ferret eyes darting from one face to another, 'you are now soldiers in Christ.'

They were in the chapel for spiritual instruction. 'In the name of the Father and of the Son and of the Holy Ghost, Amen,' Mother Clement began. 'I am the resurrection and the life. He that believeth in me shall be saved.'

Her voice rang out in the dark chapel, beautiful with its gothic windows and polished wooden floors. Hannah listening intently to the reading, let herself be moved by its soothing rhythm. There was comfort in its resonance.

'Come, oh Lord, and fill my soul with love.' Mother Clement looked at her pupils. 'Will you be able to do what the Order demands of you?

'Firstly, to bow to God's will? Secondly, to atone with sorrow for your sins and the sins of others? Thirdly, never to question your vows of poverty, chastity and obedience?

'Will your wordly bodies bend to your pure souls, which burn with unwavering love for God? Will you overcome all earthly longings? All weaknesses? I want you to examine your souls for weaknesses.'

Silence followed as each novice reflected on her personal weakness. Hannah still longed for chocolate, and rashers and sausages. She yearned to read novels sometimes instead of spiritual books and the lives of the saints. As yet she had not managed to overcome her desire to talk during meals. Often her concentration slipped during mass, and she was back home doing chores for her mother, or minding David. The austerity of the convent, where human companionship was not encouraged, the consolation of God, her only solace, made her feel lonely and isolated.

The voice of Mother Clement penetrated her thoughts. 'Behold, oh Lord, thy servant most humble.'

The novices responded, 'Take us your new family to embrace the life of this community. To burn with love for you in all that we do ...'

A feeling of belonging permeated Hannah's soul as she listened to the words. She realised she had made progress in the last nine months, despite her doubts.

She was learning to love her community like a family. Her sisters were her natural sisters now. They were all bound together in God's holy love.

'Prayers and sacrifices will still have to be made before reaching that state of mind which leaves no room for doubts and scruples,' reiterated Mother Clement.

The bell rang for the midday meal. The novices went in twos to join the rest of the community in the refectory. They stood facing one another at long scrubbed tables. Reverend Mother's chair at the head of the table was shaped like a throne, decorated with carvings of oak cherubs. Twenty nuns took their places in order of rank.

'Bless us, oh Lord ...' Reverend Mother began and the community joined in a chorus before sitting down to bowls of soup and plates of bread. Hannah folded her sleeves, bowed to the postulant who served her, and began eating.

'God often asks us to perform difficult tasks.' The spiritual reading began, and Hannah listened intently to Sister Margaret's earnest voice.

After their midday meal the novices returned to their own quarters and were given varied tasks. Hannah was sent to polish the brass with Sister Eugene. Donning her check apron, she worked, silently praying as she polished. Her beautiful face in quiet reflection gave no hint of the hatred she had for the smell of brasso. The filth on her hands and nails.

Mother Clement inspected her work.

'Smudges here and there, Sister,' and glancing at Hannah she added, 'No task is too great or too small, to be carried out to perfection for the Lord. Get rid of those finger-marks.' Hannah gratefully took the brass vase to polish it and re-present it to her all-seeing eye.

Mother Clement's control over her novices, her decisions about every detail of their lives, from spiritual direction down to when they would have a bath, or get something new, were accepted without question. The entire responsibility for the body and soul of each girl belonged to her. This, during the novices' two-year semi-seclusion in the Novitiate, was designed to strengthen their vocation.

Hannah set the table for supper. Bowl, saucer, plate were placed in symmetrical order, following the Order's Rule. Mother Clement stood watching every move, and emphasising with nods and taps on her pupils' shoulders the need for preparation for heaven, through meticulous dedication to work.

'Attention to detail is attention to God.' She reminded them of the constant presence of God in everything they did. As long as they expressed love for God they would never feel loneliness or despair.

The community-room was large and uncomfortable. Nuns sat in small groups around tables, sewing and talking. Some listened and smiled occasionally. Hannah took with her the lace she was working on and sat beside Sister Frances, the seamstress.

'It's a great honour to wear the habit of the Order, Sister. I hope you realise that.' Sister Frances's eyes darted from one face to another as she doled out bundles of stockings from the community darning basket.

Hannah put away the lace she was looking forward to working on and began darning a heavy black stocking.

As she cut off the wool she studied her minute reflection in the large cutting scissors. The face she saw elongated in the blade of the scissors looked hollow and pale. What would she look like in a black billowing veil? She imagined she would look even paler than she was.

'The habit was designed to camouflage the figure. The purpose of its uniformity is to depersonalise us. Our bodies only function as an instrument of the Lord. It is not just a question of self-control, but knowing that the forsaking of marriage and the possibility of motherhood are compensated for by the knowledge that we are living as God ordained we should'. Sister Frances said.

Hannah felt content to devote herself to God, to love him above all others. She praised the Lord with her sisters for calling her to live within her vows of poverty, chastity and obedience. Whether she was sweeping, dusting, attending lectures, her exaltations were constantly repeated while she lived and worked to an exacting schedule.

Jean Thornton, now Sister Alice, leaned towards her. 'Hannah, may I borrow the scissors?' she asked in a stage-whisper.

'From now on you'll be known only by the name you have chosen in religion, and the number given to you by the Order.' Sister Frances glared at Jean, who mumbled an apology.

Hannah began darning, listening carefully to Sister Frances as she told them about the Church's ideal of a nun. How essential prayer was. How the novices must be exemplary at all times. Soon they would study canon law, moral theology, and philosophy. Hannah had no difficulty adapting to her role of servility and obedience. She had obeyed her mother all her life, respected the nuns in school, and had always helped at home with the housework.

Each morning from the time she dressed and put on her black, laced-up shoes, she prayed. While she made her bed, and tidied her cell, she reminded herself that her struggle with loneliness, and her striving for perfection, were part of her sacrifice. That when Jesus, her divine lover, eventually called her home to the glory of the resurrection, she would bask in his light, and never feel the pain of separation again.

* * * * * *

Hannah made her bed before going to school every morning. Each day was the same. Her mother walked to the school with her, smiling at the tangled knot of women at the corner as she passed. They would stare back stoney-faced, meeting her attempt to be friendly with open hostility and a blatant curiosity that made her blush.

'She's only the one coat, and he a foreman,' a voice floated after them one morning soon after Hannah started in her new school.

'More noughts than enough after his name I'd say. Don't fuckin' spend it, though, do he? Never see them out together.'

'Oh, he's out alright. On his own but. How in God's name she ever got pregnant I'll never know.'

'According to Bridie Murphy, sure he only has to hang up his trousers and she's off.'

A skitter of laughter followed and her mother blushed.

'Come on, Hannah, you'll be late.' They hurried up the narrow street that lifted up the colourful little houses like bunting, to the bright sun on the clock tower of the cathedral. The clockface glinted gold as it chimed the hour.

Her mother collected her after school and they shopped along the sprawling streets on the way home. Hannah helped drag the groceries up the dark, musty stairs. The lashing sea, visible through the tall windows, made her mother feel sick. She would sit down with a cup of tea, her back turned to the foaming froth, while Hannah watched the screeching gulls as they wheeled and paced the boats, waiting to steal the catch. Staring out of the window, she would imagine that they were on an eternal journey, in one of the prison ships she'd read about in storybooks, going nowhere.

When her mother's turn came to wash down the stairs, Hannah helped her carry the bucket of soapy water to the top of the house. She never looked down through the bannisters in case she might fall.

'Hello,' Mrs Ryan called out as Hannah's mother dipped her mop into the suds, and wrung it out. 'I don't envy you that job this minute.'

'We all have to do it.' Resignation dulled her mother's voice.

'By the way, I saw your husband up at the top of the town last evening. I said to Pat, isn't that Missus's husband from below?'

'I don't think it was. Tom was in Cork last night, visiting a sick employee.'

'I'm certain it was himself. He was getting into a car and they were going off somewhere.'

Hannah's mother, head bent, concentrated on the thick black lino, darkening each step as she mopped away from her neighbour. There were tears in her eyes as she said to herself more than to Hannah, 'I thought I could walk surefooted now that I'm treading my own ground. Will things ever change?'

By the time the stairs were vigorously scrubbed, and Hannah had eased out the dirt from the rubber ridges with a deck scrub, the light was fading in the airless house. When they finally reached the hallway, her mother was a blurred shape in its dimness. The weak light from the only bulb in the passage highlighted the beads of perspiration that stood out on her forehead, and the grey pallor of her skin. Her breathing was rasping as she focused her attention on the job in hand. Hannah asked anxiously, 'Mammy, are we nearly finished?'

'I want to comply with Mrs Murphy's exacting standards,' her mother said as she swished and squeezed her mop, stooping, rising, reaching and lifting, until she had completed her task.

They hauled the bucket and mop upstairs.

'Tomorrow I'll give the bathroom a good scrubbing. All I'm fit for now is a cup of tea.'

'I'll put the kettle on.'

'I'm going to lie down for a while. You do your homework.'

With the restless pounding of the sea against the high wall in her ears, Hannah began to do her sums. When she had finished she went into her mother's room.

'Can I go out to play with Nancy? I'm finished.'

As her mother rose to get out of bed, she fell back and groaned in agony.

'What's wrong, Mammy?'

'Those bloody stairs will be the end of me. Still, it's not as if I'll have to do them forever. Soon we'll have our own place.' She grabbed her stomach and bent her knees.

'Oh, God ...'

'Mammy, what's wrong?' Panic immobilised Hannah. She put her hand to her mouth to stifle a scream when she saw the rusty stain on her mother's white candlewick bedspread.

'Oh, my sweet Jesus, no. Maybe it's a false alarm. I'll be alright in a minute.' Her mother stumbled to the dressing table, still clutching her stomach. 'Here, take this change and go to the call box. Dial this number.' She wrote with an eyebrow pencil on a scrap of paper. 'Tell them to send Tom Dempsey home. Say it's urgent.'

'But ...?'

'No buts. Go, Hannah. Quickly, please. Take Nancy with you. She'll show you what to do.'

Hannah ran out of the room. Nancy dialled the number and they saw the 'Red Alert' light up the factory on the island. She heard the roar of the ferry boat as it thundered on top of the waves, bringing home her bewildered father. He ran up the quay, Hannah and Nancy racing after him.

Windows rattled and banged as curious heads popped out. Tom thundered up the stairs and into the bedroom.

'I think I'm losing the baby,' Mary said before he got a chance to speak.

'Christ, no.' He banged his fist into the window, splintering the glass. Blood spouted from his hand. '

'Calm down and phone the doctor, Tom.'

Before he disappeared, he called to Hannah to mind her mother for a few minutes.

'Get me a nightdress from the drawer, lovey.'

Hannah went to the drawer where all the fancy baby clothes were wrapped in tissue paper, pressed and ready. She fingered the soft christening robe her mother had made for her own baptism, and running her hand along the fine raised threads of smocking on the slub silk, she begged God silently not to let her Mammy lose the baby.

'Now get my washbag and put my toothbrush and toothpaste in it. Oh, and a bar of soap.' She touched Hannah's face gently, her fingers outlining the curve of her jawline. 'I might have to stay in hospital for a day or two.'

Hannah's eyes swelled with tears.

'Don't you go all sad on me now, imagining the worst. Promise?' She held Hannah's head gently, forcing her to look up and meet her eyes.

'I promise.' Hannah's voice dropped to a whisper and she bit her lip to stop it trembling.

Her mother looked so tired, even her bright red hair seemed dull and lifeless.

Tom stood awkwardly in the doorway of the bedroom, trying to catch his breath. 'Doctor Moran said to get you to the hospital at once.'

He looked gauche as he steered his wife across the street, Hannah trailing after them, to the taxi rank. There was no taxi in sight. Strand Bay had no public transport and no cars passed by.

'We'd better start walking. I can't stand around here waiting for a taxi that might never arrive.' Mary's voice faltered.

A cold lump of fear gripped Hannah. She saw beads of perspiration on her mother's forehead as they began their climb up the hill to the hospital.

Slowly they went up the steep, narrow street, her father's arm encircling her mother's waist, her bag gripped in his free hand.

'Wonderful, isn't it?' His voice was bitter. 'We gave up our home in England to come back here to better ourselves. Look at us. We're much worse off in this backwater that we call home. I wouldn't mind, but we were doing alright in Birmingham.'

'Stop, Tom, please. Not in front of the child.'

He wasn't listening. 'Those stairs. Those fucking stairs.'

Her lips moved to quieten him, but no sound emitted. The steep climb uphill had left her breathless. Not a car passed them.

The little hospital at the top of the hill was quiet as they entered.

'Sit down and wait there, Hannah.' Tom indicated a bench along a wall, then took Mary to a desk, marked Reception.

'Name?' the nun in white asked.

Mary gave it.

'Date of birth?'

Mary raised her voice above a whisper to answer. 'Religion?'

'Cath...ol...ic.' Suddenly she bent forward, clutching her stomach.

'For Christ's sake, put away those fucking forms and get the doctor. Quick.' Tom pushed his contorted face into the nun's. She bolted for the door.

A flurry of activity followed with nuns and nurses and doctors all rushing Mary away. Hannah ran forward. Tom held her in his arms and they both stood helplessly gazing out of the window at the harbour below, two sad silhouettes against the orange sunset.

Doctor Moran's voice, talking to her father, woke Hannah. She had not realised that she had fallen asleep in his arms.

'The little chap didn't have a chance.' The Doctor cleared his throat.

A terrible silence followed.

'There was nothing I could do, Tom. Even if I'd had the whole of the Regional Hospital in Cork at my disposal, I couldn't have saved him. His heart wasn't strong enough.'

Tom nodded, digesting the doctor's words.

'Can we see Mammy now?' Hannah's concerned look brought Tom out of his reverie.

Doctor Moran looked at her. 'Only for a few minutes, pet. She's very tired.' He held Tom's hand in a grasp of sympathy and walked down the corridor, shoulders hunched.

Mary was asleep when Hannah leaned over her.

'We'll see her tomorrow, pet. Let's go home.' The back of the hand Tom took to guide her out of the ward was still wet from the tears she'd wiped on it.

Next day Hannah had to wait in the corridor for a while, while her Daddy went into the ward, but she hung around the door and saw and listened. Hannah's mother held the little white bundle in her arms. The tiny hands lay still against the hospital blanket. She was bent over her baby, as if shielding him from the prying eyes of the rest of the world.

'The baby must have a proper burial,' she told Tom. 'I want to dress him up.' Her eyes, wild with pain, gazed out from under a mass of stringy hair.

Tom put his arms around them both and held them for a long time. No words were spoken.

Eventually when he went to take the baby gently from her mother's now stiff arms, she shrieked. Wild animal cries rent the air. Her father held her, murmuring words Hannah couldn't hear. Occasionally she nodded and moaned softly or sighed. Finally a nurse came and took the baby away.

The room was almost invisible, with only an arc of light over her mother's head, when Hannah was allowed in to see her. She ran to her in a feverish grip of love. 'Mammy. Oh, Mammy. Are you alright?' Her mother nodded, tears streaming down her cheeks.

Soon they had to go, and Hannah kissed her goodbye.

'I'll see you later, Mammy,' she said, 'if Daddy let's me come back up with him tonight.'

'I'm sure he will, lovey.' Her mother hugged her, a preoccupied look on her face.

Next time they came, the ward was bright yellow from the electric light. Small clumps of people were scattered loosely here and there, some sitting on white-covered beds, others on chairs.

'How are you, love?' Her mother was too weak to move in the bed.

'I'm alright.' Hannah stood looking at the dark circles under her mother's eyes.

'Bring me the christening robe when you come tomorrow.'

Her father brought her to see the baby laid out in a tiny white casket, in the centre of a room, beside a table with fresh-cut lilies on it. Her mother had taken endless time to dress him in the smocked robe with handmade lace edging on the tiny sleeves. The small alabaster face of the baby was barely visible beneath the lace bonnet and flowing robe. His tiny hands were already turning blue.

Hannah put her arms around him and laid her cheek tenderly against his.

'Hello, baby brother,' she whispered, 'and goodbye. Why didn't you stay to play with me? It's lonely on my own.'

'He's gone back to Heaven.' Tom looked at the small scrap nestled in the cradle.

His infant son looked like a wax doll. Hannah hugged the little infant again, unable as yet to understand the enormity of her parents' loss, her own loss, yet grieving silently for them all. As she left the room with her father, she knew that the wild expression she saw in her mother's eyes would be indelibly imprinted on her mind.

Chapter 3

Reverend Mother ruled the Order from dawn to dusk with a will of iron, hidden behind a silken voice. Postulants, novices, and nuns alike trembled when summoned to her office. Today Hannah stood before her, her eyes fixed on the wings of Saint Michael, the Archangel, in a painting positioned behind her chair.

'Sit down, Sister Marie Claire. You look as if you're about to fly off somewhere.' Reverend Mother's sharp blue eyes gazed at her prey. 'You are with us almost two years now. Are you happy, Sister?

'Yes, Mother, very happy,' Hannah said.

'You are preparing to take your vows. Have you any doubts about your calling to the religious life?'

'No, Mother.'

'Or your ability to keep those vows for the rest of your life?'

'No, Mother.'

'As you know, it is only through prayer and devotion to liturgical practices that we get to know God better. You're an idealistic girl. You have persevered with your vocation in spite of hard work and long hours of prayer. You seem to have a slight problem with the rule of silence.' She was reading from Mother Clement's progress report as she spoke.

Hannah knew exactly the times Reverend Mother was referring to. It was during meditation, after Compline and before the Great Silence. Finding herself too tired to concentrate on the purpose of her life and how she should relate what she was learning to her daily routine, she poked Sister Immaculata in the ribs and whispered, 'I'm starving.' Mother Clement caught her eye and wrote her name in her black book. Another time she had woken up to the sound of loud sobs in the adjoining cell. Forgetting all about the Great Silence, she rushed to the bedside of Sister Alice, her favourite sister, although favouritism was discouraged among the sisters.

'What's wrong?' she asked the crumpled heap in the bed.

Sister Alice emerged from under her blankets. 'Oh, Sister, I'm sorry I disturbed you.' Hannah sat on the bed beside her. 'Tell me what's the matter,' she urged.

Sister Alice's shoulders heaved as she fought for control. 'I'm leaving tomorrow.'

'What?'

'Reverend Mother says I don't have a vocation,' she sobbed.

Hannah couldn't see her face clearly in the dark, but imagined the heartbreak in her eyes.

'I can't believe ...'

They both heard the shuffling feet at the same time and sat frozen with fear as the door opened and Mother Clement stood there.

She pointed to Hannah's cell and glared at Sister Alice until Hannah left. Because of the Great Silence, no interview took place until the next day.

'I forbid you to say goodbye to Sister Alice,' Mother Clement said when she finally sent for her. 'You should not have entered her cell and broken the Great Silence, no matter how upset you thought she might be.'

Hannah saw the taxi drive up to the back door of the convent on her way to Divine Office. She did not see Sister Alice leave. There was no display of sadness at her departure. What amazed her was the way life went on as if Sister Alice had never existed. Her name and number were erased from her cell and from her pew in the chapel. As far as the nuns were concerned she had never existed.

Reverend Mother rose from her chair and glided across the room. Hands steepled and pressed to her lips, she turned to Hannah. 'After careful consideration it has been decided by Mother General to allow you to study for a degree in social science. Your superiors feel that your future is in work in the community, and that you would best benefit the Order in that field. You will take up your studies after your profession.'

'Yes, Mother.' Volatile emotions of adolescence, long suppressed, surfaced, and were suppressed again.

Reverend Mother scrutinised Hannah's face for a reaction. Satisfied with her emotionless countenance, she continued, 'Jesus was the first social worker, and since your future is in his work, you will follow his example in administering to the needs of those in your care. You will spend a lot of your time among seculars.' She paused. 'You must never behave like one. Live by your Rule and keep the vows you are about to take foremost in your mind.'

As their profession drew nearer Mother Clement instructed her novices on the importance of confession.

'Inner exploration and the discovery of personal identity can take place only in the confessional, and only in relation to God. I want you all to make a good confession, pray about your decision, and ask God's help in the lead-up to the most important day of your life, your religious profession.'

Hannah felt the eyes of her novice mistress piercing her very soul.

'Your path will be strewn with difficulties and endurance tests. The devil will never be closer to you than at this time, and your greatest resources of physical and spiritual strength will be called upon. You have my prayers.'

All heads bowed for her blessing.

The news that she was going to college enabled Hannah to surrender completely to her life as a nun, with its contrasts of silences and splendid processional feasts, its austere cold days of darkness, then days of great enlightenment.

She responded to the rituals of the Novitiate without complaint or boredom. Not once did she resent her chosen imprisonment. She washed clothes, laid tables, sewed. The Rule obliged her to speak daily with her novice mistress about spiritual concerns. Impressed with her understanding of the spiritual life, Mother Clement put Hannah in charge of the sacristy. She loved to touch the sacred vessels and prepare the altar linens.

Decorating the altar took a long time. Each morning she placed a fresh altar cloth with its fine lace trim before the golden tabernacle. She polished the wood-block floor until it gleamed, and lined the altar with magnificent flowers on feast days.

One Sunday evening in spring Mother Clement sent for Hannah. Knocking on the door of her office, Hannah wondered what she wanted, and automatically began examining her conscience.

'Sit down, Sister Marie Claire.' Her voice was crisp.

'Thank you, Mother.'

'Father Martin is ill.'

'I'm sorry to hear that, Mother.'

Hannah was fond of the old chaplain, and had grown accustomed to his fumbling ways.

Mother Clement ignored her and continued reading from her notebook.

'Father Stephen Wall will replace him for the duration of his illness. Since he's newly ordained, you will help him to get acquainted with his duties here.'

'Yes, Mother.'

'Therefore I must remind you not to forget the Rule. Keep your contact with him to a minimum. Never engage in any conversation with him that is not pertinent to your duties.'

'Yes, Mother.'

'You looked after Father Martin well. You were patient with him. I'm sure Father Stephen won't need as much attention. He's young and healthy.' She emphasised every word.

'Yes, Mother.'

With a gesture of her hand Mother Clement indicated that the interview had come to an end. Hannah rose to her feet and bowed her head for the blessing.

Next morning she lit the candles on the altar as the nuns glided in, faces unrevealed behind veils. Hannah waited in the sacristy to welcome Father Stephen.

'Hi! Sorry I'm late. Won't take a sec to get ready.'

With a start Hannah turned to see a tall, broad-shouldered priest removing the jacket of his black suit and moving towards the vestry as he spoke.

'Good morning, Father. Everything is ready.'

He had gone ahead even as she spoke and emerged vested within minutes. Hannah silently led the way into the chapel.

During mass she kept losing concentration as she studied him, knowing she shouldn't, yet unable to stop herself. His physical presence, the texture of his skin, the relaxed smile at the corners of his mouth, unnerved her. He's better looking than Patrick Byrne, she was shocked to find herself thinking. She stopped staring and tried to attend to the mass. When she went into the sacristy afterwards, he had disrobed.

'Now I can introduce myself properly. I'm Stephen Wall. You must be Sister Marie Claire.'

'Yes, Father, I am. Pleased to meet you.' Hannah extended a hand and he shook it, smiling broadly.

'You're not local, are you?' He looked at her quizzically.

'No, Father.' She began putting things away, reminding herself of the Rule.

'I'll show you where everything's kept. You'll get used to it in no time.'

'I'm sure I will. The first day is always the worst. You're not professed yet?'

'No, Father. I've another few months to go.' She wished she could sound more friendly, while discouraging further conversation.

'What will you do afterwards? Teach?'

He's only trying to be friendly, she told herself. *Talk to him.* 'Social science, Father. It's what I've always wanted to do.' The idea of it made her smile.

He returned her smile. 'Will you be going to UCD?'

'Yes. Please God,' she added, moving nearer the door. 'The parlour is down the corridor. They'll be waiting to serve your breakfast.'

She led the way, glad to escape the direct gaze that made her blush.

The table in the parlour was set and the smell of percolating coffee tantalised her. It was years since she drank a cup of coffee. Father Stephen made straight for the coffee and began pouring out a cup. 'Would you like to join me, Sister, or is it stupid of me to ask?'

She shrank back, nodding her head, too polite to tell him that yes, it was a stupid question.

'Sister Thomas will serve you your breakfast. If you'll excuse me, Father ... I'll see you later.'

'Certainly, Sister. Thank you.'

She was not sure if the hammering in her heart was caused by her proximity to him, or the sudden void she felt as she left him. All she knew was that emotions and passions that had previously lain dormant rose now to the surface. She fought to subdue the panicky feeling Father Stephen's presence caused her, as she joined her sisters for breakfast.

That evening when he held the monstrance aloft, during benediction, Hannah stared at him. The golden globe, caught in a shaft of light from the stained-glass window, sent rays of coloured lights across his white vestments. It gave his handsome face an ethereal quality. There was a detachment about him as he officiated with devoutness. Hannah wondered how he could be unaware of his good looks. She found herself wondering what drew him into the priesthood. Was his self-assurance the result of years of rigourous training? Or was it natural, like the blonde of his hair and the blue of his eyes?

They talked in the mornings for a few minutes after mass. Hannah, remembering Mother Clement's warning, tried to keep the conversations to a minimum. He told her he had trained for the missions and was looking forward to going.

'I have to do some parish work first. Then who knows? It could be anytime. Accepting one's fate is proof of one's vocation.'

One morning he asked, 'What's your name?'

She stopped what she was doing and stared at him. 'You must have had a name before you were Sister Marie Claire.' His laugh defused her rising tension.

'Hannah.'

'May I call you Hannah?'

Seeing the petrified look in her face he added, 'Just here in the sacristy, when we're alone.'

She shrank back visibly from him. 'No one has called me by that name since I entered, except my parents.'

'I'm sorry. I shouldn't have been so personal.'

Seeing the uncomfortable look on his face she said quickly, 'It's alright. You weren't to know that it's against our Rule. Hannah, whoever she was, is dead to the world. Sister Marie Claire lives on.' She smiled at him to put him at his ease.

He said, 'I'm sure Hannah, whoever she was, was very beautiful.' There was no mistaking the warmth in his voice.

Hannah all at once felt a mixture of joy and dismay.

She was always conscious of his presence, even when he wasn't there. The novices were listening to Mother Clement reminding them that they were receptacles of the Lord, beyond the drives of the body, the weakness of the flesh. They were being prepared to take their vows of poverty, chastity and obedience. Mother Clement quoted from *De Virginibus lll 9*.

'For the younger (virgins) I think that visits, if they have to be made to parents, or companions, should be few. In these acts of dutifulness modesty wears away, boldness of manner appears and levity creeps in. Modesty goes while you are trying to be courteous. If you fail to reply to a question you seem impolite; if you do reply you are caught in idle gossip.'

Hannah was confused, accusing herself of indulging in idle gossip with Father Stephen. As time went on, walking in the grounds, praying in the chapel, whatever she was doing, she thought of him, with the self-absorption of the infatuated. When she met him she saw a kindling response. When she realised what was happening to her she tried to occupy her mind with spiritual thoughts. She read from *The Golden Legend.*

'He whom I love is nobler than thou. The sun and moon wonder at his beauty. His riches are inexhaustible. He is mighty enough to bring the dead to life and his love surpasses all love. He has placed his ring upon my finger, has given me a necklace of precious stones, and has clothed me in a gown woven with gold. He has graven a sign upon my face to keep me from loving any other than himself and he has sprinkled my cheeks with his blood. Already I have been embraced by his pure arms, already his body is with my body. And he has shown me an incomparable treasure and has promised to give it to me if I persevere in his love.

'Saint Ambrose tells us that virginity is a type of martyrdom, requiring a daily death to self. Death is the consummation of a virgin's life. In his address to the virgins of his Church in Milan, he said: This was a new martyrdom. She who was too weak to suffer was strong enough to conquer; she who could not fight yet won the crown ... No bride hurried to her bridal chamber as did the saint to her place of judgement, joyously, with hurried pace.'

No matter how she occupied her mind with prayer and spiritual reading, thoughts of him intruded. She stopped fighting her pre-occupation, and was glad of the Great Silence she had once found so difficult. Now she could have time to cherish her thoughts of Stephen.

It didn't occur to her to question her own place in all of this. His existence transformed her life, coloured her vision, heightened her perception. She looked out with new eyes on her little world. She isolated him from his ecclesiastical life, imagining him alone and separate, so that her conscious self could cope with the dawning of her love for him.

Each morning was enhanced and magnified so that she saw tenderness in her sisters which she hadn't noticed before. Things she found difficult to do in the past, like waking up, became a joy, knowing she would see him soon. Early morning bird song, the dawn breaking, gave her a heightened sense of well-being. He occupied her subconscious, sometimes vaguely, other times with staggering intensity. In her mind's eye his face was always before her.

* * * * * *

Her dreams were distorted. In one dream she was a child again screaming to her mother that her father had left home.

Her mother heated milk for her and consoled her.

'Daddy would never leave us,' she said.

Her father returned soon afterwards and, lifting her up into his arms, hugged her close. She smelt the stale beer on his breath. He carried her to her room, swaying slightly as he negotiated his way, but holding her tightly before snuggling her down into her warm bed.

'I'll never leave you,' he said, depositing a sloppy kiss on her cheek. 'You need have no worries on that score.'

'Goodnight, Daddy.' She watched his bulky shape, high and shadowy, sliding away across the ceiling towards the arc of light in her bedroom doorway.

The next night on her way up from the toilet she heard her mother's voice thick with sleep say, 'Not now, Tom.' And the exasperation in her father's reply, 'When, for God's sake? Just looking at you is driving me mad.'

'It's too soon. I'm not healed inside.'

'How long will that take?'

'I'm still raw down there.' The voice was pleading.

'I won't wait much longer. I'll go elsewhere. There's plenty only too willing to oblige.'

'Don't threaten me.' Her mother's voice was clearly angry and Hannah ran back to bed, afraid. She did not understand what was wrong. She knew nothing of the turbulence of her parents' marriage, aware only of a tension in the house from time to time. Her parents were, in fact, at this time going through a crisis in their marriage. Mary felt she had failed her husband, but her deep sense of failure was borne in silence. She crushed her emotions behind a veneer of steely armour, and the cycle of life continued its relentless rhythm.

In a dutiful attempt at reviving her marriage, she let Tom make love to her. Her ill-concealed distaste for it sent him sulking to the pub. His drinking bouts cast a shadow over everything. The raw pain of loss continued to haunt her. It grew and spread around the tenuous threads of their marriage. She couldn't bear to have the subject of their disastrous love-making broached. Tom would look at her with red whisky eyes and say in a slurred voice, 'What's the use of having a cow that yields no milk.'

Mary fell into a pit of depression.

He tried to frighten her. Sometimes he hit her. She felt he was scheming to destroy her. In her depressed state, she saw him as a tyrant. His taunts and jeers yielded up no reaction. To his friends he smiled genially, camouflaging his misery. Mary saw it as another act of deceit. She became self-righteous and almost puritanical, racing to the church for consolation after every fresh bout of cruelty he delivered. She dragged Hannah along with her, tears in her eyes. Head bowed and throbbing as she lowered it before the crucified Christ, murmuring her mantra of Hail Marys, consolation to her battered soul.

In the church she quietly summoned up his wrongdoings. She silently listed his faults and his family's, introducing and examining them one by one while she prayed. It gave her the strength to ignore his nagging and complaints, and the self-defence to remain civilised to his outstretched hand when it connected with her jaw.

When she began to feel that she was drowning in the quicksand of her marriage that had been once her rock, she began to plan a trip home to visit her mother. She decided to take Hannah to County Tipperary with her.

She was worried about the effect of Tom's querulous manner, when thwarted, on Hannah. Hannah had grown quiet since her brother's death, not seeming to notice the friction between her parents. Tom shielded her in a peculiar way, sitting her on his knee in the big armchair by the fire, giving her the affection Mary rejected.

Doctor Moran agreed that her need for privacy and solitude were a real part of the recovery process. It would do them both good to be among normal, sane people. Perhaps the tranquillity of her mother's farm might provide the sustenance needed to recover, away from prying eyes and harsh voices. Voices that belonged to people who never spoke to her directly but addressed their cadences to her affairs within earshot.

'She's delicate, God love her,' they'd say. 'Nothing you could put a finger on, just something peculiar about her.' Or 'They say her family are a bit strange. Miscarriages follow in families. Did you know that?'

'Get better or go to the undertakers and get measured up,' Tom said when he saw her packing her suitcase.

Chapter 4

The day Hannah and her mother set out on their journey, the sun shone and puffy white clouds floated apace with the chug-chugging of the train. They flashed past green and yellow trees and meadows, as they speeded toward County Tipperary and Sadie O'Reilly's farm.

Sadie O'Reilly sat in her large chintz armchair smoking a forbidden cigarette, waiting eagerly for Mary and Hannah to arrive. Since she had received the letter telling her of their planned visit, she had busied herself cleaning the house. The old pine dresser was scrubbed and polished. The blue willow-patterned plates were rinsed in soapy water and now sparkled in the morning light. She had brushed, swept and dusted and generally cleared up the muddle she lived in.

John Hanrahan, her farm manager, had to bend his head to avoid the lintel as he entered the room where Sadie sat without her teeth, her shawl or the usual clutter of books and ashtrays she surrounded herself with.

'What do you think? Is it presentable enough for my daughter and grand-daughter?'

'Perfect,' John smiled. 'It's just the way Mary'll remember it.'

Sadie surveyed the chintz chairs, the polished wooden floors.

'There's a bareness about the place. It's a bit on the tidy side, don't you think? 'She looked disgruntled.

'Stop worrying. It's fine. Will I put the kettle on?' John's easygoing ways always dispelled the old woman's worries.

'It's her first visit since she came back to Ireland. That husband of hers isn't very attentive. But she wouldn't listen to her father when he begged her not to marry him. She was far too young.'

John remembered only too well. Wasn't she the cause of him emigrating when she told him there was no future for them. Her decision to marry Tom Dempsey, a complete stranger, had shocked him.

'And you want to impress the little one?'

'I certainly do.' She smiled her toothless happy smile, but John noticed how tired she was. Days beating mats and rugs, shining and polishing and generally spring cleaning, had taken their toll. Housework was something Sadie wasn't accustomed to. She preferred to live in semi-squalor, surrounded by her beloved ornaments and books, and her noisy mongrel of a dog called Maggie, or more usually Mangy, because she smelt. She had enlisted Annie's help.

Annie Duffy had come as a live-in maid after Mrs Reilly was widowed over twelve years before, and had never left. She had been a waif of a creature with a club foot and no references. But she proved hard-working and devoted and never showed any desire to leave. Now elevated to the status of companion and in her advancing years, her efforts weren't efficient enough. Mrs O'Reilly kept finding fault and doing the chores herself, enlisting the help of a young girl from the village.

'We neglected the house for too long.' Mrs O'Reilly gazed at the freshly painted walls, a feeling of well-being stealing over her.

'Set in the heart of the country and surrounded by gorse-covered hills, the acres of well tended land stretched as far as the eye could see. The farm was inaccessible and hard to maintain, so she employed John Hanrahan as farm manager. John was the son of a neighbour who had recently returned home from Australia to his inheritance, a small farm. He had experience of managing thousands of acres of land and vast droves of sheep and cattle in Australia, yet he was glad to be home and willingly took on the extra work of managing Sadie's farm. Though it was an impractical place for an elderly person to live, Mrs O'Reilly refused point blank to be shunted off to the county home.

'What would become of Annie?' she said more than once. Annie knew that she was waiting for her beloved only son Pádraig to return from the States to claim his heritage. His mother didn't have his present address. But that was another closely guarded secret. When the neighbours inquired about him she said, 'Oh, he's doing fine,' and gave them a litany of anecdotes she had invented specially for them.

Now she was glad she had a home for her daughter to visit and she found the waiting for Mary and the grand-daughter she'd never met agonising.

Feeling the chill of the bare room, she went into the kitchen, her old knees creaking like un-oiled hinges. She slowly began to prepare a meal, calling out to John to be sure to collect them from the station on time.

'Hannah sat at her grandmother's kitchen table. The green leafy creeper made dark patterns on the window pane as it clawed its way around the old white-washed farmhouse. Mrs O'Reilly was leaning against the narrow front door, her sparse hair plaited around her ears like ear phones. A high lace collar concealed her ropey neck. Her tall straight body, clad in a long grey dress, was as frail as a twig about to break in the wind. Her deft fingers darting her crochet hook in and out of the lace she was making were the only graceful movements she made.

'Finish your breakfast, Hannah, and come out into the sunshine,' she called in a cracked voice.

'The garden was a profusion of summer flowers. Fullblown roses lived haphazardly beside drooping lupins and vivid yellow, pink and deep crimson snapdragons. Hannah had been there almost a fortnight and still savoured the smell of new-mown grass, and loved the green of the fields beyond the wicker fence. The farm was safe and friendly. And full of surprises. Obeying her Grannie's call she ran out through the fading pink, blue and white hydrangeas and followed the crazy path beyond the garden to the orchard where rooks and jackdaws rustled and called to one another from the high trees in the distance. Hannah's familiarity with the place was through her mother's endless stories. She felt she had known it always.

The hens almost tripped her up because they were in as much of a hurry as she was, wildly pecking and rustling their feathers in the heat. She went to search for Danny to tell him to hurry because they were all going fruit-picking.

Danny was Joe Morris's son. Joe worked on O'Reilly's farm in the summer and went across to England to work for the winter. They lived in a gate lodge two fields away. Danny knew everything and showed her his secret hiding places. He knew everyone in the locality and all about them.

'Danny,' she called as she ran along. Suddenly he appeared, clutching a spade twice as big as himself. His face was dirty.

'We're off fruit-picking. Coming?' Hannah called.

'I have to finish clearin' the mess outa the pig sty and hose it down or I'll be killed.'

'Ah, come on,' Hannah pleaded. 'I'll help you when we come back. Sure the pigs won't notice whether their sty is clean or not.'

'No. But me father will and I'll catch it from him.'

'Come on. We'll get Grannie to ask him can you leave it 'til later. You'd better wash yourself first though. You smell as bad as the pigs.' Hannah wrinkled her nose and turned to run off.

'Ah, get lost,' he called after her. 'Stuck-up city slicker,' he muttered and then, flinging the spade down he shouted, 'Wait for me.'

'We'll take a picnic,' Mrs O'Reilly said and called out to Hannah to come and help. Her voice in the distance sounded as crackly as an old gramophone record.

Mary cut thick slices of soda bread and buttered them with golden blobs of homemade butter. She sandwiched slices of home-cured ham between them, and wrapped them in a large white napkin. She cut up cucumber and tomatoes and radishes from the vegetable garden, adding chives for colour and flavour.

Granny O'Reilly took down a tin of rich fruit cake and sent Hannah into the pantry for the sealed stone jar of cider.

'Oh, and bring a siphon of lemonade,' she called after her. She thought of everything.

The eggs bubbled on the stove and Hannah put salt and pepper into the huge shopping basket they used for a picnic hamper.

'Now, let's see. Cups, spoons, plates, knives. Yes, that's everything. I'll make a flask of tea. It's such a hot day. Bring the sun bonnets or we'll be roasted alive.' Mary finished packing the basket.

Grannie O'Reilly sent Hannah flying off to find the hats in the big chest in her bedroom. Hannah wore a straw boater and ran ahead. Grannie walked slowly with Mary, her feet wobbly and unsure in the long grass. Hannah stopped ever so often to sink her knees into the grass and smother her face in daisies and buttercups. She by-passed the gate and, sure-footed, climbed the fence.

'Hurray,' she shouted, jumping.

'The answering birds chirped in the still fields. There was an everlasting feeling about the pine trees that grew up the sides of the far hills. Hannah wanted to explore them. With a child's impulsiveness she wanted to do everything at once, yet she knew instinctively she must restrain herself. Grannie was very old. If Hannah had an accident, the shock might be too much for her.

The apples in the orchard hung like golden globes. Cox's pippins, cox's orange pippins and brambleys for cooking. Hannah reached into the branches and plucked the delicious fruit at random, tasting, deciding. She flung the scab-marked or cracked ones to the ground in careless abandon, for the birds to eat. Joe Morris would pick them up later and wheel them away in his barrow to the compost heap at the far corner of the lower meadow.

Gooseberries on prickly stalks bordered the apple trees.

'We'll make gooseberry jam and gooseberry tart and gooseberry fool,' Mary said, catching up with Hannah.

They picked the ripe fruit into large white basins.

Hannah painted her lips rosebud red with the juice of redcurrants and blackcurrants and loganberries.

'Victoria plums for plum pie. You'll have so much to eat during the winter, Ma, you won't have to cook a thing. Just heat everything up.' Mary worked eagerly.

'Sounds good to me,' Grannie said, winding her fingers around the gnarled branches, while plucking expertly as she moved through the rows of bushes. Her lopsided hat was secured with a big bow tied under her chin. She looked like an ancient china doll.

Danny observed them with a twist of a smile.

'Wouldya look at your grannie?' he whispered to Hannah, stifling a laugh.

Hannah looked.

'She can't risk getting her head sunburnt. Her hair is very thin and it would hurt like mad.' She was indignant, seeing nothing amusing about her grannie.

'Lunchtime,' Mary called out eventually and went to the shaded oak tree to unwrap the picnic basket.

At the far end of the field John Hanrahan was digging up potatoes from their drills.

'John, John', Mrs O'Reilly called in a thin wail which sounded more like 'Help, Help'.

He stopped what he was doing and came to join them. He smiled at Mary who stood tall in the panorama of fields and hills and sky. Their silhouettes merged. Hannah, up in the branches of the apple tree, tried not to stare. She felt shaky inside watching them. A fragment of inexplicable fear gripped her, and made the watching compulsive.

Danny stuck out his tongue at the squinting, curious Hannah.

'She knows him for years and years.' Authority was in his voice and Hannah's face reddened.

'How do you know?'

'Because John's from here and everyone knows everyone else.' It sounded reasonable.

'I never heard of him before.' A puzzled expression crossed Hannah's features.

'She probably never thought to tell you. She can't remember to tell you everything.'

'Yes, she can.' Hannah was defiant. 'What would you know anyway? You just think you know everything.'

'I know more than you. You don't even know the difference between a cow and a bull.'

'Stop squabbling, you two, and come on for your picnic,' Grannie called.

The sun swung high up into the sky as John moved the heavy rustic table under the shade of the oak tree, and placed the chairs around it. Mary set out the picnic.

'You'll have a bite to eat with us, won't you?' she asked him.

Hannah, finally defeated by the blinding sun, reluctantly joined them. She had a sudden feeling of being an intruder.

Mary unfolded the napkin of sandwiches and poured out the cider from the stone jar into a mug. She handed it to John. Their eyes held and Hannah shivered while Grannie looked on in innocent fondness.

The farmhouse was small. Miles away from anywhere, its rutted lane was shaded by trees, its entrance guarded by snarling stone lions who sat uneasily on pillared iron gates. The backyard was flagged outside the kitchen door. There was a stillness about the place. Only birdsong, and the gurgle of a stream that flowed through the fields down to the duck pond in the lower meadow, broke the silence.

Hannah sat on a pile of freshly cut logs, warmed by the hot sun. She had explored everywhere. Exhausted, she dabbled her aching feet in the sedgy pond, scattering the ducks. They swam away straight and motionless, their movements unseen beneath the water. The sun mellowed and cast long shadows over the fields. Cattle grazed peacefully. Only ducks and duckling scrambling up the muddy banks in great confusion at the invasion of their privacy, and small birds fluttering and settling in the trees, stirred the stillness.

Hannah left them and wandered back across the grass picking forget-me-nots and buttercups on her way. She stood gazing at the ripening wheat-field as it rose to meet the dark pine trees in the distance. Suddenly she recognised this place as the kingdom she had wished for ages ago, before her baby brother died. Some fairy knew she was unhappy and had granted her wish. Here in the safe comfort of the farm everything was alright. In the daytime. It was during the night that she became distressed, her dreams peppered with ominous shadowy people. Black witches stalked with hooting owls and Grannie turned into a cackling hen. She would cry out and Mary would come and stay with her until she went back to sleep.

Mary rolled and shaped the pastry into a pie dish, then tipped in the gooseberries, covering them with pastry. She sealed in the edges with neat fork patterns. All the time watched by Hannah and John Hanrahan. Finally she removed her long apron, uncovering bare brown legs, and a slim body in a faded cotton print frock. His eyes were intent on her. 'You're very quiet this morning.'

She looked away.

He brushed his bare elbow lightly against her as she cleared the table. She moved back.

He said, 'Sorry.'

Hannah said, 'What's wrong?'

'Nothing. Eat your porridge.'

'About this evening?' He was much taller than her mother, Hannah noticed.

'I'll talk to you later,' her mother side-stepped him and concentrated on pouring Hannah's tea.

Later, hiding in the trees in the orchard, and eating an apple any time she was hungry, Hannah decided she would like to live in the trees, like they did in the jungle. Away from prying eyes and fighting parents. Danny showed her how to climb the trees.

'Tuck your dress into your knickers.'

They had crawled along the grey branches, Danny surefooted as a monkey. Then they played hide and seek and made Indian calling sounds to one another.

'Wa Wa Wa Wa Wa,' they cried, sending birds flying into the sky.

The jackdaws caw-cawed in unison. From the trees they could see into the distance, past the old red barn and the hayrick. They sauntered along in the heat to the duck pond to bathe their feet, annoying the ducks with their presence.

'Whoosh whoosh,' Danny clapped his hands, sending them flurrying off in all directions.

'You're cruel.' Hannah lay back on the grass dreaming about knights in shining armour coming to her rescue in this wilderness, and fairy princesses and castles in forests.

When it became too hot, they climbed into the shadowy rafters of the hayrick and slid down the cool side of the newly saved hay.

'We'll catch it if we mess up this hay,' Danny warned.

Her child's instinct knew Grannie would not say a word. She rolled and rolled in it, covering herself in hayseeds.

'I never want to go back to that horrible flat.' She was lying on top of the hayrick.

'Don't then.'

Even as she said the words she knew she would be going home soon. Her mother looked better. Sitting there, surrounded by the summer smells and buzzing bees, Hannah remembered her father and missed him again.

When it became unbearably hot, they slid down the far side and hid under the corrugated roof where hens nested and pigs snorted impolitely from their pens.

Hannah recognised her mother's laugh before she saw them. She moved into the shadows as they passed. John was holding her hand. Hannah nudged Danny to keep quiet. Silently they watched as her mother and John walked down to the lower meadow, talking softly and clinging together and laughing helplessly, before falling into the long grass.

Hannah raced back to the farmhouse and clambered upstairs, locking her bedroom door so as not to be disturbed. They would have to go home before something terrible happened. She wasn't sure what that something terrible might be.

But it was only at Grannie's party that Hannah realised that there was something strange going on between her mother and John.

'Let's have a bit of a do and invite in the neighbours,' Grannie had suggested.

'What neighbours, Grannie?' Hannah surveyed the endless fields from her perch in the deep sill of the kitchen windows.

'You'd be surprised. There's old Duignan from the next farm and Mr and Mrs Russell over at the cross. There's Father Breen and his housekeeper Nellie of course. She's been with him forty years and never an unkind word between them. There's Liam O'Brien, the grocer, and his wife May. They supply us with everything we need. The Ormonds from the far side of the hill. They're protestants, mind, but very neighbourly. They brought provisions last year when we were flooded. Sent their son to help with the clearing up.' As she spoke her fingers flew, weaving her neighbours into her silken web.

'You were flooded?' Mary lifted her eyebrows in surprise.' You never told me that.'

'It rained so much that the river burst its banks. The drains got clogged up with mud. Look at it now. Hard-baked from the sun. We could use a drop of the rain we had then'.

'That's the way it goes. Either a famine or a feast,' said Annie.

'Well, it'll be a feast tomorrow. Now let's make out a list for John to take to the village.' Grannie loved making lists.

They drove to the village in John's lorry. Hannah and Danny sat in the back seat, Mary high up in the front beside John. They bounced over rough narrow roads, with John expertly negotiating every familiar twist and turn. Dust rose up from under the huge wheels coating the windows in a thin brown film, almost blocking out the view. They slowed down as they approached the village and drove slowly up the wide street. John pointed out familiar landmarks along the way.

'Remember Flanagans?' He pointed to the huxter shop jammed up against an end wall.

'The best toffee apples in the county. And do you remember ...' Hannah stopped listening.

They parked outside 'General Grocers and Provisions'. Two petrol pumps guarded the long shop windows.

'If Liam hasn't got it, then you don't need it. That's the motto here,' John informed them as he helped Mary down from the lorry.

Danny and Hannah climbed down the side of the huge mudguard. They got covered in dust.

'The inside of the shop was dark after the glare of the sun. It took Mary a few minutes to adjust her eyes to the tightly packed shelves. Beeswax candles, glue, twine and shop cake were jammed together on higher shelves. Fruit and vegetables were stacked in wire racks under the window. Open sacks of meal and chicken feed were heaped in corners. A big sack of sugar, with a silver metal scoop inside it, sat beside a chest of tea with Ceylon written on its side.

Rows of dimpled jars full of sweets and lollipops, all the colours of the rainbow, caught and held Hannah's and Danny's attention. John went through an open door into a smaller shop where forks, spades, brushes and wellington boots hung from the ceiling. Bulbs and seed packets with instructions on the back were stacked in crates.

'Did ye ever see anything like the beautiful weather we're having?' Liam O'Brien looked cheerfully at Mary.

'It's glorious. We're so lucky.'

'Not so glorious for the poor unfortunate farmer.' John came through the door laden with packages.' We could do with a drop of rain now. It's too dry.'

'You can never satisfy farmers,' Liam laughed. 'They're always complaining.'

'You're the spit of your mother,' the kindly lady in flowery overalls said to Hannah. 'What's your name?'

'Hannah.'

'Would you like a biscuit and a drop of lemonade?' she asked. 'Sure you must be as parched as the ground outside.'

Danny smiled and Hannah said, 'Yes, please,' shyly.

'Is your Daddy not with ye?' She squirted red lemonade from a syphon into two large glasses.

'He's too busy to take his holidays now. He'll be joining us later on.' Mary looked uneasy as she spoke and Hannah's face turned crimson.

'Bread, tea, sugar, jelly, fruit for trifle, flour, a side of ham,' Mary read from her list and Liam began packing a large cardboard box.

John bought Hannah and Danny a selection of sweets in a brown bag. They went outside to share them out evenly. On the cool stone step they drank their lemonade, and let the fizzy bubbles break against their noses.

John bought supplies for the farm, then loaded up the lorry with several enormous cardboard boxes.

They drove home, deviating along cracked and dusty tracks to outlying farms to deliver verbal invitations.

After a cup of tea Mary and Annie began the preparations for the feast.

'Is Daddy coming to the party?' Hannah asked.

'No, love, it's too far.'

'I'd like to see him.'

'You'll see plenty of him when we go home.'
Mary said.

Hannah felt uncomfortable in the pink and white
cotton dress with puffed sleeves and a big bow
tied at the back.

'Don't get it dirty and don't forget your
manners, please and thank you and all that.'

As evening approached, friends and
neighbours arrived in dribs and drabs. Grannie
stood at the door, tall and serene in black, a white
crochet shawl covering her thin shoulders.

'Ye're welcome.' There was delight in her
greeting and pleasure in her smile.

'Is it yourself?' they said to Mary or 'You left it
long enough to come back for a visit' or 'Where
were you at all, at all?'

Healthy women in Sunday-best frocks
embraced Mary and then Hannah. Large work-
rough hands of workworn men shook Hannah's
small proffered hand with unexpected gentleness.
Men clapped one another on the back, their
muddy boots causing criss-crossing trails on the
clean stone-flagged floor, as they gathered in
groups. Annie served whisky to the men and
sherry to the ladies, her affability reducing her
limp to a light hop. Nothing was too much
trouble.

'Come and eat. Sure ye must be starving.' Mrs O'Reilly called them to partake of the feast spread out before them with a sweeping gesture of her hand.

They ate as if they had travelled a great distance, and drank with a terrible thirst.

Later there was trifle and cream, and piled high plates of fruit cake. The women drank tea from delicate china cups. The men drank the beer and porter.

They talked about the land and the weather and old times. About their dear departed and their emigrants. How the new rich in America were so rich, with several jobs to pay for what they had.

'I don't envy them one bit,' Annie observed, the tot of whisky she was drinking reddening her cheeks. 'Sure you can only use one thing at a time.'

They all talked at once.

From her favourite perch, Hannah observed them. Then all of a sudden she noticed her mother's absence, and looking around, she could see no sign of John either. A wave of fear gripped her then.

Eventually the visitors left, their thanks as abundant as the hospitality they had received.

'It's always a pleasure to visit Sadie O'Reilly,' Mrs Liam, the grocer's wife, said. 'The most respected neighbour in the parish,' Liam rejoined. Annie said 'Praise the Lord' and 'Thanks be to God', and 'Glory be' as each one left. If they did not know her so well, they might have mistaken her aspiration for a sort of thanksgiving at their departure.

Annie attributed everything to God. The weather, nature, the events of the day. She praised him when she was scrubbing with the washing board, her wiry body lopsided as she vigorously worked, her hands calloused and red from the carbolic soap. Every morning she limped two miles to mass to thank God for the strength he gave her, and drank a pint of stout every night to renew that strength. Because Annie was not a fool. As long as she could work she could survive. She had a simple method of dealing with her life. By obliterating her past she lulled herself into a false sense of happiness. The milking of the cows at dawn on cold winter mornings when she was only seven and eight, was the only reference she ever made to her childhood. She had no connection with her family anymore. How her foot, encased in the ugly high boot, had become so badly mutilated, could only be guessed at.

Now she cleared away the last of the dishes and folded the hand-embroidered tablecloth, a family heirloom. Mrs O'Reilly had gone to bed after 'The Cualin' played by Danny's father on the violin, and Mrs Russell's rendition of 'The Lark in the clear air'.

As the last car droned into the night and Annie folded away the tablecloth she said to Hannah, 'I think you'd better go to bed, love. It's very late.'

'I'll wait for Mammy,' Hannah said sleepily from her perch in the deep sill of the kitchen window. 'Where did they go?'

'Hmm,' Annie cleared her throat, and ignoring the question suggested again that Hannah go to bed. Eventually she did, reluctantly and sleepily, only dimly aware that there was some anxiety gnawing at her heart. She was not to know what her mother was experiencing that night and could only put some of the jigsaw pieces together years later as she herself faced the same dilemma.

Mary and John had disappeared from the party and were walking now, hand in hand.

'It's a long time since this little house rang out with singing and laughter like that,' she said.

'Touch of the old days.' His arms encircled her waist. 'Do you know the first time I ever saw you, you were wearing a blue dress too.'

'Hardly like this one.'

'Your hair was in plaits. I was dying to pull them.'

'How can you remember that far back?'

'I've never forgotten anything about you.' He kissed her suddenly.

It was pitch dark with only the light from John's small torch to guide them. An owl made a hooting sound nearby that sent Mary into his arms with fright. They stumbled along to the haybarn, holding each other closely, unable to see in the blackness.

Wordlessly, in the shelter of the rafters, she lay down with him on the hay. There was an urgency and purposefulness in his kisses.

'I'm desperate for you,' he whispered.

Mary, not recognising herself, helped him remove her clothes.

'I've wanted you for so long ...'

'Don't talk ... please ... '

She closed her eyes and let his body grind against hers. Suddenly she came to her senses.

'I can't ... I'm not ready.'

'Sorry.' He held and stroked her hair and kissed her mouth.

'I got greedy,' he said in a half-apologetic whisper. Slowly and patiently he stroked her body until she could bear the waiting no longer. He moved her hips with his hands so that she was comfortably aligned beneath him. Finally, when he knew she was ready he entered her. Matching her rhythm to his own they became one. She screamed as he climaxed, waking the roosters in frenzied protestation, the realisation of what she had just done dawning on her.

Gradually she moved away from the sated and contented John and lay there. Guilt crept over her. Adultery, the pleasures of the flesh. Words preached from the pulpit tumbled around her head. Words that could never apply to her. With one transgression she'd stepped from her world of marriage and respectability into a world where no rules applied, where no commitments were guaranteed. The thought terrified her.

They dressed in silence. He waited for her on the path. Silently they walked back to the farmhouse. At the kitchen door they parted with a kiss. He went into the darkness whistling a fragmented tune. There had been no inquisition, not even a few reassuring words. She wondered if he'd thought she'd climaxed when she screamed. That would have made him feel good.

She crept up to her bedroom and removed all her clothes, shaking them vigorously before hanging them over the chair. She filled the basin with tepid water from the kettle. She soaped a small towel and washed away the semen that trickled down the inside of her thighs. She scrubbed between her legs until her skin was raw.

As she lay in bed she didn't even try to make sense or meaning out of what she had done. She convinced herself that Hannah's accusatory stares were all in her imagination. That what happened was harmless. John had seduced her with his attention. With his laughter and good humour. Above all with his genuine interest in her. That had never wavered since they were children. She took it for granted years ago when he followed her everywhere. He was more of a nuisance then. Little did she realise how starved she had been for all the things he was giving so generously. She would never take him for granted again.

He invited her for a meal in Cashel. He told her he knew somewhere quiet.

'I want to show you the house I'm building in Corry's field.'

'Are you planning on getting married?'

'Someday.'

'John's giving me a lift as far as the Ormond's house. They invited me over for a game of cards,' Mary said to Grannie.

'Good. Are you taking Hannah?'

'She'd be bored stiff and anyway she's still exhausted from the party.'

She spent a long time getting ready. Hannah was waiting for her when she came downstairs.

'You look nice,' she said.

'Thank you love.'

'Will you be long?' Hannah couldn't hide her anxiety.

'Not too long. Anyway, Grannie is here to mind you.'

'Yes, I suppose.'

'Do what you're told and go to bed on time. Oh, and clear the table for Annie.'

She was gone, sinking deeper and deeper into the lies and deceit, unwilling to confront it.

They ate medium rare steaks in a small hotel outside Cashel, then drove back to his farm in the fading light.

'I've got great plans.' He took her by the hand and led her from room to room, elaborating as they went.'

'It's a fine house. Certainly big enough.'

'I hope to be in for the winter.'

'What's the rush?'

'Wait till you see where I live at the moment.'

His home was a converted barn, untidy and cramped. He lit a fire and shifted bundles of clothes from one corner to another in awkward embarrassment.

'I can't stay too long ...'

'Come here.'

He took her into his bedroom. They made love slowly as if time was theirs, knowing that it wasn't.

'I never wanted this to happen,' she told him.

'It has happened and I want it to last forever.'

'That's impossible,' Mary began but he covered her lips with his and kissed away her protestations.

He kissed every part of her body until she dug her nails into his back and begged him to make love to her again. Mary knew she'd changed irrevocably and while he was beside her she didn't care.

Hannah was asleep when Mary crept into her room. She kissed her damp red curls and went to bed. The light of the full moon flooded the patch of sky in her window. She lay in the bright darkness, watching the shadows of the outside trees sliding down the sloping attic wall. Even with its flaky paint and old casement window, it was the prettiest room in the house. The bedroom where she grew up safe and secure. Now as she pondered her plight she realised she wasn't in control anymore. Her course was being steered by a force greater than either herself or John. The strange thing was that for the first time in her whole life she was truly happy. She was also frightened and guilty. Tom had a terrible temper and Hannah was unhappy. She imagined the eyes of the world staring accusingly. 'You look wonderful,' or 'You're radiant'. Were there any tell-tale signs of the sexual gratification she'd never experienced with Tom? Was she sending out messages like, 'I'm sexually satisfied,' or 'We're having an affair.' She knew she was being watched by Annie and Hannah. She also knew that her mother was the only one who was oblivious to it. Her mother at eighty-two was oblivious to most things except making people happy.

If there was gossip and Tom heard it? But that was ridiculous because John had a perfectly legitimate reason to be there all the time. Supposing they were careless and laughed too much, or looked at one another for too long the way lovers do? Finally she fell asleep.

The farm seemed cramped now, with danger lurking in every corner, and still Mary couldn't help herself. She'd wait for him impatiently and be on tenterhooks until they were together. Nothing was said to either of them and even Hannah stopped staring.

Mary never felt happier and more alive than during those long hot idyllic days in the country. The heat intensified their longing.

They made love like starving animals, their sense of danger adding to their excitement. She lived from day to day. She wrote to Tom with one excuse after another for not returning. Her mother wasn't so well. Hannah was thriving. There was so much to be done on the farm.

One evening she walked up from the lower meadow covered in hayseeds. Her skin was brown and glistening, her face happy and alive. Hannah came running to meet her.

'Daddy's here, Daddy's here,' she chanted jumping up and down with excitement. 'He's in the kitchen with Grannie.'

Mary slowed down. She tried to regulate her breathing. She wiped her hand across her mouth in an unconscious effort to wipe away any traces of John's kisses. Then like someone in a trance she moved to the kitchen door, asking herself over and over how he found out.

'Hello, Tom,' she heard herself say.

'Hello, Mary.' He stood up from the table and came over to her. He was wearing his Sunday suit. His hair was neatly brushed, his dark curls slicked back.

'You're looking fine and well,' he said.

'Thanks. So are you.' She moved away to put the kettle on. 'What brought you all this way? Is something wrong?' Again she heard her own voice as if it came from a great distance.

'No. Nothing's wrong. Everything's fine. It's time for you and Hannah to come home.' Relief flooded through her whole being obliterating the sickening feeling the word 'home' caused her.

Mary packed and went to look for John to say goodbye. All the times she had enacted their parting she never imagined how painful it would be. What began as an innocuous flirtation was breaking her heart. Their lovemaking had drawn her into depths of emotion she'd never experienced before. Like the sedges and the reeds in the duck pond, she was drawn to him by a need she didn't know she possessed. He loved her, she was sure. But that knowledge was no consolation. Her love for him denied her the ability to think well of herself and what she was doing.

Hannah kept away from the house. She stayed hidden in the soft grass under the old grey trees in the orchard. She hoped Danny wouldn't find her. She wanted to avoid the almighty row her father's appearance would cause.

If only her brother had lived she mightn't have been the focus of so much attention. She was always the reason they gave each other for their actions. John had changed her mother. She had noticed their secret smiles and private jokes. Hannah hoped that John would stay out of the way while her father was around.

Hidden in the long grass she dreamed John and Tom fought a duel to find out which was the strongest, wisest, and most handsome. Before the duel was over she fell asleep. When she woke up the sunset had mellowed the orchard. Only the edges of the grass were visible in the twilight. Everywhere was deadly quiet and the sky had changed to a smoky grey. There was a storm brewing. Her legs dragged stiffly as she made her way back. The yellow globe of light shone from the kitchen window. The house was quiet. Her mother was upstairs packing.

'Where's Daddy?' Hannah asked her grannie. 'He's gone to the pub with John for a drink. He won't be long. Now, you get ready for bed. You've a long journey ahead of you tomorrow.' Grannie's face was impassive, only her darting crochet hook slipping in and out of her lace indicated her agitation.

'Damn,' she muttered to herself, 'I've dropped a stitch here somewhere.' She began her unravelling as Hannah kissed her goodnight and went upstairs.

That night Hannah dreamed that she was back home sitting on the steps, watching the rise and fall of the rough grey sea. The sea horses foamed at the mouth from the exertion. Clouds cleared and the wind rose. The waves were fuller and whiter than ever.

She picked out the biggest wave, imagining it was a prince come to take her away over the sea. They held hands as they walked on the uneven waves, their feet hardly touching the water. He tapped his gold-tipped cane and tipped his topper to the rhythm of the sea. Hannah was scared and happy all at once. They went so far away that her old shambles of a house was only a speck in the distance. They sailed on top of the waves. Hannah was exhilarated and happy. Then, without warning, when they reached the horizon, her magic prince dropped her unceremoniously into the sea and she was drowning, drowning, drowning. Just as she disappeared under the waves for the last time her daddy was beside her, pulling her up. He held her for a long time above the water. She was safe, safe, safe.

'Now, no more tears, lovey,' her father said gently. 'We'll be going home tomorrow and everything will be alright.'

Hannah didn't want to tell him that she didn't want to go home, because she knew it would upset him. Her mother never left her like her father did, yet sometimes in a peculiar way she wasn't really there either. Since her baby died her mother was often in a trance, her mind elsewhere. She would cry silently to herself too. Hannah was afraid to disturb her on those occasions for fear she might dissolve and sink in her own tears.

Once she asked her was she crying and her mother denied it, saying in a robust voice, 'Don't be silly. Of course I'm not crying.' Hannah knew otherwise and felt compelled to do something to make her mother happy again.

Chapter 5

Sometimes in the long evenings her mother allowed Hannah to wait on the dockside for her father. A great part of her world was connected with the island that sat in green waters, fire spitting from its yawning mouth, while it distilled its steel and guarded its secrets. Hannah christened it 'Dragon Island' and longed to go there. It was forbidden territory to everyone apart from the men employed there. The ferry unloaded them every evening at six o'clock. Men with granite faces, men with scarred faces. Tired and shabby men who respected the island and its secrets. Hannah decided she would get a job on the island and look into the mouth of the dragon who sucked her daddy into its molten heat each morning and disgorged him, charred from the smoke and exhausted, in the evenings.

As a long beam from the lighthouse lit up a strip of sea, her father disembarked, surrounded by a group of workmen. The sight of him always delighted her. His strength, his bigness. The pleasure of seeing him in the distance, head and shoulders above the crowd, was renewed.

'Daddy,' she called out, running to plant a kiss on the dark side of his face.

'Hello, lovey. How was school today?' He took her hand as they walked home together.

When they were together like this Hannah did not want any brothers or sisters to take his undivided attention from her. This was her time and she guarded it like a jealous lover. He was all she wanted when they were together, only her time with him was precious little.

She knew she had the power to draw her parents close because she was the centre of their little circle. When there was an upheaval she blamed herself and felt the enormous weight of her responsibility. Then she longed for a brother or sister. Her father drew close to her when there was trouble between her parents. He would take her for walks along the rocks, explaining their formation, telling her their names. They gathered coloured shells, different shaped stones, birds' feathers, treasures the sea delivered up to them. Her parents had rarely spoken to each other since the baby died. Their silence often made Hannah want to scream. It was worse than the terrible rows they had when her mother blamed him for her losing the baby.

In the dull kitchen her mother leaned out the window to take the washing off the pulley line.

'Here, take these, Hannah.' She searched blindly for her daughter's outstretched hands.

Hannah took the dry clothes from her.

'I'm afraid to look down in case I fall into that dirty coalyard.'

There was a knock on the door.

'I'd better shut this window first before the ceiling caves in with the draught.'

Mrs Ryan stood there, her black hair half-hidden in a red chiffon scarf, her knitting needles flying in and out of an intricately patterned sweater. Her wool was tightly secured under her elbow.

'You shouldn't be leanin' outa the window like that. Get himself to bring them in. Why don't ya?' Her needles flew as fast as her tongue. 'Mind you they make themselves scarce when they could be useful around the place.'

'That's right,' her mother agreed.

'Feelin' any better after the holiday?' Mrs Ryan scrutinised her mother's face while her fingers raced through the stitches.

'Much better, thanks.'

'I suppose you'll be off again soon.'

Her mother looked puzzled. 'I wasn't planning on going anywhere ...'

Mrs Ryan gave a raucous laugh.

'I mean that you'll be pregnant again before long. A young healthy one like you will have a clatter of them.' She stopped to readjust her wool. 'Anyway, I really came down to apologise.'

'Apologise?' Her mother was astounded.

'For keeping ye awake at night.' Lips pursed tightly, she started a new row of frenzied knitting.

'But you're not keeping us awake.' Hannah watched the incredulous expression on her mother's face.

'Ah, go on. You're too polite. I said to Pat, Mrs below is very polite. She wouldn't complain about it. Too much of a lady.'

Hannah mentally thought through the night sounds that kept her awake. The shunting trains, the whining foghorn. All the while she kept watching the puzzled look on her mother's face.

'I hear the baby's bottle falling out of the cot,' she said and her mother nudged her to be quiet.

'It's Pat's fault. He has to have it every single night. I keep telling him to go easy. Takes no notice.' She burst out laughing.

Hannah's mother's face reddened as Mrs Ryan's dark eyes caught hers again and held them.

'It's all because of the accident.'

'Accident?'

'He was hit by a hurley in the balls and had to have one of them removed. The surgeon, a top man in Cork, warned me mind that he'd be very sexy with only the one ball left, like. Being young and foolish I thought that was grand. Begod I've stopped laughin' this long time.'

'Hannah, go up and start your homework. I won't be long.' Hannah ran upstairs and hid behind her bedroom door, listening.

'The worst of it is I'm frigid. Can't stand sex at all. I just lie there until he's finished. That don't bother him. It's not me who's makin' all the rumpus. Still I hope we're not disturbin' ye.'

'I ... no ... never... honestly.' Even from where she stood Hannah could feel her mother's embarrassment.

'Don't know where he gets the energy. After the last baby, I said, "No more," but sure he don't know the meanin' of the word. It keeps him good-humoured, I suppose.'

'That sleeve is nearly finished,' her mother said.

'We'd move into the back bedroom only it's damp. The oul house is so shaky, 'tis a wonder we don't fall through the ceilin' down on top of ye.'

'You've wonderful hands. How do you knit so fast?'

'Years of practice. The faster I knit the quicker I get paid. A shillin' an ounce. Comes in handy when you're rearin' children without a proper job. Keeps me occupied. Pat don't say much at the best of times. There's no need for words in that game. It isn't like Scrabble.'

'I'd better get their supper.'

'Don't get depressed. Call up anytime.'

'Thanks. I will.'

Hannah watched Mrs Ryan from the half-open door as she went up the stairs. Her dark hair, caught in a sunbeam from the landing window, shone glossy. Her skin was milk and honey soft. When she smiled she was beautiful.

'The shoal of herrin' will be in soon. Would you like to come down to the harbour?' she called back.

'I'd love to.'

They went to the beach on sunny days, walking two miles along the coast road. The diffused light played magic tricks on the little islands strewn out across the bay. The colours changed from emerald to blue to grey in a minute. Hannah made sandcastles for her imaginary king and queen, their extended family and servants. She stuck a flag made out of sweet wrappers on top of the centre turret, to indicate that the royal family were in residence. There were hundreds of rooms.

Children from the next village approached her, eyed her surreptitiously, the bundles of seaweed they were gathering to sell to the local fertilizer factory tucked securely under their arms. Some were barefoot. Others wore rotten boots.

'What's that?' They looked aggressively at Hannah.

'A sandcastle.' She glanced over to the rocks where her mother was sitting.

'It was, you mean.' Laughing loudly they kicked it, sending the carefully crafted turrets flying in a flurry of sand.

Hannah started to cry.

'Go away,' her mother shouted.

Hannah never made sandcastles again. She made tiny cups and saucers for her doll's picnic and hid them under the rug.

The fishing trawlers finally came into the little port early in November. Their arrival was heralded by gulls screeching, their raucous cries signalling to the women that the shoal of herring was here at last.

Traders came and fish were weighed, dead-eyed, their skin glistening silvery green in the light. Hannah watched the men seal bargains with spitting handshakes, over huge weighing scales, before trudging home. Mrs Ryan's pram was full. Hannah could tell by the way her mother looked longingly at Mrs Ryan's baby in his pram that she envied her.

'These are gorgeous fried, or baked, or even stuffed with oatmeal.'

'We'll be eating them forever,' Hannah's mother said, looking at the pile of skins in front of her.

'What harm! They're nutritious and free.'

They were in Mrs Ryan's kitchen watching her bloodied hands dexterously gutting the herrings.

'Himself might have a job down the docks,' said Mrs Ryan.

'That's great news.'

'Says he'll buy me one of the houses up at the top of the town, so I can look down on everyone,' she laughed. 'The new ones with the fertility room out the back.'

Her mother looked aghast. 'Oh, you mean utility?'

'That's what I said. I could put all the washing and vegetables there outa the way. Get a washing machine.'

'I wouldn't mind a fertility room myself.'

'What's a fertility room, Mammy?' Hannah asked.

'Go and play with the lads and don't annoy me.'

'Mr Murphy below isn't well.' Mrs Ryan was coating the fish in flour. Hannah lingered to watch.

'What's wrong with him?'

'According to Mrs Lee, it's his heart. Not surprising when you think of the size of her. She'd crush him to death in a fit of passion.'

'Hannah, I told you to go off and play.'

'Pat thinks he's got vagina of the heart because he's on painkillers. He goes very purple betimes.'

Hannah's mother burst out laughing.

'It's no laughing matter. I hope he doesn't drop dead climbing those stairs. I'm squeamish.'

'You're not squeamish when it comes to gutting herrings.'

Hannah watched the gulls wheeling in disarray across rooftops and trawlers, their mawkish cries carrying in the wind. Defiantly they closed in on the huge Dutch trawler docked at the opposite pier. It was there when she woke up, massive and solid, like a building, the gulls challenging it to unleash its cargo. The rain swept over the sea and lashed against the vessel. Still the ravenous gulls weaved around it, relentless in their pursuit of food. Watching them tear the scrap the squat Dutch fishermen flung them, and listening to their din, Hannah felt scared. They had called and cried from early dawn, evoking an unexplained fear in her.

Her mother was reading a letter. 'I have to go away for a few days, Hannah. Mrs. Ryan is going to mind you in the daytime. Daddy will be here in the evenings.'

'Where are you going? Grannie's?'

'Yes. She's not very well. I want to see her.'

'Why can't I come?'

'You can't miss school. Anyway I won't be away too long.'

Hannah didn't mind staying up in the Ryan's flat. She liked listening to Mrs Ryan, and the boys played with her. She felt again that gnawing sense of anxiety, but it was only later, from hints and guesses, that she was to have any inkling of where her mother went and who she met there.

Mary hadn't slept since she had got the letter from John inviting her to join him in Connemara for a few days. She hadn't expected to hear from him again. Their parting and her guilt were still open wounds waiting to be healed by time. Cowardice prevented her from casting off the shackles of her life. And fear of losing Hannah. There was a telephone number for her to contact.

She took the train to Galway, still dazed by the lies and the upheaval that had made her journey possible. Her deception caused her the greatest unease. As the bus took her through the narrow Connemara roads she became nervous of meeting John again. The mountains loomed large, their peaks hidden by clouds that threatened rain, and gave the landscape a wildness and harshness that Mary had never seen before. Small thatched cottages were scattered here and there, turf stacked neatly to one side.

The bus negotiated bends and dips around lakes dotted with islands. Further inland, the barren, desolate and rainwashed countryside, where sheep and cattle wandered aimlessly, caused Mary to reconsider the wisdom of her decision to come.

The bus stopped suddenly.

'This is your stop, Missus,' the driver called to her.

She walked past tall hedgerows up a narrow hill to the Post Office.

'I'm looking for Slíabh Bán cottage.' She extended the piece of paper for the elderly woman behind the counter to see.

'About a half mile further up the hill.' She adjusted her glasses, and returned the piece of paper to Mary.

'Are you here for a bit of a holiday?' Her eyes were fastened on Mary's small suitcase.

'Just a day or two.' Mary began to retreat but her inherent politeness stopped her at the door when the postmistress said, 'I've seen a few strange faces around. Hope the weather picks up.'

'Yes. Thank you.'

The smoke curled up out of the chimney of the little whitewashed cottage that squatted into the hill. Mary almost ran to the red painted door. The rain began to spatter down as the door opened. She fell into his arms.

'Mary.' He held her tightly. 'I thought you'd never get here.'

He drew her into the warm kitchen.

'Let me take your coat. You're frozen.'

'It's so isolated. I was beginning to wonder if I was in another country when the bus stopped.'

'Isn't that what we want?'

They kissed, unleashing a violent passion with their embraces. He started undressing her before they got to the bedroom, unlocking a whole new sensual world with some secret key. For the next few days they lived in a state of permanent arousal. They worshipped one another with their lovemaking and blunted their guilt with continual passion.

'If we were married you'd have real sex all the time,' he said.

'Don't say that. It only makes it worse.'

'Lovemaking is another form of art. It needs practice to perfect it. We haven't time ...' He looked sadly away.

When they weren't making love they lay in each other's arms in the double bed and kissed. Mary told him about losing her baby.

'Why didn't you tell me before?'

'It was too soon. I went home to forget. I thought the pain would go eventually.'

'And did it?'

'No. It's always there. Even when I'm engrossed in something else or talking to someone it is there at the back of my mind. The only way I'll get over it is to have another baby.

The way things are with Tom ...' Her voice trailed off.

He took her in his arms and rocked her gently like a baby. She basked in his adoration of her, feeling both tantalised and captive.

The rain clouds cleared and the newly washed countryside looked fresh and clean. They walked along the little grey road that ribboned the sea and padded through the sandy beach. The sun came up edging the water in a silvery light as they picked their way between jutting rocks. They undressed and swam together, naked and uninhibited. Only the sheep grazing on the nearby slopes noticed them. Afterwards they sat and watched the sea, a sheet of silver, rhythmic and undulating, cocooning them in gentle unreality.

'I hate the sea at home. It unnerves me. Always outside the window, roaring like a raging lion. Here it calms me,' Mary said.

'Because here it's magic.'

They swam again next day in the cold waters and he towelled her dry with longing in his eyes. They ate prawns and Galway Bay oysters in a tiny restaurant with a flagged floor in Cleggan. They drank in the local pubs, integrating themselves with the people.

She never mentioned Hannah, but she thought about her. What if she woke in the night? Would Tom be there for her? Was what she was doing worth it all? Sometimes, in her euphoria with John, she was convinced it was. At other times despair over the life she had to go back to overtook her. All the time she knew she couldn't help herself. Her emotional pendulum swung crazily from one extreme to the other. When John asked her to stay with him and not return to Cork, she became manic. He saw the recurring tides of her conflicting emotions.

'Leave him. Come and live with me. I don't care about the gossip and scandal.'

'Hannah matters more than anybody else in the whole world. I have to go back to her.' She saw the pain in his eyes, he saw the fear in hers and didn't persist.

'I'll always love you,' he said when they were parting.

Hannah was waiting on the steps for her. Nancy was a discreet distance behind.

'Mammy, Mammy.' Her thin arms entwined Mary in a grasp that nearly choked her.

'Daddy's home.' She loosened her grip.

Mary looked at her watch. 'It's only four o'clock. Why is he home so early?'

'I don't know.' Hannah ran ahead.

Mary climbed the stairs with the same feeling of revulsion she always got when she returned to this place.

Tom was waiting at the living-room door.

'Hello,' she said.

He looked past her at the children.

'Go up to Mrs Ryan's and play. I'll call you in a while.'

'But Daddy, Mammy's only home. I want to talk ...'

'Do what you're told at once,' he shouted.

They backed away, incredulous, then turned and ran.

'That's a bit harsh. I'm only ...'

'Only what?' His eyes bore into hers.

'I'm only back.' She put down her suitcase.

Suddenly he caught her arm and pulled her into the living-room, slamming the door.

'You'd better start talking.' His voice was low, his eyes ablaze. 'Where were you? Don't give me that shit about your mother either.'

'I don't know what you're talking about.' She tried to free herself.

'You're a liar and not even a good one,' he spat out.

'How ... who ... what ...?' Her voice faded every time she tried to form the words.

'You may well ask. What a damn fool I've been to have ever believed a word out of your lying mouth.' He slapped her across the face.

Her hand went involuntarily to where he'd hit her.

'I thought I married a decent girl. You're nothing but a lying, cheating slut. You're no better than the whores out there parading up and down by the trawlers. Look at them.' He dragged her to the window by the hair forcing her to look out at the Dutch trawler moored below.

'You're hurting me,' she cried but she didn't try to pull away.

He wasn't listening. 'How's Hannah going to like it when she finds out what her mother really is? Answer me, slut.'

He pushed her from him. The impact of her head against the wall sent her sliding slowly to the floor.

'Don't ...' she whimpered trying to focus her eyes.

'Can't bear to face the truth? You still haven't told me where you were and who you were with?'

He pulled her to her feet.

His face was dangerously close.

'I want to know.'

She froze for a second, then slid under his arm to escape behind the settee.

He leaned across the settee and grabbed her.

'Who?

'John.'

'I thought so. The bastard. Where?'

'Where?'

'You heard me. Where?' he shouted.

'Galway.'

He hit her again. The blow from his fist caught her on the side of the head. She slumped dizzily to the floor.

'Have your bags packed and be gone by the time I get back.' His face was unrecognisable with temper.

After what seemed like ages, Mary recovered sufficiently to crawl on her hands and knees upstairs.

'Oh, sweet divine God. What happened?' Mrs Ryan helped her into the kitchen.

'He lost the head,' Mary whispered, sipping the water Mrs Ryan gave her. Hannah was crouching in the corner, an ashed-faced waif. She had heard the shouting, uncomprehending.

'He's been acting strange all day. Ever since the telegram arrived.'

'What telegram?'

'Didn't he tell you? There was a telegram last evening to say that your mother had passed away. He went frantic, looking everywhere for you.'

Mary fainted.

Mrs Ryan put her arms around her and called to the gaping children, 'Get another glass of water. Quick.'

When Mary came to, her limbs felt like jelly. She was propped up in bed, the Ryan family gazing down at her in wonderment, Hannah among them white and snivelling.

'Mammy what happened? Did you fall?'

'Those stairs are lethal,' Mrs Ryan obliged. 'I knew someone'd get injured on them.'

She didn't unpack. She put Hannah's clothes in a separate bag and they left that evening for Tipperary.

Chapter 6

The novices went into retreat for the week leading up to their profession. During that time they maintained complete silence, listening to the advice of their spiritual director, Father Joseph, a Jesuit from Miltown Park, and to Mother Clement's final instructions. They prayed and meditated all day, even during meals. Hannah used this time to clear her mind of all doubts about her life as a nun, and deepen her love of God.

Mother Clement read from Genesis. 'It is not good that man should be alone. I will make him a helpmate.' Then she went on to deal with the vow of chastity. 'The guideline on how to handle the vow of chastity is simple. Mortification of the flesh. The early virgins dressed like men to renounce their femininity. Saint Joan wore a soldier's uniform and protected her femininity with a shield. Our habits are our shield. Almost all the saints were virgins. It is a higher calling. Virginity gives us independence and autonomy and enables us to concentrate on God's holy will, without earthly distractions.

The virgin knew no pain of pregnancy and childbirth, Saint Ambrose pointed out, so she was freed from the curse of Eve. Few people are natural celibates. Only by celibacy and virginity can we conquer our bodies. From now on they will be dead to the world. We will adopt the role of the Virgin Mary, celebrating the glory of virginity with the most illustrious virgin of the Church, the mother of God.'

Hannah was thinking of Stephen. He had written to her from Dublin where he was doing parish work while waiting to be called to the missions. He was well and wished her great happiness and joy in her life as a nun.

She was remembering back to the day he had left the convent. He came across her planting shrubs in a discarded part of the garden, where the path narrowed.

'I didn't know you had green fingers,' he said, surprised to see her digging vigorously, veil pinned back, face red from exertion.

Hannah's laughter carried in the wind. 'I haven't the faintest idea what I'm doing. I'm following Mother Agatha's instructions.' She stood back to survey her work.

He lifted a plant to place into the hole she had dug.

'That rhododendron should thrive in this soil.'

He filled the soil in around it and pressed it down with the toe of his shoe. 'That'll do the trick.'

'You're no stranger to planting.'

He shrugged. 'Farmer's son. Have you time for a short walk?'

Hannah said yes, giving time and the Rule no consideration.

They walked along the path.

'I wanted to talk to you.'

'Yes?'

He stopped and reached for her hands, but unable to circumvent the conduct of years, released them as if they scorched his own.

'Hannah, I'm leaving tomorrow. They're sending me to a parish in Dublin.'

She saw the fire in his eyes and the dampness on his brow, as he raked back his hair.

She gazed steadily at him, then looked away and said, 'I'll miss you.'

'I have to get away, Hannah. Do you understand?'

'Did you ask to be transferred?'

There was silence before he said, 'It wasn't easy. Discipline and self-control have kept me going these last couple of months.'

'I know. You're the only one I've been close to since I entered the convent.'

'Why did you enter?' He watched her intently as she spoke.'

I come from an unhappy home. My parents rejected one another, and fought battles over me. It was one struggle after another. I entered to do something useful with my life, perhaps help people like my parents in their struggles and rejections.'

'Are you sure that's what God wants from you?'

'I'm sure I have a vocation. God will show me what he wants of me as time goes on, if I listen to him.'

'I think what's happening to us is a test of our faith.'

'Yes.'

'I have wondered about my vow of celibacy. Is it worth the struggle? The loneliness? Knowing I can never share in another person's life, or do the ordinary things other people take for granted.'

'God wants you. There are people out there in Africa waiting for you to help them. You're doing something you didn't choose to do. You were chosen. He wants you to work for him. You can give him your undivided attention only by remaining celibate. You're hardly going to say no to God now, Stephen?'

'Damn it. Does God know the extent of the sacrifice he's asking? That we have to give up everything for him?'

'Yes, he does. That's why he only asks his friends to follow him.'

He looked straight at her. 'I had no trouble with my vow of celibacy until I met you. Now it's the most difficult part of my life as a priest.'

Hannah's face went crimson.

'I'm sorry. I don't mean to upset you,' he said.

'You need to talk to someone more qualified than me about your life.' She hesitated. 'Your vocation isn't something you can disregard from time to time. It's a life-long commitment. Celibacy is part of it.'

'I admire your strength. My problem is that I think I've fallen in love with you, Hannah.' Their eyes met.

'You can't, Stephen. Neither can I. I would make you very unhappy. How could you live with your conscience?'

'Maybe I'd rather be with you and settle for unhappiness with my conscience.'

'You're not making sense. You're not in love. You hardly know me.'

'I know enough to know that I'm happy when I'm with you. You're lovely.'

'I'm honoured and flattered and I care for you.' Hannah blurted it all out, then turned away, hiding her face so he would not see the emotions evoked by her words. 'Don't throw it all away, Stephen,' she said. 'You have to give your vocation a fair try.'

He shrugged. 'Thanks for your strength, Hannah. Thanks for everything.'

'Good luck.'

There was an awkwardness between them.

'I'll write.' The words were barely audible.

She stood before him, a silent captive of her own human frailty. Young, beautiful, her transparent skin sprinkled with freckles, the red-gold hair that framed her veil shining in the sun. He was sick with love for her as he walked away.

Hannah lifted her spade and began digging, digging, digging.

She did not watch him go. Afterwards she thanked God that he did not try to touch her, because she would not have had the strength to resist him.

After he left she had several harrowing days with Mother Clement. Stitching her way through endless patches of darning, her fingers bled from the pricks of her unskilled needle. She was thinking of him, riveted by an intense desire to be with him, a desire that prevented her from concentrating on her duties. She told herself that he was firmly anchored in his vows, as she was in hers. That his declaration of love for her was infatuation, moving in that familiar pattern where the person one wants is always beyond one's reach.

Mother Clement's looks of frustration made it unbearable for her to face each day. Finally she sent for her.

'Have you any reason to give for your general inertia, Sister?'

'No, Mother.' Hannah bowed her head.

Steepling her fingers, Mother Clement looked sternly at her and said, 'I think you are aware, Sister, that you are not living the life required of you. Unless your approach to the religious life and your commitment to God improves, we may be forced to reconsider your vocation. Dismissed.'

The magnitude of the whole appalling mess suddenly burst open and Hannah found herself weeping at Mother Clement's feet, begging forgiveness for her sins. Not once did she mention Stephen.

Used to sleeping coffin fashion, she lay still, her hands joined, thinking of him. She found no pleasure in her recollections. Only distorted pain, and a paralysis of the senses. Confused and unrecognisable to herself, she worried about never seeing him again. She wept without sound or movement, and tried to pray.

In the morning life seemed normal, but the walls crushed her in. Hannah realised that she loved Stephen, and from then on life took on a new dimension. Each moment was enhanced and magnified so that she felt tenderness for all around her. Simple things like early morning bird song, the dawn breaking, heightened her senses. In her mind's eye she could see his face. Over and over she would describe him to herself. Silently, at prayer, she felt the loneliness of her decision, and with it the unbearable pain of their parting.

During recreation she took no part in any of the conversations. Mother Clement noticed her silence and the inhibited expression on her face.

'Sister Marie Claire barely speaks a word,' she reported to Reverend Mother. 'She was always so full of life.'

'I'll talk to her. Perhaps she's having doubts about her vocation.'

Hannah walked alone in the grounds on autumn evenings. The distant lights of the town quivered in the wind. It was enough to know that he existed, she told herself. Looking down through the barren gardens she could visualise him. As long as he inhabited the world she was not alone. She imagined him kneeling, his head resting in his hands, praying. The lamplight would reflect the gold of his hair. His features would be perfectly still in his contemplation of God. She missed him, his nearness, his presence which she had grown dependent on. Even in the silence she missed him.

'If thy right eye scandalise thee, pluck it out and cast it from thee. For it is expedient for thee that one of thy members should perish rather than that thy whole body be cast into hell.' Mother Clement closed the book.

Eyes cast down, faces expressionless, the novices knelt in a circle around the room, each one waiting with dread for the final confession of her faults in public before her profession. Hannah felt tense as the first novice approached the centre, knelt before Reverend Mother and began, in trembling voice, her list of faults committed during the week. When it came to Hannah's turn she knelt down, and with her face withdrawn into the darkness began, 'Dear Mothers and Sisters in

Christ, I accuse myself of having committed many faults.' She quoted from her prepared mental list. Faults committed against charity, patience, humility. Sins against her vow of obedience.

All the time her mind was focused on the real sin she had committed. 'I accuse myself of many faults against modesty ...' She wanted to scream aloud that she had fallen in love. That without Stephen life was meaningless. How could she make a good nun after this encounter with love? This was a real sin and she wanted them all to know about it. The tiny boring faults she was confessing were futile compared to her sin against chastity. She wanted to say, 'God is not the only one I love. I love someone who is flesh and blood. Someone I can see, talk to, listen to. Someone human.' Instead she said, 'I ask to be forgiven for speaking out of turn, not keeping the silence, making too much noise when I walked in the corridor. For these and for all my faults I am sorry and ask your pardon.' Her voice shook as she waited in the interminable silence.

'You may be seated.'

Tears stung her eyes as she returned to her place. How could she ever say she was sorry for feeling something as beautiful as the love she had for another human being?

She went to her last confession as a novice.

'Bless me, Father. I have fallen in love with a priest.' Her voice trembled as she waited in the darkness for the response.

'When, my child?' The voice humoured her gently.

'Recently, Father. Several months ago.'

'I see. Have you overcome these feelings of ... ahem ...' the priest coughed, 'love, whether real or imagined, by now, Sister?'

'No, Father.'

Silence.

'You realise, Sister, that it is the easiest thing in the world for a nun to develop let's say, a crush, for want of a better word, on another person. Loving God is lonely. Say three Hail Marys for your penance and put all thoughts of him from your mind.'

Hannah kept her eyes on her plate while she listened intently to the words of the reading delivered that evening at supper. 'In order to triumph more effectively over the unruliness of the flesh, we must renounce even lawful pleasure.'

She had no appetite and began to lose weight. Reverend Mother sent for Her.

'You look wretched. Are you ill, Sister?'

'No, Mother. I'm alright, thank you.'

'It's your duty to report to matron any sign of fatigue or illness. You know that, dont you?'

'Yes, Mother.'

'Your parents are alright? No problems at home?'

'No, Mother.'

Reverend Mother knew better than Hannah how things were at home.

'You haven't changed your mind about your vocation?'

'No Mother.' Their eyes met.

'Come and talk to me anytime if there's something troubling you, my child. These last weeks are crucial to your future as a nun.'

'Yes, Mother.'

Reverend Mother searched her face. 'Remember, Sister, the devil is at his most active now.'

'I will, Mother.' Hannah rose, bowed her head for Reverend Mother's blessing and left.

Reverend Mother's eyes followed the gaunt figure, lost in the long black robes, and wondered what had happened to the lovely bright girl who had come to them less than three years before. The fact that she was about to be professed hardly caused the anxiety that had reduced her to a waif-like creature whose spirit seemed crushed under the weight of her habit. She would keep an eye on her and if her appearance did not improve she would send for the doctor.

'Watch ye and pray that ye enter not into temptation.'

'The spiritual life consists principally of love.'

'Mortification of the body must be practised at all times.' Reverend Mother's eyes followed Hannah, whether she was walking in the corridor, scrubbing tables, or polishing endless wooden floors.

Hannah kept her eyes averted and worked harder than ever, convinced that Reverend Mother knew her secret. Life seemed normal but she felt threatened. The distant lake squinted knowingly at her. Hannah felt lonely and vulnerable, her secret withdrawing her from her community. Her training in discretion and tact were too ingrained in her to even let a flicker of a smile or a blink of an eye give away her feelings. There was too much notice taken of her movements as it was.

During mealtime there was no head turning, no talking, no looking at other novices. Not even in a crisis. Everything had to be eaten. Sometimes Hannah took a second helping of the monotonous food because she was being observed. During spiritual reading they were told that Saint Therese ate the leftovers. Her sisters said she would eat anything; the truth was that she hardly had any appetite at all. Hannah often wondered if she herself would ever be transformed from a girl to a nun.

The organ played softly in the background as the novices approached the altar in single file. There was silence and then the bishop entered the packed chapel from the sacristy, accompanied by his assistants.

The organ burst forth as the voices in the choir rose in joyful unison. All eyes were riveted on the four young women, dressed as brides, each carrying a bouquet of flowers.

Hannah approached the bishop.

'In the name of the Father and of the Son and of the Holy Spirit,' she blessed herself.

'What do you wish for, my daughter?'

'Consecrated to God in Baptism, I dedicate myself to Him totally in religious profession for the Church and all people, following Christ in his poverty and obedience. In a life consecrated to celibacy, lived in communion, under the special protection of Mary, Virgin Mother of God. In the presence of my community gathered here, I commit myself to God and vow to observe celibacy for the sake of the Kingdom. To embrace voluntary poverty and to offer the gift of total obedience for my whole life according to the Constitution of the Sisters of Good Counsel and so share in Christ's healing mission to the world.'

'Do you intend to persevere faithfully in all the rules and constitutions of this Order?'

'I do.'

'What God has begun in you may He Himself make perfect.'

The bishop made the sign of the cross on her forehead. Her solemn interrogation was over. He then placed a silver ring on the third finger of her right hand, a symbol of her betrothal to Christ. The choir sang the 'Magnificat', as the newly professed nuns prostrated themselves on the altar.

'I know that my redeemer liveth,' intoned the bishop.

The incense enveloped her as she lay with her forehead touching the ground, inwardly beseeching her new bridegroom to make her a perfect lover.

It was over. In the vestry they were clothed in their black habits. Hannah stood still as Sister Gerald attacked her beautiful hair with a scissors which was almost the size of a sheers, and hacked it off. The burnished curls fell to the floor, dull and lifeless. She never flinched as the wimple was placed on her head, then the hood. Blinkered, she returned to the chapel to receive the veil from the bishop, another symbol of her marriage to Christ.

At last she was really a nun, committed to a life of dedication and sacrifice. Mentally she ran through her vows. Poverty, chastity, obedience. They released her from earthly responsibilities, to allow her to pursue a life of striving for spiritual perfection.

When the ceremony was over, she followed the other brides out of the chapel, clumsy in her new habit. The sunlight struck her face and she blinked as she moved further into the cloistered garden. She closed her eyes against the stark light and when she opened them her father was standing there, an embarrassed smile on his face. He touched her cheek with his finger. This gesture more than anything made her realise that he had finally accepted her decision to become a nun.

Looking at him she thought of the time he had lived away from home. How she had imagined him lonely and lost, waiting to be sent for, waiting for her mother's acceptance again. Now she felt that same isolation in him and her heart lurched. The sun danced behind the trees and reflected its yellow light off her silver crucifix, making it dazzle.

Her father moved away from her, allowing himself to endure this torture for her sake, and she almost cried at the realisation of the pain and sorrow she had inflicted on him by entering the convent.

Her mother was talking to the nuns, her young brother David hopping from one leg to the other, impatient for the promised feast. They were being introduced to other families, her mother unaware of her father's heartbreak. They looked so divided. Hannah moved towards him and he leaned forward.

'Well, Hannah, you look beautiful.' He gazed at her shining eyes and looked away, an unhappy smile on his face.

'I'm happy, Daddy. It's what I want.'

'I know.' He gave her hand a squeeze, almost begging her not to say anything.

She was near enough to him to smell his aftershave. Today it gave her no comfort. His loneliness separated them. Hannah, suddenly aware of the light banter and laughing voices around them, realised how isolated his sadness at the loss of his daughter made him.

The three-storey over basement house in Waterloo Road was Hannah's new home for the duration of her university studies. With its three-bedded dormitories, refectory, and tiny chapel, it was referred to as a mini-convent by its six occupants, all students, except for Mother Terence, their Reverend Mother. Hannah's day started at half-past five with meditation, mass, and then breakfast. At half-past eight she left to join the queues of people, pushing and jostling for buses. It was a different world, one her convent training had not equipped her for.

Now two months into her degree course she was becoming acquainted with her subjects, psychology and social administration. Next year she would take politics and economics. The long-haired, noisy undergraduates were distant at first. Gradually they smiled and began to draw her into their conversations. She was glad to have shed the billowing veil for a short blue one, and the long skirt of the habit for a neat blue suit.

Later, listening to her tutor discussing the merits of social administration in the social structure, she felt as confident as her peers. In the convent she could think things out peacefully. It was the coffee breaks which paralysed her with fear. Everyone around her chatted and laughed and gave her embarrassed smiles, not knowing whether to rush past her, or engage her in conversations she was not supposed to participate in. Running for the bus to get her back to her convent for lunch at one o'clock, which was followed by prayers, exhausted her. As time went on there never seemed to be any opportunity to relax, or think, with more lectures in the afternoon, then study, supper, Compline and bed.

Sitting in front of Reverend Mother for instruction on religious life, Hannah's eyes began to close.

'Sister Marie Claire, you're falling asleep. That won't do at all.'

Hannah was jolted into an upright position and gripped her hands tightly together to make herself concentrate on what Reverend Mother was saying.

'You must make sure you don't lose sight of your ideals. The development of spiritual maturity is your primary concern. Your social studies, Sister, come second. Remember that at all times.

As Hannah became more integrated in college life she found it more difficult to concentrate on the spiritual side of her life.

Reverend Mother called her into her office.

'You seem to be in a spin, Sister. Always rushing around. Late for meals, prayers.'

'I'm sorry, Mother. It's a very tight schedule.'

'I realise that. Perhaps if you took a sandwich with you. Would that give you more time?'

'I'd miss prayers, Mother.'

'I think we can rely on you to say them yourself, at your desk. As long as you don't see too much of the students, waste time talking. Your dependence is on God, on him alone.'

'Yes, Mother. Thank you for your consideration.'

Hannah bowed her head for Mother Terence's blessing and found to her surprise that she really liked this quiet, considerate nun.

After her first term she returned to her convent in Wicklow and was consumed with loneliness for college life and its companionship.

'Let us think about the blessing of loneliness. Your silence isolates you from your community so you can contemplate God, your master.'

Hannah, listening to the spiritual reading, felt a deepening sense of loneliness. She had no one to discuss her studies with. Stephen's letters from Nigeria were her only consolation. She answered each one of them, giving details of her studies, her spiritual life, and any information about current affairs she thought he might be interested in. Never once did she say anything that could be considered personal. He always wrote back immediately, so there was a constant flow of correspondence between them. He wrote:

'The malaria has returned so I'm on large doses of Nivaquine. This means I have to take life a little easier. The parish is so widespread that without my motorbike I couldn't get around it. There's no traffic problem. I can shoot along endless miles of dirt tracks that pass for roads. Last week Father Martin and I went to Lagos for a conference. We hit a go slow that backed up for miles into the city. Here traders run through the traffic selling brushes, mops, matches. It was so long since I had seen crowds of people that I couldn't get used to it.

'The women do all the work. They carry huge baskets of wood on their heads. The men tend their cattle, buffalo mostly. Tomorrow I go to Tarkwa Bay to see an old priest who wants to return to Ireland to die.

'Life is hard. It makes it easier to cope with the loneliness when you have someone of your own to love. Write to me and tell me all about college.'

She folded the letter into her pocket. It made her feel less alone and helped her through her day. Deep down she worried that her contact with him was dangerous, then dismissed the notion as nonsense. It was only an occasional letter sent across thousands of miles. She was glad he was far away.

College was waking Hannah up to a different kind of life. A worldly one. Watching girls her own age, confident, bursting with enthusiasm, arms entwined with their boyfriends, fascinated her. So did the mini-skirts that barely concealed their bodies. She realised how much she wanted to continue her life as a nun. To follow Jesus, her beloved friend. To be passionately involved with him and no other. She prayed for acceptance of her self-imposed exile from life. Her studies gave her solace in her world of isolation.

Chapter 7

That summer in Wicklow one of the old nuns died and Hannah's mind was catapulted back to the time she had gone with her mother to her Grannie's funeral. Nothing about the farm was the same. Red and gold leaves mingled on the muddy lane. The cows were housed in the byre, the horses moved to a neighbour's paddock. A cold wind whistled around the farmhouse bringing fog and rain in its wake. Remnants of the once luscious roses blew limply in the wind.

The biggest changes were inside. The neighbours greeted her mother with tears in their eyes. They spoke to her in whispers, making her cry in sudden bursts.

Annie threw her arms around Mary. 'She was the heart and soul of the place. What are we going to do without her?' She let the tears flood her face and Hannah wished she would make an effort to wipe them away.

'No one like her in the parish,' said Liam, the grocer.

'A wonderful neighbour,' his wife reiterated.

The men removed their caps before entering the bedroom. The women crept into the room and knelt at the foot of the bed. Her Grannie's wrinkled face was marble smooth, her hands joined together, her rosary threaded through her fingers. Only a slight indentation under the white counterpane marked her body. She reminded Hannah of a statue.

'In the name of the Father and of the Son and of the Holy Ghost.' John began the recitation of the rosary and Hannah gazed at the picture of the Sacred Heart that hung over her Grannie's bed.

Afterwards Annie served sandwiches on the blue willow patterned plates. Her mother and John served drinks. The wailing woman came later and began her keening, low and mournful, then rising to a crescendo as the pints were sunk, and pipes were smoked, in near silence.

'She's going to the church tomorrow evening, to lie under the stained-glass window she paid for,' Annie told Hannah. 'She loved that window. It was her pride and joy.'

Hannah burst into tears, thinking of her Grannie all alone in the cold church.

'What are you saying to upset the child so much?' Her mother threw Annie a look of fury, before marching Hannah off to bed.

People in their Sunday going-to-mass suits came to the village church to walk with the mourners behind the coffin. The priest spoke of the wonders of God, of his wisdom in taking Mrs O'Reilly out of her misery.

'It's not for us to question his will,' he concluded.

'Amen.'

'I didn't know she was miserable,' Danny whispered.

'She wasn't. Just old.' Hannah poked him in the ribs to shut him up.

He giggled and Annie glared at them.

The organ played 'Abide with me' and Hannah's mother cried into her handkerchief.

'It'll never be the same without her,' Annie said as they left the graveyard, her body lop-sided from her pronounced limp.

The neighbours returned to the farmhouse and the eating and drinking began all over again.

'I wonder who'll take charge ...? 'I suppose the brother in America or Australia' ... 'If they can find him'... 'Mary's husband's not here again ... At least she had a bit of time with her mother' ... 'neglected for too long'.

Hannah sat in her niche in the windowsill, listening to the babble of voices when she felt like it. She was watching out for her Daddy, sure he would come to take them home.

The farmhouse was not the same golden happy home of the holidays. Damp green patches on the whitewashed walls replaced the clinging creeper that had retreated into the earth like her Grannie.

She overheard Annie say to her mother, 'Your mother would never see you stuck for a roof over your head,' And her mother's remark, 'We don't know what's going to happen to this place ...'

Hannah moved away from the voices all buzzing together like bees in summer, greedy for the pollen of scented flowers.

She went to a dry part of the barn and sat in her old haunt, an empty feeling in her stomach.

'There you are. I was looking for you. Come down and tell me what's the matter.' John called up to her.

She shrank back.

'It's all your fault,' she shouted at him, and circled her skinny arms around her bent head so he couldn't see the tears falling down her cheeks.

'Don't be upset, love.'

'I'm not.' The answer came from deep within her sleeves.

'Your Grannie died of pneumonia. The doctor did everything he could. It was nobody's fault.'

His words evaporated into the air.

'I've got something for you.'

She pressed her arms tighter against her ears so that she couldn't hear a single word he was saying.

'Oh well, please yourself.' His footsteps faded into the distance.

Hannah waited until he was gone before running back to the house.

'Are you alright, love?' Annie hugged her. 'You're getting very pretty, you know. Just like your Grannie.'

Hannah was too polite to tell her that she thought her Grannie was dead ugly!

There were too types of magic. Good and bad. The good magic was the holiday in Grannie's farmhouse. The bad magic involved witches who cast evil spells on people like her mother and John, making them forget that her mother was married. Her father had become some sort of monster, only referred to in whispers, who sent important letters to her mother, written by someone else, the address embossed in heavy gold lettering. They made her mother cry.

Hannah began to dread the letters in long white envelopes.

She overheard John say to Mary, 'We've got to talk.'

'Things are bad enough without making them any worse,' she'd replied, wiping away her tears with her apron.

'Tom wants her back. Says she needs a regular, secure life. Says I'm not a fit mother and he'll prove it in court.'

'Oh, my God.'

Hannah, listening in the windowsill, understood the word court. Her kings, queens and fairies held court where they drank tea from delicate china cups, and ate fairy cake made of fine sponge buttercups and daisies. She wasn't afraid of court. Court was friendly. The king and queen go courting. 'Don't worry.

Let him cool his heels,' Annie advised her.

Her Daddy had hot heels. Probably from climbing up and down ladders all day, in his metal-toed shoes.

When Hannah was in bed Mary and John sat in the kitchen talking late into the night. But standing on the landing, she overheard snatches of their conversation.

'What if he comes for her?'

'He won't do that. Even he knows she needs her mother. She's only a child.' John's voice, patient and reasonable.

'He'll do anything to get back at me. He's mad as hell over what happened. He'll stop at nothing to make me suffer and he'll use Hannah as bait.'

'Mary, I think you're exaggerating. How can he look after a child and go to work? He won't jeopardise her happiness. He knows how to behave. He'll be reasonable.'

'Then why am I sitting here in my dead mother's kitchen, if he's reasonable? Was what he did to me reasonable? I admit he had cause to be angry but there was no excuse for what he did. He can talk eloquently enough to fool any judge. He's capable of passing himself off as a caring, hard-done-by husband and parent. He'll get his friends to back him up and go witness for him.

He's nothing but a loudmouth. When it suits he can charm the birds off the trees.'

Mary lost weight. Annie tried to build her up with fresh milk, egg flips with a drop of whisky in them, and a bottle of stout in the evenings. Mary hated the stout and made a funny face when she forced herself to take some.

She told Annie to stop complaining and leave her alone. She sewed. Hannah kept out of her way when she heard the whirr whirr of the old sewing machine and the squeek of the foot pedal. She cut out with a big scissors, her movements quick and jerky as she pulled the material away from her. She made a dress for Hannah and a shirt and blouse for herself. She finished off the blouse with one of her mother's lace collars.

'Take a break. Have a cup of tea,' Annie begged, but Mary sewed on relentlessly.

'I think she's gone berserk,' Annie said to John.

Hannah was disappointed with her new dress. Her body was long and shapeless in it. Danny had called her thin legs 'two straws hangin' off a loft'. She reddened with embarrassment at the thought of him seeing her now.

'It makes me look thinner than I am. Look at my arms and legs.' She put her arms out in front of her.

'If you ate your dinner instead of picking at it you'd soon cover those bones,' Annie said.

'You're skin and bone alright,' her mother agreed and Hannah was furious with her for saying it in front of Annie.

She took off the new dress, put on her jumper and skirt and sneaked off.

Everyone was either silent or angry. Annie and Mary argued quite a lot. Annie told Hannah to sweep the floor and feed the chickens. She was glad to have something to do.

The weather was bad. It rained a fine misty rain that clung to trees and hedges, and obscured the view of the mountains. The ducks had left the pond. Even the hens had stopped laying.

Hannah didn't bother going down to the orchard. The apples had either been sold or stored in a deep sandy pit.

Danny came over during the mid-term break. He was rough and show-offish.

'Watch where your goin',' he called as she rushed ahead to keep up with him. She fell in the caked mud and twisted her ankle.

'I suppose you'll go snivelling home to tell them it was my fault,' he teased, standing over her. 'Just to get me into more trouble.'

Hannah picked herself up and tested her ankle.

'I won't tell anyone.'

She hobbled home.

Danny laughed when he saw her limping. Mary, coming to the door, thought she was imitating Annie.

'How dare you mock the afflicted?' she hissed, giving Hannah a resounding slap across the face.

Hannah stared at her in astonishment, as the stinging pain spread along her jawline.

'I wasn't,' Hannah began, lower lip trembling.

Danny ran off laughing. Hannah shouted after him. 'I hate you, Danny Morris. I hate you.'

'Come inside at once. You've gone to the dogs. Too much idleness. You'll have to go to school.'

'School. Here?' Hannah cried.

'It's as good a place as any,' Mary retaliated.

'But aren't we going home? What about Daddy?'

'What about him? And don't refer to that god-forsaken place as home ever again.' With an outburst of temper Mary flung the bucket of meal she was carrying against the fence and flounced off down the path.

Hannah ran to her room and bolted the door. She ignored Annie calling her for dinner. She didn't understood her mother anymore. There was no kind word or softness in her these days. She gazed at the purplish tinge of her swelling jaw in the mirror and felt sorry for herself. Her mother didn't deserve to have her. Her father wanted her home desperately. What if he were sick and alone and couldn't get a message to her? She decided to go home, home to take care of him. Her money box was full since the funeral. She lay on her bed for a long time planning her escape. 'You'll be starting school on Monday,' Her mother said when Annie had finally coaxed her downstairs for her tea. 'It's all arranged.'

Hannah hung her head and said nothing. On Monday morning she bolted her bedroom door, dimming her mother's exasperated voice with pillows piled over her head.

'Come out at once,' she heard faintly, then footsteps on the wooden stairs and louder, 'You'd better open up, or else ...'

Something about the timbre of her mother's voice made Hannah afraid so she unlocked the door. Her mother marched into the room and dragged her across the floor to pull her into her dress. Silently she brushed her unruly hair. Hannah let herself be got ready, her head aching as the strong hairbrush was pulled through the tangled mass. She held on to the dressing-table to steady herself, her eyes watering.

'Don't send me. Please don't send me,' she begged in a small voice.

Even as she spoke she knew she was wasting her breath.

John drove her there in the lorry, rattling along the rutted road. Singing, cajoling, whistling, he refused to let her sullenness insinuate his good humour. The more he sang, the more annoyed she became until her anger spread throughout the lorry to manifest itself in stubborn silence, in answer to his questions.

Eyes diverted, jaw set, she sat stiffly, trying to prevent threatening tears from falling. Slowly he drove through the school gates and stopped. Hannah sagged back in her seat as he opened the door. He lifted her down gently.

'I'll be here at three o'clock sharp,' he said, leading her to the school door. 'You'll be waiting for me, won't you?'

She nodded, eyes diverted.

'Come on, chin up,' he whispered as a tall nun came to greet them and take Hannah into her new classroom.

The school was dark and cold inside. With swishing skirts and rattling beads the nun led her to her classroom where another nun stood in front of her class, stern-faced, lips compressed.

'Sister Celia. This is our new pupil, Hannah Dempsey.' Ice-blue eyes peered from behind steel-framed spectacles, cutting into Hannah's soul.

'Luckily you haven't missed much of this term's work because we were doing revision. Nonetheless, you'd better sit up here in the front row, until I ascertain what standard you are. Thank you, Sister.'

The other nun left without a word and class began.

Hannah shivered and took her place.

'What do we know about Wolfe Tone?' Her expressionless face was met with silence.

'Have you done Wolfe Tone yet, Hannah Dempsey?'

'No ...'

'Stand up.'

Hannah stood up and plucking up courage said, 'Miss Carey is gone to get a baby so we had no history for a while. We did drawing instead with Sister Mary.'

There was a titter around the classroom.

'Silence,' Sister Celia hissed, spraying the children immediately in front of her.

'It's a matter of complete indifference to me why you are not up to standard with your history. You'll have to learn it at home. Now sit down and pay attention,' she said with relish.

From that moment on Hannah sat in petrified silence and renewed her vow to run away as soon as the opportunity presented itself.

In the playground the children chattered in groups, or played hop-scotch on the grey concrete, calling out to one another. Their voices still retained the freedom of the long summer, as their laughter rose high above the school. Hannah hung back, watching from the shelter of a tree, wishing someone would invite her to take part. Nobody did. When the bell clanged summoning them to their classrooms, they filed silently into the dark corridors of the school, Hannah straggling behind.

At three o'clock they spilled out again, shouting and running to the freedom of the spiked railings, and their waiting mothers. Babies cried, prams were rocked as mothers chatted and dragged unwilling toddlers to them, coaxing them with sweets, or a slap across the legs. The lorry waited obediently down the road for Hannah.

The days passed in a blur of fear and bewilderment. Hannah made no attempt to make friends with anyone. She spent her lunchbreak eating her sandwiches in a corner of the yard, while the others played tig, nudging and whispering whenever they looked in her direction.

John collected her each day.

'Well, how's it going?' he'd ask, knowing the question would be met with a shrug.

He bought her lollipops and bubble gum. She blew shapeless bubbles that billowed transparently over her face and burst with a smack across her nose and mouth, in a sticky pink mess. He watched her in his rear-view mirror.

'Get that off quick before your mother sees it,' he warned.

Hannah obediently wiped her face and concentrated on the grey October sky, the light already fading as the lorry trundled back to the farm.

One morning Hannah was late because John had slept it out. The classroom went silent as she entered and went to her seat. Everyone stared at her with censorious interest.

'You're late,' Sister Celia said contemptuously.

Hannah froze.

'And what is your excuse? Let me guess. You had to milk the cows,' she sneered.

'No, Sister. We only have dry cattle on the farm.' Hannah's voice was barely audible but loud enough to cause a laugh.

'Anyone who is late for class gets the cane. You're no exception. Hold out your hand.'

In a daze of helplessness Hannah shot out her hand. As the cane made its descent she snatched it back, only to be caught across her bunched fingers. She howled in pain.

'Stand in the corner for the rest of the morning. Let that be a lesson to you and everyone else in the room. I will not tolerate lateness.'

Cringing, Hannah cowered in the corner, her eyes focused on the far wall. Her exposure made her feel like a plucked chicken. She passed the time planning her escape.

When the whistle blew after the lunch break and the children filed back into their respective classrooms, Hannah sneaked out of the school gates. She hid behind the school wall, exhilarated by the sudden sense of freedom. When the last child left the yard she sneaked along by the wall, head down. Once out of sight of the school she began to run out the Cashel road. She ran fast at first to put as much distance between herself and the school as possible, then slowed down to conserve her energy.

When she looked back the school had disappeared. Before her was the endless road and a vast expanse of countryside. At last she was going home. The young garda at the corner dispersing the last of the mothers cast her a sidelong glance. Hannah kept her eyes down, her head forward, her face hidden by a curtain of flame-red hair. She ran some of the way and walked aimlessly when her breath caught in her throat. The cold wind on her face calmed her flushed cheeks and dried her hot tears of misery.

She was never to know fully what went on back at the farm when it was discovered that she was well and truly missing. Only the odd comment as years went by indicated to her the misery she had caused her mother and father.

When John had arrived home without her, Annie searched everywhere. Disgusted at Mary's hysteria, and the pervading atmosphere of gloom that hung around the house, she decided to go and search for Hannah herself.

Taking her man-size raincoat and the stick she rarely used, she limped across the fields. Her disfigured foot, encased in its ugly boot, thumped against the ladder as she climbed heavily into the loft calling, 'Hannah, Hannah'. Her breathing grew raspish as she went from place to place looking sharply around her.

Annie hadn't scoured the farm like this since her younger days when she went searching for a missing animal. She poked the duck pond with her stick, making patterns on its scummy surface.

Her mania grew and she waded into cold, muddy water. Realising the stupidity of her dilemma, she continued over the fields, watched by the big sad eyes of the farm animals. She rested against a rock, too exhausted to continue. Finally she returned to the farmhouse, defeated.

Mary saw her coming into the yard alone and flung her hand to her mouth to stifle a sob.

Annie's whole body sagged into the nearest chair, defeat woven into every crease of her lined face and the pouches around her sagging mouth.

'I should never have sent her to school,' Mary said in a choking voice.

'I knew that but there was no point in saying anything. You wouldn't have listened.' Annie pushed back the straggly strands of hair from her forehead.

Mary burst into fresh sobs.

'Ah, shut up, for God's sake. Crying won't bring her back. Do something useful.' Annie hunched her lowered head in her hands.

'Like what?' Suddenly Mary realised that Annie couldn't care less about her. Hannah was her only concern.

'I'm old,' Annie cried. 'It doesn't matter what happens to me. But she's only a little girl. Not even able to stand up for herself. She could be in real danger.'

A breathy sigh slipped from her lips. A blue vein throbbed in her temple. Her hands plucked feverishly at the tablecloth.

'We've contacted the guards, we've contacted Tom, and we've contacted everyone who ever knew us.' Mary levelled red-rimmed eyes at her accusingly.

Annie hauled herself out of her chair and lumbered across the room. Bending stiffly she pulled open one of the drawers of the dresser and extracted a copybook. She put on her glasses and scrutinized the pages, kicking the dresser shut behind her.

'I'll contact Madge Byrne. She'll know what to do.'

With trembling hands Mary reached out to take the screwed-up old copybook. Annie snatched it back.

'Who's she?' Mary asked in a high pitched voice, the skin drawn tightly across her cheeks.

'She was once recommended to your mother when she was searchin' for Patrick. She's a fortune teller.'

'Oh God, no.' Mary looked terrified.

Annie's watery eyes flickered over her coldly. Resolutely she moved to the door, one hand on the handle, her hair already dishevelled before she'd even faced out into the wind again.

'Dry your eyes and make a bit of supper. If she comes back she'll be hungry. You should have thought of the poor child when you were carrying on with John. You thought no one noticed. You didn't make much of an effort to conceal it in front of the poor child. It was disgusting.' She drew her too large coat around her. 'You let her down.' She stood unflinching, defying Mary to deny it.

'You're just a jealous old crone. You've always been jealous of anyone who came between mother and you, even Hannah. All you're worried about is your own security. Now that you've served up your usefulness, you'll have plenty of time to brood over your misfortunes when you're in the county home.'

Annie ignored the malicious outburst. She wrapped her coat around her, a protection against the onslaught of Mary's anger as much as the cold wind. She gazed at Mary for a long moment before she left, slamming the door behind her.

Mary watched the frail shrinking woman hobble away, face set against the elements, murmuring to herself. She fell to her knees, shoulders drooped with guilt, and she began to pray. God was punishing her for what she'd done. But she felt Annie had exceeded her position in her mother's home by speaking to her like that. Even if she was right. She went into her mother's room and knelt before the picture of the Sacred Heart. If God would find Hannah she'd make some sort of compromise with him. There and then she vowed never to have anything to do with John again.

'Where is she?' she wailed pitiably to the exposed heart. 'Where is she?' Her voice rose but only the silence echoed her words.

Meanwhile Hannah trudged along. Soon she heard the engine of a car in the distance but resisted the temptation to look over her shoulder. It slowed down to a bumpety bump behind her. She walked faster.

'Hello there. Want a lift?' a gruff voice called.

She turned around.

'You're in a hurry.' The curly-haired man behind the wheel smiled, showing large teeth.

Hannah stared at him. He had a lot of hair on his head and horn-rimmed glasses.

'I live here,' she heard herself say in a high-pitched voice.

Her eyes fastened on the hair that sprouted from the curl of his ear. The hands that gripped the steering wheel were also furred with hair. His heavy eyebrows lay over the frames of his spectacles like a pair of dormant caterpillars. The more Hannah stared, the more the hair seemed to spread. It even grew in tufts across his ruddy cheeks.

Her terror rooted her to the spot.

'Well?' he said, yawning, his teeth protruding. 'Has the cat got your tongue? Where d'you live?

Are you lost?' His attendant ears seemed to grow bigger as they listened for an answer.

'I live over there.' Pulling herself together she pointed to the clump of trees in the distance. 'My mother's waiting. I have to go.'

She turned and ran towards the trees, thoughts of her mother bringing a lump to her throat.

The engine of the car spluttered into life and drove off. Hannah didn't turn to look back.

It was getting dark. The mountains had disappeared. The wind rose and carried the leaves to gather them up in heaps at corners and tree stumps.

Across the fields Hannah found a barn hidden among the trees. She ran to it for shelter. The chaff whirled around her as she climbed the rickety wooden ladder. The disused barn was shabby, but she was glad of the shelter it provided.

The wind howled. The sagging barn groaned its protest and woke Hannah.

'I'll huff and I'll puff and I'll blow your house down,' the whistling wind seemed to sigh.

Hannah resisted the temptation to get up and leave. Despair rose within her like a cold hard lump. Her earlier resolution crumbled. Images of Sister Celia stifled the sob in her throat. What was she doing in here? She hadn't done anything wrong. Her parents had rejected one another and she was the innocent victim. Unchecked tears slid slowly down her cheeks. She erased them with her tongue, their warm, salty taste comforting her until eventually she fell asleep again; but before she did, she made a solemn promise to herself that she would never return home to her mother.

Dawn light streaked in through a hole in the roof. Rubbing the sleep from her eyes, Hannah straightened her clothes and ran her fingers through her hair. She picked her steps carefully through the semi-darkness, making her way down the crooked ladder. She cautiously crossed the field, afraid she might be confronted by a bull.

When she got out on the road she walked faster.

'That child seems to be lost,' an elderly woman, on her way to the shops, remarked to her younger companion, a cross-looking woman.

The companion, unperturbed by the spectacle of a child walking alone when she should be in school, shrugged indifferently.

'She's not from around here. I've never seen a head of hair like that before,' the older woman said and, to pacify her, the companion crossed the road to interview Hannah. The old woman squinted into the morning sun, curiosity screwing up her face into papery wrinkles.

'Are you lost?'

Hannah wheeled around. Her face reddened. She stood still in front of the granite-faced woman who had barred her path.

'Are you deaf? I asked you where you're headin' for.' The impatience in the woman's voice and her interfering questions spurted Hannah into action. Suddenly she came to life and dived past her, fleeing off down the road as fast as her legs could carry her, muttering 'busybody' on her way.

'Children nowadays,' the old woman clucked. 'Ungrateful little brats.'

When Hannah finally reached the town centre, she was hungry. She went into the first sweetshop she saw. The large woman behind the counter smiled at her.

'What can I get you?' she asked, scrutinising Hannah.

'A pound of loose biscuits please,' Hannah half whispered.

'Plain or mixed?'

'Mixed.'

Her mouth watered as she watched the shopkeeper twist the corners of a brown bag into ears. Then she filled it with a delicious selection of chocolate biscuits, coconut creams, and flat nutty ones with raisins in them. When the bag was full, she weighed it, and holding it by the edges, twirled it.

'That'll be a shilling, please.'

Hannah took her purse from her coat pocket where she'd kept it all week, and carefully took out some coins. The woman handed over the bag of biscuits.

'You won't lose any of them. Unless you eat them on the way home.' She shot Hannah a meaningful look.

'Thanks,' Hannah said.

'Does your mother know where you are?' The unexpected question deflected Hannah for a second.

'Yes. These biscuits are for her. We're having lots of visitors today.'

'Did she keep you home from school to help her?'

Hannah surveyed the face, pinched with curiosity, the calculating eyes, and was suddenly frightened.

She ran to the door and pushed it open with all her strength. A bell tinkled and a small bald man appeared behind the counter from nowhere.

'Strange child,' remarked the woman, her eyes following Hannah's retreating figure.

'And hungry too.' The little man was watching Hannah already dipping into the bag of biscuits as she rounded the corner.

She walked along the path, wondering if it would be safe to ask where the train station was. She munched her biscuits and moved into the grass verge to let someone pass. She heard running footsteps and walked faster, not daring to look round. The footsteps sounded closer. She broke into a run.

'Hey. Stop.' She turned suddenly to be confronted by the little man from the shop.

'You forgot this,' he panted. 'It's your change.'

She stared at him, grabbed the money and ran like the wind.

When Hannah arrived at the station she glanced at her reflection in the black shiny pane of the door as she entered. She looked exhausted and dishevelled.

'I want to get a train to Cork,' she said to the man behind the ticket barrier who squinted out at her.

'All by yourself?' He trained suspicious eyes on her.

'I'm meeting my father.' She spoke with conviction, because she knew she was going home.

The man looked at the soft young face crowned by the flaming hair and said, 'Train's over there. Leaving in a few minutes.' He punched out a ticket.

'One pound, please.'

Hannah counted out the money. She pushed it awkwardly under the grid, then returned her last nine shillings to her purse.

'You're a wealthy lady, faith. Were you playing poker?' She felt his glance was suspicious.

'Confirmation money.' Her tongue tripped over the lie with an agility brought on by her relief.

She ran to the train before he had finished counting it.

'You've given me too much,' he called after her, his voice dying in the hiss and splutter of the train.

White vapour blew out from its sides as the engine grunted into life, and pushed its length crankily out of the station.

Hannah leaned back into her seat, the rough material scratchy against her face. She closed her eyes. The train lulled her into a trance-like sleep. She slept for most of the journey.

When the train slowed down Hannah moved to the door, watching the approaching grey city through sections of windows. She wondered if she'd remember where her bus stop was.

She was amazed to see two policemen waiting on the platform for her.

'Are you Hannah Dempsey?' One of them scanned a notebook.

'Yes.' She was frightened.

'You were reported missing yesterday evening. You'll have to come to the police station with us. We'll contact your parents.'

The police station was cold and dreary. The walls were covered in a film of dust. Hannah sat in a black plastic chair, uncomfortable and afraid. Her feet ached and she felt sick from the smell of the cocoa the Sergeant had given her to warm her up. Her father came into the station in a loping stride, still wearing his boiler suit.

'Hannah!' Thank God you're safe.' He hugged her to him. 'Why did you run away? Do you realise the state we were in?' His voice was cross even as he held her.

He looked tired and uneasy; his hair was untidy and his face was darkened by the shadow of a beard.

'You don't seem to realise how dangerous it is to travel alone at your age.' The Sergeant's voice was low and gruff.

Her father nervously ran his fingers through his hair.

'I wanted to come home.' this time the tears refused to be checked.

He remained constrained, undelighted to see her. 'We were all worried sick. Your mother is frantic.'

A cord of rejection registered in Hannah.

'I can't understand why she did it. Her mother was overprotective, if anything.' Her father sat opposite the social worker at home. Hannah hung around outside the living-room door.

The stout bespeckled woman wrote in a notebook.

'So you think that because of her deep attachment to her mother she sees this other man as a real threat?'

'Without a doubt. Mary mothered her too much after she lost the baby...' As he continued on, relentlessly blaming Mary for everything that had gone wrong, Hannah shivered on the cold dark stairs. Everything was eerily the same.

Finally the social worker left.

'There's a new chip shop in the town. Would you like fish and chips for tea?' Her father asked Hannah.

'Oh yes, please. I love chips.'

They ate them from the newspaper they were wrapped in as they walked home. Later on her father's friends called. There was shouting and back slapping and cheers, until they saw Hannah.

'I don't know how I'm going to manage.' Hannah sensed the exasperation in his voice. 'She's unhappy, moping about the place...'

Grunts and murmurs of understanding reached her ears. She got into bed and pulled the blankets over her head.

There was a new awkwardness between herself and her father. The eagerness that had always been in him was gone. It was as if he was punishing her for returning to him. She felt unwanted by the distance he put between them, by the encumbrances her presence imposed on him. She had misjudged him, and he intended to make her pay with a long deliberate repentance.

Hannah was lost.

'I'm taking you to your Grannie Dempsey for a few days. Until I sort something out.'

'Why can't I stay here and go back to school?'

'Because I've a lot of overtime for the next few days. I can't look after you properly.'

'Couldn't I stay with Mrs Ryan?'

'No.' His voice was rough.

Chapter 8

Eventually Hannah's mother returned home. Again, Hannah as a young nun ruminated over the seeming harmony that had gradually enveloped her family, but of course she could never know the whole story.

What actually happened was that one morning Mary got on a train and headed for home. She sat opposite a middle-aged woman with dark fuzzy hair and leathery skin. The train swayed her from side to side, speeding her back to chaos. Every now and again she glanced at the woman opposite. There was something familiar about her face, but the woman gave no sign of recognition. So Mary gazed out the window, seeing nothing.

While she waited in the queue for the connection bus, she silently rehearsed her speech for Tom.

'I only came back to talk to you ... I'm only here for ... I want what's best for Hannah ...'

He mightn't listen. He might shout and tell her to go back to where she came from. He might tell her to fuck off.

Exhausted and sick of the contradictory life she was leading, and tired of all the lies and deceit that constituted her marriage, she boarded the bus. Hannah's rejection was her worst fear.

The bus creaked and rattled to a final halt at the junction. The air blowing up from the harbour had the same fishy smell it had had the first day she arrived in the town. Her stomach heaved as she looked defiantly at the cold swell of the sea.

'I'm back,' she said aloud to the sea. 'And I didn't want to come. Damn you.'

Mary stood in the cold bare flat surveying the heaps of clothes and the few discarded toys. She felt disconnected and dazed at the unreality of the whole place. There was no sign of anybody. Not even Mrs Ryan or the babble of voices from upstairs.Where was everybody? She checked her watch. She made a pot of tea and lit the fire.

She heard footsteps on the stairs and went to the door. Mrs Ryan was carrying a heavy shopping bag upstairs.

'Is it yourself? You're back?' She looked surprised.

'Hello. Where's Hannah? Where's Tom?' Mary's desperate need for information wiped out all other considerations.

'I think they're gone to his mother's. Hannah said something to our lads about having to go to her Grannie Dempsey's. Didn't he know you were coming back?'

'No'.

'I'm sure he'll be home soon. Oh, and by the way I'm off again. Joe didn't believe me because I'm on this new type of mini-pill Doctor Moran prescribed for me. But me mother knew right well when I went for the sour apples in her orchard. She's better than any Doctor.'

'When are you due?' Mary tried to control the surge of rage she felt at Mrs Ryan's insensitivity. Didn't she know that she herself wanted a baby more than anything in the world?

'I don't know. Doctor Moran told me to bring down a sample to the surgery. I was that nervous I couldn't produce enough so I added a drop of tonic water that was in the cabinet. When he tested it the stick turned purple. He said there was something wrong and put me in the hospital for tests. I was there three days and not a damn thing showed up. I mentioned the tonic water when I thought I'd never get outa the place. He nearly had a fit. Said 'twas the quinine that set the sample crooked. Sure as long as it's healthy isn't that all that matters? Joe's been promised a job on the new buildin' site. Call up later for a chat.' She continued on upstairs, strenuously heaving her shopping, her legs infested with varicose veins.

'Congratulations,' Mary called after her.

Envy was Mary's next strongest emotion. The hardship Mrs Ryan endured trying to maintain her increasing family suddenly seemed preferable to the possibility of spending the rest of her life alone. The emptiness of the flat engulfed her in a wash of self-pity. She tidied away the scattered cups in the kitchen, put away colouring books and discarded pencils and went to bed. She woke up cold and cramped. A heaviness surrounded her heart. The silence was magnified by the wind blowing in from the sea, rattling the windows half-heartedly. Where was he? What if he'd taken Hannah away for good?

There was a knock on the door and Mary ran to open it.

Tim Ryan stood there, taller now and thin as a blade.

'Me Ma wants you to come up for your tea.' He gazed past her into the room. 'Any sign of Hannah yet?'

'No. They're not home yet. Tell your mother I'll be up in a few minutes, and thanks.'

He ran upstairs and Mary tidied her hair and put on some lipstick, glad of the respite from the loneliness but hoping 'himself' wasn't home yet.

'Sit down there and make yourself comfortable.' A film of perspiration covered Mrs Ryan's face as she turned rashers and sausages and black pudding on an enormous frying pan.

'I bet you haven't eaten for days. You look gaunt. Course the shock of Hannah running away. Who'd have thought such a good little girl would do a thing like that? Come to the pictures tonight. Me and the girls are going to see Gigi. I'm not sittin' beside Betty Mooney. The last night she

168

she spent the whole of the film polishing the seats. Her nerves are gone.'

'Where?' Mary was only half-listening.

'I don't know where but I know why. Ned's on the booze again. I know she's houseproud but cleaning the cinema after payin' to get in! She's the same at bingo. They daren't let her get her hands on the balls. She'd be shinin' them and the game'd niver get goin'.

'She's the cleaner at the factory, isn't she?'

'That's the one. Cleans in her sleep I think. She polishes her hedge, according to Tutsie Brown. There's a brillo pad in the gate so she can wipe the finger marks off when the visitors are gone. Especially the mother-in-law's. She don't have many visitors nowadays because no one wants to remove their shoes at her door. And the smell of disinfectant would make you heave. Especially if you were in a delicate condition like me and sensitive to smells.'

Mrs Ryan's newly polished floor was shining.

'You can see your reflection in that,' Mary said. 'How do you keep the place so perfect?' she continued, eyeing neatly piled ironing in the corner. 'And you still have the energy to go out.'

'If I didn't get out I'd go mad. Simple as that. You should come with me. Do you good.'

'I'll wait for Hannah if you don't mind.'

'Suit yourself but you could have a long wait, girl.'

Early the next morning Mary put on her coat and went shopping. A Russian ship had crept stealthily into the harbour in the night and loomed large in the shelter of its mouth. Her travelling companion on the train was sitting on the harbour wall, her low-cut dress gaping to reveal huge globes of breasts, their flesh as weathered from exposure as the skin on her face. Mary remembered that she'd seen her there before when the Dutch trawler was in.

'Come on, fellas. We've got all the time in the world and I know what you like to do best in your spare time.' She stood up to follow the sailors, her movements loose and sensual, her voice a lazy drawl.

Mary walked on, thinking of Tom. He'd promised before they left England to give up the drink. She had been naïve enough to believe him. She walked through the park. The trees were gaunt and ghostlike, leaves long vanished. She watched the uneasy water rise and fall and looked up and down, keeping a vigil. It was quiet except for the sailors straggling up from the harbour in pairs. A quietness that intensified and held its breath as if waiting too for something to happen. As she returned home with her small bag of groceries she heard the low rumble of thunder in the distance. Mary went home to make beans on toast and wait. The house was as silent as a tomb. Mrs Murphy was working in the canteen in the factory. In spite of herself Mary had to admit she missed the sounds from their living quarters.

The stairs was dirty and neglected. The half-shuttered windows looked blindly out at cracked pavements, and bundles of papers and dead leaves gathered in the corners of the steps.

In the evening Mary rang Mrs Ryan's bell. No one came thundering to answer it. No sounds emitted from within. It was late and the deserted house mocked her.

'Hannah,' she called out. 'Hannah,' hoping the house might throw back some answer. Only the silence returned her echo and she thought she was going demented.

She walked again, preferring the streets and the roads outside the town to the empty shell of a house. She walked along the narrow path towards the harbour. Then, to her amazement she saw Tom in the distance coming towards her. She couldn't believe her eyes.

She took a deep breath and waited for him. As he drew nearer he gave her a casual glance and might have passed on, ignoring, her only that she barred his way.

'Hello,' she said.

'Hello.' There was a chill in his voice.

She felt the awfulness of the situation but stood her ground and slowly retraced her steps with him. He walked ahead, eyes diverted, mouth shut tight.

The shadows of the tenements lengthened across the road, sending a new wave of depression over her as she faced into the dark hallway again. Was the bastard going to talk at all? Or was his punishing silence to be measured out in slow killing doses? Her own fatigue pulled her upstairs and while he put the kettle on she went to the window. The dark sea was dotted with bobbing trawlers and fishing boats. Further out the Russian ship lay like a beached whale. The town was stirring into life. Russian sailors walked in twos in impeccable uniforms, some already with girls in tow. Girls sat on the sea wall gazing in their direction. Their cheap made-up faces beckoned with smiles and artificial laughter. They gathered in increasing numbers, loitering, calling out in high-pitched voices, their cheap gold jewellery glinting in the setting sun. 'Hiya boyos,' they called out, their tight mini-skirts and masked faces giving them a clownish appearance.

Blatantly and wordlessly their assets were offered to the sex-starved sailors who strutted with exaggerated movements and made rude gestures.

The excited chatter heightened as they laughed and cajoled and paired themselves off. Bargains were sealed with banter. Sailors were ready to pay for their pleasures in the fleshpots of the city night.

'Let's go to the pub first,' a shrill girl voice rang out.

'You stay here.' He lifted his foaming glass, slopping some of it over the side before it reached his lips. 'Not much to ask, considering,' he added.

'Considering what?' she asked crossly.

'Considering you're bloody lucky I'm letting you back after what you did.'

'What concessions are you prepared to make?'

'You must be kidding. Hannah needs a mother. That's the only reason I'm sitting here talking to you.

'You cold, calculating bastard.'

'Thanks,' he said sarcastically. 'There is one bright spark on the horizon. We're moving to Dublin, always assuming that is that you're coming with us.'

'Dublin?' Mary couldn't believe her ears.

'Correct. I've got a job with a construction company there. The money's good and I intend to buy a house somewhere in the suburbs.' His words were clipped, brooking no argument.

'I'll go with you on one condition,' Mary said.

'I thought I explained. It's unconditional. Take it or leave it.'

Mary gave him a direct gaze.

'I want Hannah to have stability in her life from now on ... '

'I thought it was the drink you were going to mention.'

She ignored the interruption. 'I also want her to have the best education money can buy and that

'Hey, lady up there. Come down. Join in the fun. I've got just the thing for you.'

More guffaws of laughter.

'Why don't ye?' Tom was standing beside her. 'It's the best offer you'll get around here.'

'Ah, fuck off.' Mrs Murphy's voice rang out from below.

Laughter followed as her window slammed, shaking the house nearly out of its foundations.

'Wouldn't you think she'd have the sense by now to keep her stupid head out of the window when the ships are in,' Tom said. 'Or maybe she's living in hope.'

'We've got to talk.' Mary turned to him and he gave her a freezing look.

'Then talk.' He shrugged.

'When'll Hannah be back?' She held her breath.

He shrugged again. 'Why?'

'Because I've been out of my mind with worry. Why do you think I'm here?'

'I don't think anymore,' he replied sarcastically. 'You were too busy fucking with your Australian cowboy to bother about Hannah.'

'Tom!' Mary went white.

'So you weren't fucking. I only imagined it?'

She turned away.

'I have to go out for a while.' He walked out of the room, slamming the door.

Mary returned to the window, keeping well back in the shadow of the ragged curtains. She watched the Russian sailors showing off, encouraged by their audience. They moved off slowly as the sinking sun reflected itself in a gold crumpled trail across the water.

Mary put on her jacket and went out again.

'Hey lady. Come 'ere.'

She looked at the face of the weather-beaten sailor who smiled at her.

'Lady sad?' He gave her the routine once-over she'd seen so many times before.

'I buy you drink.' He gestured to the pub, his outstretched arm tattooed beneath dark fuzzy hair.

Mary moved away, lonelier than ever. The uglier the sailors were the more they wolf-whistled.

Children scrambled to collect the pennies they threw to them.

On a sudden impulse she went into Tom's local. She chose a table in a corner and ordered a lemonade. She watched the door nervously, her underlying annoyance giving her the stamina she needed to confront him on his territory.

The bar hummed with noisy Russians. The locals, distracted from their everyday morbid curiosity, didn't even notice Mary.

Finally Tom walked in and looked around. Surprise flickered on his face when he saw her, then composing himself he came quickly to her, dodging among tables, extended legs, arms and handbags. 'What are you doing here?' His expression, diffident and distant, made a strange out of him. The very bond of their marriage seemed at that minute to distance them. He presence embarrassed him.

He drew up a chair.

'I couldn't stand the flat,' she said in a dead voice reiterating the very words he so often used himself. He said nothing, letting the silence between them grow until Mary snapped, 'Are you going to talk at all?'

'This isn't the place.'

'I thought here on neutral territory you'd more at ease ... '

He leaned forward. 'Right. Talk.'

'Well,' Mary hesitated. 'What I wanted to you was ... '

'Just a sec ... ' Tom caught the barman's eye called across.

'Pint, please. What'll you have?'

'Nothing, thanks.' She felt a rush of fear in postponed second. She hadn't a leg to stand her mother would say when a neig presented her with a useless argument.

'I want to see Hannah. I want her back.'

'Depends,' he said, concentrating on hi wetting his lips with its froth and licking savour their taste before taking a long dra it.

'Depends on what?' Mary asked, see delaying tactics as a ploy to drive her o mind.

means that you start saving now for a university education for our daughter.'

'You always had delusions of grandeur, Mary Dempsey, but I'd go along with a good education myself. Hannah is the whole world to me.'

Chapter 9

Hannah saw the greyish tinge on her mother's face, and heard her slurred voice, 'It's a boy.'

She also saw a new radiance in her eyes.

'You're exhausted, Mammy. I'll make out a list and do the jobs.' She spoke close to her ear so her mother could draw comfort from her words. Hannah could be relied upon. Her father worried about that aspect of her personality which drove her on to new heights of perfection.

'Don't take life so seriously,' he would say or, 'Stop striving for perfection. It doesn't exist.'

Hannah said, 'I only want to do my best.'

'Well you should try to enjoy life a little too.'

Hannah did not listen. She did the washing before she went to school, and ironed when she came home. In the evening she shopped in the corner shop and cooked simple meals. She wanted everything to be right for her father while her mother was in hospital.

Finally she was allowed to see her little brother. She gazed at him in the incubator, sleeping, his tiny body crumpled in the cot, the sheen of his hair gold in the light, one tiny fist exposed.

'You're a little fighter, you beautiful baby,' she whispered through the glass bubble. 'You won't die on us.'

David's birth transformed the family. Her father had been withdrawn for so long after her mother's return from Tipperary, that Hannah had developed a sense of desolation and loss. With the birth of David, the coolness between her parents seemed to evaporate. She would try to ensure that everything would stay alright between them from now on.

In retrospect the events in Hannah's childhood changed. Her perspective of important milestones differed from her mother's version, in her timing, her interpretation of events and their meaning. One thing she was certain of: that there was something complicated and painful between her parents. On reflection, Hannah remembered the feeling of being an intrusion in their lives. Yet she was also their only cohesion. Without her their lives together were meaningless. The only thing she was sure of was that they both loved her. Separately.

Her mother's love was intense and uneven, with bearhug embraces, and the quick gathering up of her into her arms, telling her how precious she was. Sudden anger would make her shout, usually because of some outside force, beyond her control. Hannah could never tell how her mother would be and spent a great deal of time trying to gauge her moods. All she was certain of was that her mother's emotions ruled her, Hannah's, life.

She felt that her father was more reliably connected to the world, perhaps because he led a routine life. His way of dealing with her mother's moods was to get out of the way. One day he moved away altogether. Hannah was in secondary school. David was only four.

Her father had got a job in Dublin and they moved from Cork to the outskirts of Wicklow. The new house was uncluttered because it had three separate bedrooms. Hannah had her own bedroom, where she could lay out her precious belongings. A room uncrammed with the awful cardboard boxes that had earlier held the strands of their temporary lives because there was never any place to unpack them. Her father painted David's room in primary colours and her mother carefully selected furnishings for it.

Although their new house was small Hannah loved it. She attended the local convent secondary school and settled down quickly.

Kilgarragh was a small town with an enviable community spirit. Hannah's mother was soon immersed in community work and the care of the elderly. When Father O'Keefe's housekeeper ran off with the milkman, she cooked for him until he found a replacement.

Her father worked in a construction company in the city. He still came home late. Sometimes he had a few drinks on the way. Her mother hardly noticed. She was too tired after a busy day or she just didn't care.

Until one day her father arrived home and told them he had been made redundant. 'Staff cuts,' was the only reason he gave.

'You'll get another job,' her mother said. 'You're good.'

He had never been out of work since he had left school at fifteen to serve his apprenticeship. Wherever he was employed he worked his way up, never allowing his fondness for drink to intrude. He did not share his wife's optimism about finding work.

He was conscious of friends' and neighbours' reaction to his redundancy. Defensive, shrugging his shoulders, he'd say, 'It's not my fault. It's happening all over.' People were careful of his feelings because they knew he loved his work. All his life he had worked. It was a challenge that excited him and bought him the possibility of spending time relaxing with his friends in the pub.

He changed. First he was shiftless, drifting in and out of the house. They all sensed his discomfort and when he said he was off to London to work as a barman with a friend, no objection was raised. They needed the money. The redundancy pay had gone on the mortgage and other outstanding bills.

Hannah never could remember his leaving. She had blocked out the pain and only felt it as a hollow loss within her. He sent money home regularly at first. Then the cheques dwindled and Hannah's mother accused him of being his own best customer in the bar.

Hannah missed him intensely. Missed his jokes. The comfort when he held her silently if she was upset. The tears he wiped away when she fell, or someone called her names. The laughter. The stories he told her when she could not sleep. How he coped when her mother could not. Now life with his family had become impossible for him because he was redundant.

Her mother collapsed after he had gone.

'I can't think straight,' she would say and return to bed.

Hannah was left to fend for David and herself alone. Her mother's eyes were swollen from constant crying. When she spoke she sounded as if someone was trying to strangle her. She lived in her dressing-gown. Hannah organised what they needed and took David to school. She stayed at home with him on days he couldn't attend and cooked simple meals: beans on toast, scrambled eggs, potatoes and rashers. While her mother slept she kept him quiet.

It was a frightening time in Hannah's memory.

Sometimes she thought her mother was lost to her forever in her darkened bedroom. One day it dawned on her that it was her responsibility to get her out of her room and back into their lives, before she forgot their existence.

'Are you coming down for something to eat?' she asked and was shocked at her mother's vicious retaliation. 'Get out and leave me alone.'

That moment was a nightmare Hannah often re-lived in her dreams. Her mother's weeping was her most vibrant memory and for years afterwards had the power to make her feel sick. The vicious accusations she had directed at her father in fits of temper was another memory that haunted Hannah. Her shrill voice sounded almost jubilant as she scored points against him, weaving her hands in the air like a bookie at the tote.

Gradually, with Hannah's coaxing, she recovered. She became part of them again. Her thinness made her jawline more defiant. She began to gain strength. She resumed her life, peaceful and lonely, David's affection and obvious need of her giving her the strength to cope.

Hannah's father had not come back to see them since the spring and when he wrote to say he could not come home for Christmas either, explaining the problems of a barman in London at the busiest time of the year, her mother said it was a flimsy excuse. Hannah was heartbroken.

They shopped early for Christmas and hid the presents. While Hannah fried sausages and set the table, her mother sat over a cup of tea and said she wished it was all over. She counted her change and planned her Christmas strategy. The club money had provided most of the shopping and presents.

'I still haven't got David's bike, or the turkey. I suppose I could borrow from January's children's allowance, and forget about the turkey.'

'Christmas isn't Christmas without a turkey, ' Hannah said, thinking that she would far prefer to have her father home than any turkey.

David was looking forward to Christmas with the blissful innocence of a child. He had started school and the previous week in Clery's had told Santa that he desperately needed a bike. Santa, watching his earnest little face, agreed, promising him one without fail.

'Down the chimbley it'll come, even if I have to ride it meself,' and David's eyes had rounded in astonishment.

'Oh no, Santa. Don't do that. You'll break it.'

'I'm only coddin', child. You go to sleep like a good little boy on Christmas eve and when you wake up it'll be there beside your bed.' He patted the little boy's curls.

'Thanks,' Hannah's mother said sarcastically to Santa. 'It's no skin off your nose. The nightmare to provide it is mine.'

'We all have our problems.' Santa smiled genially behind his fluffy beard and called 'Next'.

'Mammy, I'm starving,' David came into the kitchen eyeing the sausages on the warming plate and the table set for supper.

The doorbell rang. Hannah answered it.

'Mammy, it's Demented for you.'

Her mother threw her eyes up to heaven. 'I'm tired telling you not to call her that,' she hissed, then, 'Hello, Sister De Santus,' she said in her more respectful voice, marvelling at the perfection of the nun's timing. She always managed to arrive at the busiest time of the day. Time was measured at the convent by a different bell-toll.

'Mary,' her voice trilled, 'I'm sorry to disturb you but I have a slight problem.' She smiled at the children.

Mary said, 'Sit down, Sister,' and steeled herself. Mary helped out at the convent, cooking for them on special occasions. With dwindling vocations they could not afford a permanent cook, and there was only one lay sister Mary's secret dream was that Hannah would join them soon and become a nun.

'Mother General is coming for the great feast. She's bringing four other sisters and the bishop.' Her voice rose, and hung, like a rag on a rusty nail, hysteria and excitement pushing it into a crescendo.

'How marvellous,' Hannah's mother said.

'Yes. I suppose. But we're very stuck, Mary. Can you help out?'

'Christmas day?' Mary was incredulous.

'I know, dear. I thought of that. Even prayed about it, and I think I've found a solution.'

'I'm sure.'

'If we have dinner at 1.00 p.m. sharp, that leaves you free to make an evening meal for the family.'

'Ingenious,' Mary said under her breath.

Sister De Santus said, 'I'll make it worth your while.'

Hannah said, 'I'll help, Sister.'

'That's very kind of you, dear.'

'Who'll mind David?'

'Bring him with you.'

'He's a holy terror. The only way I could manage is if you were to put the turkey in the oven very early.' Hannah guessed her mother was thinking of David's bike and the leftover turkey from the convent.

'What temperature?'

'High. Then reduce it. Of course you'll have to stuff it first and spread plenty of butter over the breast.'

'Where will I get the stuffing?'

'I'll make it fresh and we'll bring it over.'

'God bless you, Mary, but you're a marvel. What would we do without you?' Sister stood up to leave as Hannah echoed her sentiments.

'Your father has run away from his responsibilities,' Hannah's mother said later. 'He isn't fooling me. Staying at home stifled him. So he fled.'

Hannah felt her bitterness and disillusionment at his not coming home for Christmas. She hoped he would phone on Christmas day.

On an impulse her mother took them into Moore Street on Christmas eve. For all the coloured lights and illuminated trees, there was a cold bareness about the streets. They walked among the stalls, watching the vendors packing up, listening to cries of, 'Last of the Christmas trees. Goin' for a song.'

They gazed at the large plump birds hanging in rows over the butcher's shop. Finally her mother settled for a small turkey, pinching its clammy skin.

'Seems fresh enough. I have a tin of chestnuts somewhere. That with the sage and onion stuffing should do.'

'Special price for you, dear,' the old woman behind the stall coaxed.

Hannah, looking at her sitting in the cold, felt sorry for her.

'Take it, Mammy' she said.

At 11.00 am sharp on Christmas morning, Sister De Santus floated to the door to greet Mary, Hannah and David, the smell of sherry wafting in her wake, as she led the way to the kitchen. Sister Veronica was sweeping up the debris from the stuffing, her ample bottom swaying from the exertion, her face beaming like a beacon.

'Mary, my dear, you're welcome,' she called.

She'd been at the sherry too. In the kitchen she waved towards the oven.

'I did it, Mary. I succ...eed..ed.' She laughed gleefully. 'The turkey is ... is ... in the ov ... en.' Her hand flew to her mouth to stiffle a hiccup.

The smell of singeing alarmed Hannah.

'Better check it,' she told her mother.

The stuffing lay in a lump on top of its belly, its splayed legs stiffly protruding.

'It looks like a poor creature in the advanced stages of labour. Where's the tinfoil and butter?'

'Oh, I forgot.' Demented put her hand to her mouth like an errant child.

'Lucky the oven is low, or the damage would be irreparable,' her mother whispered to Hannah.

'Happy Christmas, Mary,' Hannah Demented poured two scooners of sherry.

'I wonder will David be alright on his bike? Hannah, go and see.' Her mother lifted the brimming glass and toasted the nuns.

Finally Mother Superior arrived with her entourage. She despatched the bishop to the parlour with a large whisky and a couple of nuns to ensure his comfort. Then she came to unload her bounty in the kitchen. Smoked salmon, sides of ham and beef, another turkey. Cakes, chocolate biscuits, chocolates. Demented handed her a sherry and Mother Superior proposed a toast.

'To a happy and a holy Christmas.' She looked at each one of them solemnly.

'And a bountiful one,' said Demented, looking at the mouth-watering food.

'Here, have a warm up.' Mary was handed another overflowing glass by a now shaky hand.

A fleet of nuns scurried and fussed, setting tables, uncorking wine, chilling wine, and chatting warmly. Delicious smells wafted from the kitchen as Mary flexed her professional muscle, through a cloud of alcohol. Demented doctored the sherry trifle once again.

'For what we are about to receive,' the bishop intoned, 'may we be truly grateful.'

Gazing at the splendour of the table as she helped serve the soup, Hannah thought of the poor unfortunates who would go without a meal today.

They left after the main course was served. Sister De Santus escorted them to the door, pressing bags and parcels into their hands, and money in a envelope.

'We're so grateful,' she repeated over and over again.

'Anytime,' her mother said.

On the way home she said to Hannah 'I'm glad Christmas comes round only once a year.'

Hannah's father was waiting for them.

'Daddy, Daddy,' David shouted, hurtling himself into his arms.

Hannah's greeting was more subdued. 'I'm glad you came,' she said, giving him a hug.

'I've missed you all.' He looked from one to the other, awkward and bashful and said to Mary, 'I brought you a turkey.'

Her mother prepared another dinner. Her father pitched in, helping and telling them stories about the pub in London.

'It's lonely over there,' he said.

'Would you find work here?'

'No. I want you and the children to come back to England with me.'

Hannah's mother pursed her lips and said nothing.

Her father was in a bad mood.

'I want my children to be educated here. Hannah's doing well. The nuns are putting her in for a university scholarship.' Mary shot him a defiant glance.

'A lot of good that'll do her. Who'll provide the rest?'

'I will if I have to.' She left the room.

'She only wants the best for me,' Hannah explained to him.

'I know. She wants you to rise above your background and succeed. Have a profession. I don't hold that against her. It's her determination to keep me out of it, as if I had some disease or something.'

'That's not true.'

'Never mind,' her father's voice softened. 'You're growing into a beautiful young lady. I'm proud of you.' He admired her russet hair and long graceful limbs. 'I wish I could provide you with the life you deserve.'

It was on the tip of Hannah's tongue to tell him that the life she craved would cost him nothing. Something in his eyes stopped her.

'I hate going back to London. The only thing that keeps me going is knowing that by working there I can provide for you, at least.'

Outwardly Hannah seemed unaltered by the loss of him. Inside she was troubled and sad. She could only measure his love on reflection so that the gratitude it deserved was never spoken. The pain inflicted when he had first left returned, the memories still tangible. By now Hannah could see clearly her parents? failure to one another. Their will for her to succeed was the focus they used to salvage the wreckage of their lives.

Her father sent money home regularly, making it clear that he did not want his wife to go out to work. But when she was offered a job as cook at the Castle Hotel, she took it and saved every penny for her children's education.

Chapter 10

Hannah walked past the presbytery, along the footpath, to the tall house that stood alone among barren fields. She hoped her friend Katie would be ready for school for a change.

Mrs White greeted her with a frosty smile and called upstairs, 'Katie, Hannah's here.'

'Coming,' came the instant reply as Hannah was ushered in out of the cold.

'How's your mother, Hannah? Is she over the flu?'

'She's grand this morning, thanks.' Hannah's eyes strayed anxiously upstairs.

'Katie!' Mrs White's exasperated voice floated upwards just as a tall, dark-haired girl came bounding downstairs.

'What's all the fuss about? I'm ready. Hello, Hannah,' she said shrugging her shoulders into her coat.

'Don't forget to say a prayer before you go in.' Her mother gave her a peck on the cheek. 'Good luck, both of you.'

'Don't fuss, Mother.' Katie frowned impatiently.

'Thanks, Mrs White.' Hannah waved goodbye.

Katie sighed as they walked up the road. 'God between us and fussy parents. That mother of mine will drive me to drink before I'm much older.'

'You can't blame her. My mother's up the walls. If I don't get the scholarship she'll go mad.'

'We can only do our best,' Katie mimicked Sister De Santus as she walked nonchalantly beside her best friend. They had been best friends since Hannah's first day at Saint Mary's convent secondary school, and had shared all their hopes and dreams, and now their fear of the Leaving Certificate Examination.

'If I don't pass I'll do hairdressing,' Katie said.

'Of course you'll pass.' Hannah was thinking of the high standard her mother and Sister De Santus had set for herself. 'Anyway you're doing dress designing, aren't you? You're cut out for it.'

They both laughed.

'Did I tell you that you've got a date with Patrick Byrne tonight? He said to be at Riordan's corner at eight sharp. I'm meeting Joe. It'll look more casual if we're together,' Katie said.

'What about the maths paper tomorrow?'

'Sister Ignatius said if we don't know it by now we never will, and to give our brains a rest.'

'Your mother'll go mad.'

'I'll tell her I'm going to your house to revise with you.'

She gave Hannah a friendly poke with her elbow. 'You can say you'll be in mine.'

Katie sneaked out to a lot of parties and dragged Hannah along as often as Hannah's mother allowed. Hannah did not raise any objection because she liked Patrick Byrne.

'She's irresponsible,' her mother said of Katie, 'though God knows her mother's strict.'

Patrick Byrne went around with a bunch of Elvis Presley lookalikes who hung around corners, stormed streets and sat for hours in Bimbo's, the one café in Kilgarragh. He was the most fanciable of the sleek sultry-looking lads who lolled around talking about girls and their own mode of attire. His thick hair was lifted high off his forehead and cut in a bebop. Sometimes he held a kiss curl in place with Brylcreem. He laughed and smoked with his gang, and adjusted the scarlet handkerchief in the breast pocket of his drain-pipe suit.

Patrick stared out at the world with gimlet eyes that glinted in sullen silence. He took a comb from his top pocket and sleeked back his black hair while he waited for Hannah. It shone like newly polished boots. His imitation diamond-studded tie caught the evening sun and dazzled off the wall of Riordan's pub. As he glanced furtively up and down, he hoped nobody would notice that he was being kept waiting.

He was nicknamed Elvis because of his baby-face resemblance to the great star. He nurtured his nickname with clinging desperation. He now checked his watch and stamped his brothel creepers to keep out the chill. His light suit only narrowly covered him. Hannah felt sorry for him because his father had abandoned himself and his mother, leaving Patrick to look after her in semi-squalor in Parnell Row. Tenements behind a dump of broken bottles and old tyres. Patrick's pride in his appearance was a credit to him, considering they had only a tin bath and an outside lavatory.

His mother was slowly disintegrating, even though his wages as an apprentice electrician had lifted their meagre lives out of starvation.

'Sorry I'm late.' Hannah came up behind him, Katie trailing her.

'Where's Joe?' Katie asked.

'He'll be up by the river.'

'Let's go then before some oul bag tells on us.' Katie walked ahead.

They left the outskirts of the town and headed towards the river. The early summer air was chilly. Buttercups, amassed along the bank, bent their timid heads in the stiff breeze.

'You look well.' Patrick was looking at the elaborate beehive Hannah had made out of her hair.

She shrugged with pleasure and embarrassment, while he stopped to comb his own hair once again.

Joe was waiting for them.

'Let's sit down here,' Patrick said when they reached a stretch of lush grass.

Hannah removed her cardigan and spread it out for Patrick and herself to sit on. He stretched out beside her and hung his arm on her shoulders. She shivered and drew closer to him.

'Pity it's too cold for a swim.' He nuzzled her ear.

'Swim! Are you mad? Look at my hands. They're turning blue,' Hannah said.

'I'll warm you up. Come here.'

They merged together, Hannah's inherent dignity forgotten as he hitched up her skirt and moved his hand familiarly up and down her legs. Casually he placed his hand between them and she slapped it hard.

Katie was further up river, with Joe. Her mother would have been furious if she knew her only daughter was dodging study. She had academic ambitions for Katie and planned that she would marry a rich businessman.

Katie had other ideas. When her mother spoke about her bright future to her she yawned and said, 'Those rich business men sound boringly dull.'

Katie longed to be a dress designer and design for the rich and famous, who could afford to give her carte blanche to make the magnificent creations that she constantly dreamed about. Her other ambition was to take Patrick Byrne away from Hannah without losing her friendship. Since Hannah had come to live in Kilgarragh, they had found solace in each other from the isolation enforced on them as only daughters.

Hannah was rolling up her new polka dot bikini into her towel when her mother announced that she would be starting work in the hotel next morning. The exams were only over. She longed for a summer of languid days lazing on the banks of the river with Patrick Byrne; lying on the beach; nights at the hop down at the Beach House, the sound of the tide washing in over the blaring rock-n-roll. Most of all she yearned for leisurely mornings in bed after a year of slavery, which had culminated in the Leaving Certificate exam.

'What about the holidays?'

'I don't want you parading around the town in front of those sex-starved teddyboys. You're going places, so you might as well get some valuable experience now. I promised Mrs Cunningham you'd be available after the exams.' She spoke the name with reverence, conceding Mrs Cunningham a superiority that seemed rightfully hers, by virtue of her position in the community as the hotel owner.

Hannah did not argue. Her one consolation was that Katie would be working at the hotel too.

'Good morning.' Mrs Cunningham looked her up and down.

Hannah said, 'Good morning' and waited for her to speak. She was a tall, imposing woman in a black dress that added a severe look to her appearance. A bunch of keys dangled menacingly from her waist.

She led Hannah into the bar. 'You can clear this first.' She indicated the previous night's debris with a sweeping gesture, and departed.

As Hannah gathered dirty glasses, and emptied the dregs of coffee cups, she wondered where Katie was. They'd agreed to meet at the hotel at nine o'clock. By the time she had stacked bottles neatly into crates, hoovered and polished, she was exhausted and it was only eleven o'clock.

Mrs Cunningham appeared from nowhere.

'It's time to start upstairs. The sheets and towels are in the linen cupboard.' She extracted a key from the bunch and gave it to Hannah. 'I'll get Dolly to show you where everything is.'

Dolly was the most senior member of the staff, the only permanent one. She was pretty in a garish way. Hannah thought her name suited her because she looked like a doll.

'We'll clear the breakfast dishes first,' she said, piling the trolley which miraculously flew to the nether regions on a pulley. Then she showed Hannah how to set the tables for lunch.

'I'll show you the ropes. You'll be an expert in no time.' She led Hannah upstairs, hoovering and cleaning, confounding Hannah with her energy.

Katie appeared just as Dolly announced the coffee break.

'You look the part.' Hannah laughed at the cleaning cap perched on her head, and the dirty smudge on her cheek. 'Where were you?'

'Mrs Cunningham wouldn't let me up to see you when I got here. Made me clean out the fireplaces for being late.'

'A bit of hard work won't kill two strappin' girls like yourselves,' said Dolly. She made the coffee in the pantry.

'What's Mr Cunningham like?' Katie asked. 'I haven't seen him around.'

'Distant,' Dolly shrugged. 'I suppose he's not bad-looking in a way.' She wrinkled her nose. 'He's the relics of old decency, as they say. Still fancies himself no end. I can see why she married him.'

'I can't see why he married her.' Katie made a face.

'Money. The root of all evil. Her father owned the hotel and left her everything. He didn't approve of the marriage though.'

'Why?'

Dolly lowered her voice. 'He had a bit of a reputation with the women. Anyway it's time to stop gossiping and get on with the work.'

Dolly drained her cup and straightened her uniform.

She had not done Mr Cunningham justice, Hannah thought when she met him. He was tall and dark, with fine-boned features and a penetrating gaze.

'Another new one,' he said. 'It's great to see a bit of life in the place again.'

She watched him out of the corner of her eye. His slight paunch denoted his fondness for excesses, and although he wore a good suit, something about his slick smile gave him an air of depravity. He confined himself to the bar and Hannah kept her distance.

Dolly had a boyfriend. She preened herself and became more important when he was due to call for her. She talked about him endlessly, Séan this, Séan that, until the girls were sick of the mention of his name. He christened Hannah 'Miss Prude' because she did not encourage any conversation.

One day as she was leaving the hotel he almost collided with her.

'Sorry,' she said, moving aside.

'You know what you need, don't you?' He lowered his voice and leaned towards her. 'A good fuck, that's what.'

He didn't notice Mrs Cunningham standing at the hotel entrance, a thunderous expression on her face. Hannah ran home, determined to leave the hotel.

'You'll have books to pay for if you get into college,' her mother said. 'You'll need pocket money.'

'I don't like it and I never see Katie. We work different shifts.'

'You'll get used to it. I did.'

One evening when Hannah was in one of the bedrooms turning back the bedspreads, Mr Cunningham appeared in the doorway.

'Where's Dolly?' he inquired.

'Gone out with Séan. It's her half day.'

'Oh, that's right.' He barred her way as she tried to leave.

'Excuse me, sir.' She tried to side-step him, but he detained her with his hand.

'How long have you been with us now?' His voice was slightly hoarse.

'Three weeks.'

He moved his hand across her shoulders, touching her bare neck, letting it wander to her throat. His glazed eyes did not seem to register her. Then he turned abruptly and left. Trembling with fear, she made a hasty retreat to the kitchen.

A few days later he came up to her and placed his hand on her buttocks as she was hanging tea towels on the line.

'You're beautiful,' he said, his beery breath fanning her hair.

A knot of disgust gathered in her stomach.

'Please, Mr Cunningham,' she pleaded, shrugging him off.

He smiled a slick smile and left.

Another day she was on her hands and knees cleaning a bathroom floor when a shadow fell across her. She turned to find him standing over her, his lustful eyes fixed on the curve of her buttocks.

As she rose, he grabbed her, stumbling in his eagerness.

'Leave me alone,' she shouted, trying to push him away.

They both fell backwards against the wall.

'You want it too. I know you do.' His face was purple.

Suddenly the door flew open and Mrs Cunningham stood there, staring at them.

'Out,' she roared, her index finger shaking as she pointed towards the door.

To Hannah's amazement her mother did not attach much importance to the matter. 'You should be able to keep that fool at arm's length. He's harmless.'

'I never want to set foot in that place again,' Hannah protested.

'I'll have a word with Mrs Cunningham.'

When Hannah told Patrick Byrne about Mr Cunningham's advances, he narrowed his eyes and looked away. 'You probably led him on,' he said.

'What do you mean?'

'You're the *femme fatale* of Kilgarragh. All the boys fancy you.'

'Rubbish. You're jealous!'

'Jealous! I can have you any day of the week.'

'Oh, really? You're nothing but a conceited teddyboy, swanning around in your fancy gear, trying to impress the girls. Look at you, standing there preening yourself.'

'Drop dead.' He spat into the gutter and walked away, hands stuffed into his trouser pockets, yellow jacket swinging, head high, polka-dot tie flying back in the breeze.

Hannah stormed off, swearing never to speak to him again. 'He's got a nerve,' she said to Katie. 'A nobody like him.'

'I don't know. I like Patrick.'

'Well, you can have him. I never want to see him again,' she said robustly to disguise her shaky voice.

Hannah thought he would seek her out and apologise. Instead he became distant. His features were harsh and knotted with tension whenever she saw him with his gang, or standing at corners, whistling and jeering at passing girls.

Katie began seeing him. He wore a leather jacket, bought a motorbike, and tore up and down the main street, his face screwed up as he unleashed his fury at the world, in the speed of his souped-up engine.

Katie rode pillion passenger, and delighted in terrorising the town with the roar of the engine. People stood in fear waiting for something awful to happen.

Katie's mother ranted at Katie, 'You're a fallen angel in God's eyes as long as you mix with the likes of him. You're doomed.'

Summer brought swarms of people out to swim in the river. Semi-nude bodies lay in a row, Patrick's and Katie's among them. One day they went to Dublin shopping. When they did not return Katie's mother went frantic, phoning the police and all her friends. Gradually, as time went by and there was still no sign of them, word spread that they had eloped.

'They couldn't have.' Hannah defended Katie, hiding her fury for her desertion of her.

Patrick Byrne's mother went demented. She searched for Patrick through fields and woods, as if he were a little boy whom someone had stolen. Each day she went to the river, where midges hung in the air, and flowers kept their own council, nodding to her pathetic cries of 'Patrick! Patrick!' She refused to believe that he would leave her of his own volition.

The women whispered to one another outside the chapel, 'God help the creature. Sure she was never right since her husband left. Now she's no one.'

Her anguish cut into her face. She looked like a sculpture in her grief. Sometimes she got lost, her wanderings taking her far from the town. Eventually the mental hospital sheltered her, while she waited for her son's return.

Katie's mother, cursed her daughter and called Patrick Byrne all the foul names her well-bred background could think of. She took to her bed, only leaving it to light candles and press envelopes of money into the priest's outstretched hand. Katie's father went to London to search for his daughter and so pacify his wife.

'Wait till I get my hands on her,' she shouted at Hannah. 'I wanted a future for my daughter. One that did not include Patrick Byrne.'

'They mightn't be together at all.' Hannah's words had a feeble ring to them, even to her own ears.

Hannah missed Katie desperately. She prayed and lit candles and attended the confraternity with her mother every Tuesday night, in the hope that Katie's whereabouts would be revealed to them. She continued working at the hotel, while she waited for the results of her Leaving Certificate. Mr Cunningham had gone to Dublin to stay with his sister for an extended holiday. She went for walks in the evening, ignoring the cat calls and wolf whistles from the boys. The weather had broken and clouds scudded across the sky, sending shadows fleeing over the fields, darkening the river. The rain came suddenly, wetting the shoulders of her jacket. She did not retrace her steps. She walked along the steep bank, looking at the dampened reeds that edged the shimmering water. She plucked a blade of grass, chewing it thoughtfully.

The beauty of the summer had disappeared, taking the warmth of the fields, the abundance of flowers, the glint of mica on stone, the excitement of buzzing bees. As Hannah trudged along, she wondered how her parents would react when she told them that she was thinking of entering the convent; in fact had decided on it.

Chapter 11

Hannah wanted to be a nun for as long as she could remember. Her mother's dependence on her own faith, and her encouragement to her children to develop their spirituality, was the driving force. The teaching of the Catholic faith from the nuns reinforced her thinking. Hannah liked the security her beliefs gave her. She eagerly embraced the values the nuns taught her, love of God, love of the neighbour, christian charity. Acceptance was encouraged by those priests and nuns who counselled their young charges. To question the doctrine taught to them was considered blasphemous. The power of absolution in the confessional she considered to be the greatest miracle of all, and went to confession every Saturday because of the feeling of well-being it gave her. After she confessed her sins and the priest meted out her penance, giving her absolution with the sign of the cross, declaring her free from sin, she felt cleansed. 'You are a shining white soul for God now,' Father Murphy would always say as she rose to leave the dark, narrow box, and that's what she felt.

It was to Sister De Santus she first spoke about entering the convent. Her father was in England and the loss of him was like a raw wound in her heart. She remembered him most when she was in the chapel. His voice calling her name, the scrape of his key in the hall-door, his footstep as he entered, her running to meet him, helping him off with his coat.

'Are you tired, Daddy?' she would ask, searching his face anxiously.

'Not too bad today,' he'd say, his face creasing as he smiled. 'We were kept going. The time flies when we're busy.'

'Have you heard from your Father?' Sister De Santus asked her, noticing her sad face.

'Oh yes. He's very well and working very hard,' Hannah attempted at cheerfulness, casting Sister De Santus a shy smile.

Sister De Santus often inquired about her father. One day during lunch-break Hannah approached her.

'How are you, Hannah? How's everything at home?' Her smile was encouraging.

'Fine, thank you, Sister. Mammy's busy at the hotel and David goes up there after school.'

'That's good. Your mother's a wonderful woman, you know that of course.'

'Yes,' Hannah said, turning to Sister De Santus she said, 'Sister, I'd like to talk to you privately about something important.'

The kind nun who was nicknamed 'Demented' by the girls, stooped to give Hannah her full attention.

'If there's anything on your mind Hannah I'd...'

'I think I have a vocation, Sister,' Hannah blurted out.

Sister De Santus looked at her, then asked guardedly. 'How much thought have you given it, Hannah?'

'I've thought of little else this last year, Sister.'

'Have you considered what it's really like to be a nun? To live a life of prayer? To renounce your own identity and give up everything for God. To pray for others, to serve others, to put yourself last at all times?'

'Yes, Sister.'

Sister De Santus was not listening.

'Have you considered what it would be like to work without payment, teaching or nursing or whatever your calling demands of you? Never be able to marry? Never to have children of your own? Or a special person in your life to love and cherish?' Sister De Santus's eyes probed Hannah's.

'I don't ever want to get married, Sister.' Hannah's voice was resolute.

'Is this because of your parents, Hannah?'

'No, Sister. Marriage has never appealed to me. Even when the others talk about what their future husbands might be like I can't imagine wanting a husband. Entering the convent seems satisfying enough for me. I want to help people who are in need or in trouble.'

'You're a thoughtful girl, Hannah, and a spiritual one. I have no doubt that you have a real sense of your vocation. Nevertheless I want you to talk to your parents about it fully before you make a final decision.'

'Daddy isn't here to talk to.' Hannah's eyes filled with tears.

'Then I suggest you go and see him. The break would do you good. I'm sure he'd love to see you.'

Hannah looked at her in amazement. 'In London?'

'Why not?' Sister De Santus smiled. 'It's not that far away. If you're thinking of becoming incarcerated in a convent for the rest of your life, now is a good time to see a little bit of the world.'

A slow smile edged the corners of Hannah's lips. By the time Sister De Santus's suggestion had sunk in, her face was beaming. Then she was serious again. 'Mammy wouldn't hear of it. She'd never let me go.'

'Do you want me to have a word with her?'

'Would you, Sister? She'd listen to you. I haven't told her anything about entering yet, Sister. What'll I do?' Her excitement brought her words out in a rush.

'Tell her this evening when you go home. Leave the rest to me.'

'Thank you, Sister. I'm so grateful.' Hannah turned to leave.

'By the way, Hannah, what order were you thinking of entering?'

'Yours, Sister. I don't know of any other.'

'Bless you, my child. May God enlighten you.' Sister De Santus smiled with pleasure as she watched Hannah walk away. Did she imagine the lightness in her step, as if a heavy burden had been lifted from her.?

'I was talking to Sister De Santus today,' Hannah said to her mother as they washed up after dinner.

'That reminds me she asked me to give her a hand with the garden fete at the end of the month. I must write it down. I'm becoming very forgetful. How is she anyway? It isn't anything to do with the scholarship, is it? What does she think your chances are?'

'I told her I thought I had a vocation.' Hannah concentrated on the plate she was drying in order to avoid her mother's eyes.

The silence deepened and grew as she continued washing the dishes and stacking them neatly on the draining board. Hannah searched her mind for something to say, something apt that would comfort her mother, but nothing came to mind. She wished her mother would speak, say something, anything. Her silence gave her a strange feeling. A feeling of something unfamiliar, of alienation. This was the last reaction she had expected. When she looked at her mother again she saw that her shoulders were shaking.

Finally Mary said, 'If that is the life God has chosen for you, Hannah, you are truly blessed. To serve him and others through him is the highest calling. I would be the happiest mother in the world to think that I had given birth to one of God's labourers.' She left the dishes and sat down, tears pouring down her face. In all her imaginings of this scene Hannah never dreamed that it would be she who would take her mother in her arms, to console her. Her mother repeated over and over, 'This is what I have prayed for,' as Hannah pleaded with her not to cry.

Two days later Mary said to Hannah, 'Sister De Santus thinks it would be a good idea for you to go to London to visit your Daddy. Under the circumstances it's probably the best thing to do. He's hardly going to come home and if you're going to enter the convent it wouldn't be any harm for you to spend some time with him.'

Hannah was surprised at her acceptance of the situation but remained silent, in case she might say something to make her mother change her mind. Quietly she prepared for her trip, keeping to herself her delight at the prospect of seeing her father again.

The earliest sailing she could get was the evening boat to Holyhead. Its decks were swarming with holidaymakers returning to England. From the upper deck she watched with fascination the night sky over the sea and the trail of lights strung out along the coast, growing fainter and fainter as the boat sped along, leaving a trail of light on the churned-up sea. She was wondering what her father's reaction to seeing her would be. What he'd say when she told him her news. Her mother saw Hannah's vocation as a direct missive from God, the only good, positive thing to come out of their lives, out of her union with her husband. Hannah knew her father's reaction would be different. As she stood on deck, the wind from the sea billowing around her, tossing her hair, she tried to picture his face and could not.

'All alone?' Hannah whirled around, hugging herself against the cold night air and growing darkness.

A figure swung his feet down from the upper deck, and jumped, landing in front of her. She opened her mouth to scream, then instinctively put her hand up to stifle it, feeling foolish.

'Sorry. I didn't mean to frighten you,' he said softly.

Hannah could see that he was tall. The white trousers and shirt he was wearing broadened his silhouette against the dark sky. As her eyes grew accustomed to the darkness she saw the slow, teasing smile on his face.

'My name is Tommy. I'm part of your friendly cabin crew. At your service.' He bowed low and Hannah, mortified, stepped backwards.

When he straightened himself up he was grinning broadly.

'You should see the look on your face! I'm not going to eat you. Are you travelling alone?'

'Yes. I'm going to visit my father.' She moved away, blushing, trying to think of a way to extract herself without seeming rude.

'And who let a child like you out on your own?' With feet planted firmly apart, he was gazing at her, watching every nuance of movement.

'My mother, and she told me not to talk to strangers. I'd better go.' Shivering she turned to walk away but he caught up with her, and walked in unison with her.

'I told you I'm part of the crew. If you want to check out my credentials I'll escort you to the Petty Officer. Ask him.'

Hannah stuck her head in the air. 'I don't need to check your credentials. I don't intend to waste any more time talking. I'm frozen stiff.'

'Let me buy you a cup of coffee. Hey, don't go so fast. Watch your steps on the gangplank. Let me at least show you where the lounge is.'

Hannah kept walking, ignoring him.

She was level with the floating water, making her way hesitantly now into the slowly filling lounge. She sighed with relief as she moved among people who were talking loudly and drinking. Following in the direction of the smell of food, she kept moving until she was certain she had lost him. She was breathless when she reached the bar. As she waited to give her order he appeared from nowhere holding two steaming mugs of coffee in his hands.

'Would madame like anything to eat?' He smiled his teasing smile and Hannah couldn't help smiling back at him.

'That's better. Now drink up. You looked parched.'

Obediently Hannah sipped her coffee and felt the hot liquid spread all over her body, warming every inch of her. He found her a space among the crowded tables and beckoned her to sit down.

'That better?' He leaned towards her, touching her shoulder, his breath fanning her face, making her skin tingle.

'Hey you! Aren't you supposed to be on duty?'

They turned to see another young man approach them, dressed like Tommy.

'Yea. So!' He turned to Hannah. 'Listen, this is my mate, Pop-eye, I mean Pete. I'll have a word with him.'

He stood up and whispered in his pal's ear, then said aloud, 'Give us a break. Cover for me, will you?'

Pete rolled away through the moving crowd. Hannah watched him until he disappeared.

'We're alone again,' he said sipping his coffee with satisfaction. 'Tell me about yourself.'

Hannah looked at him, then shrugged. 'There isn't a lot to tell. I've just left school and I'm going to see my father.'

'Did anyone ever tell you that you're beautiful?' His earnest face made Hannah laugh. 'No,' she answered trying to think of something bright or witty to say that would disguise her sudden shyness.

'No boyfriend to tell you how gorgeous you are? How much he desires you?'

Hannah went cold inside as sudden fear gripped her. She wanted to die, disappear, anything but be there. Silence came over her and she wished she was smart enough to know how to reply. It occurred to her for the first time in her life how socially inadequate she was, how gauche, how inexperienced in the ways of the world. Just as she was mustering up the courage to say, 'Mind your own business,' he moved closer and slid his arm across the back of her seat.

'I'm sorry,' he said. 'I've embarrassed you. It was stupid of me.' He looked upset.

'It's alright,' Hannah said and it was.

'You're not used to compliments from strange men.'

'I'm not used to compliments. Or strange men.' They both laughed.

'That's a shame because you are beautiful. I mean that.' His eyes told her he was telling her the truth.

Suddenly her self-consciousness left her and she said, 'Thank you. I believe you do.'

'Let me get you a sandwich.'

He moved off among the crowd, and she missed his presence instantly. She hoped he would come back, and felt foolish for wanting to be with him. She caught his eye as he edged towards her, balancing plates of sandwiches and cakes high above his head, to protect them. He winked at her, and she smiled.

'Eat up. You must be hungry.'

'I am. Thanks.'

They ate silently. Several times he caught her eye and grinned shyly at her. When they finished he stood up, took a deep breath and said, 'Let's go for a walk along the deck. The moon's up.'

Before she could answer he took her hand and led her through the lounge and out on deck. She was trembling.

He kept her hand in his until they reached the upper deck where she had first met him. Then he stopped and turned to her in the darkness, looking at her for a long time.

She shivered and he smiled and said, 'We can't have you cold like this, can we?' and took her in his arms.

She let herself be held, let him rub her arms and her back like her mother did when she came in cold from school.

'Alright?' he asked. 'Are you all warmed up?'

They both laughed and suddenly they were still, gazing at one another, his arms around her, his face close to hers. He stepped back. 'Good God, I don't even know your name.' He seemed surprised at that sudden realisation.

'My name is Hannah,' she told him.

Haltingly she told him a little more about herself, her desire to go to university, to become a social worker. She never mentioned her vocation because it was the last thing on her mind. He listened with interest and she began to relax.

He reached for her, took her in his arms again and touched her cheeks with his lips. The cold wind whipped around them as he folded her into him and kissed her. His mouth was warm, his lips gentle and coaxing all at once. Hannah let herself be kissed and when he stopped and let her go, she almost staggered backwards. He took her hand and they walked along the deck. Her eyes were smarting from the wind.

'You're lovely. Has anyone ever kissed you like that before?' he asked suddenly.

Hannah, thinking of Patrick Byrne's sloppy kisses, suddenly laughed and quickly apologised.

'No. Never. I wish you would do it again.'

He smiled at her and, leaning against the railings, hugged her tightly to him. 'I don't know you,' he whispered 'but I'd like to get to know you more. Is that possible, do you think?'

A rush of panic seized her and in the silence she could hear the churning of the engine and the lapping of water. Her stomach heaved, forcing her to turn away from the sea.

'It wouldn't be fair. I have nothing to offer.'

He grinned. 'You could make me very happy.'

He took her hand and lifted it to his lips, then he kissed her again, slowly at first, then more urgently, his tongue touching her teeth, gently opening them. She felt happy, glad to be kissed, to be with him.

'Oy!' They stopped and stepped back from one another, looking in the direction of Pop-eye, sprinting along the deck.

'You're wanted below this minute or there'll be trouble. Can't cover for you any longer.'

Tommy gave Hannah a defeated look and said with a shrug, 'Duty calls. Best go. I'll see you when we dock if you wait around until the boat empties. Will you wait for me?' His face was eager and expectant. 'I'll take you for something to eat. I know a nice little place down the quay ...'

'I have to get the connection train, don't I?'

He nodded. 'Wait as long as you can. I want to see you before you go.'

She lifted her face to him, waiting for him to kiss her once more. But he just hugged her and left, running as fast as he could.

She went below and sat in the corner of the lounge where they'd eaten. With her eyes closed, she thought of him and the way he kissed her. She yearned for him to come back to her, to kiss her again. The emotions he had aroused in her were new to her, and the power they had over her frightened her. She touched her lips with her fingers, feeling where his lips had pressed against hers, and wondered if she would ever be the same again. How would it be when she became a nun? Never to experience the warmth and excitement of being kissed by a man for the rest of her life. Tears trickled through her tightly shut eyelids and she brushed them away self-consciously, telling herself how foolish she was. She didn't even know this man. When they docked at Holyhead she was at the head of the queue for the train, afraid to look over her shoulder in case she might catch a glimpse of him.

As Hannah searched for her father's flat among the maze of flats in Notting Hill she felt conspicuous, walking alone, past endless 'To Rent' or 'For Sale' boards, in the early morning. No one answered when she pressed the bell marked T. Dempsey. She sat on the steps in the sunshine watching black children playing, their bright clothes making a rainbow of colour, as they chased in and out of the streamers they held aloft in the wind. Their high-pitched voices sang out rhythmically as they played, making her feel vulnerable. An all-pervasive loneliness threatened her. Her father wasn't there. What would happen if he didn't turn up? Where would she go? Her emergency money would provide for one night's accommodation, but that was all. She imagined her father's face coming alive with pleasure at the sight of her. But what if he didn't want to see her? Supposing for some reason it was not convenient for her to be here? Why had she not thought of that sooner, and waited for his reply to her letter? What if he had not received the letter?

Suddenly the sky became overcast and Hannah shivered with the cold. The children yelled to one another and ran off down the road, leaving her alone on the quiet street. Then she saw him in the distance, his loping stride as he came quickly up the street. She ran to meet him and saw the intense love in his eyes for an instant before he wrapped her in his arms.

'I was afraid you might not have got my letter.' Her voice was trembling as they walked up the steps, arms entwined.

'I got your letter, lovey. But I'm on nights this week. They let me off early and I came as soon as I could. The damn tubes are crowded this hour of the morning.'

He inserted his key in the lock and let her into the dingy hall. His bedsitter was dark, and when he pulled back the heavy curtain, it was still dark with oak furniture, dull wallpaper and dirty rugs. A lump rose in Hannah's throat as she took in the cheerless, airless room.

She turned to her father. 'Aren't you lonely here, Daddy?' It was all she could manage without breaking down.

'I'm alright. I don't spend much time in the place. Joe gives me plenty of overtime and,' he looked at her, 'it's peaceful here. No one to fight with but myself.'

She wanted to ask him if he missed David and herself, if he missed her mother, but he'd turned toward the cooker and was busy piling rashers and sausages on a black frying pan. She felt any more questions would be considered an intrusion.

'You must be tired,' he said as he sat down opposite her. They were both hungry and settled in to the breakfast he had cooked for them. 'What was the crossing like?'

'Lovely.' Hannah felt herself blush as she thought of Tommy and wondered what her father would say if she told him she had spent a good deal of the journey letting a stranger kiss her, and kissing him in return.

'The good thing about working nights,' her father was saying, 'is that I'll be able to show you a bit of London.'

'Aren't you tired? You look tired.'

'I'll be alright in an hour or so when I've had a wash and a rest. Then we'll be off.'

He took her to Madame Tussauds to see the wax works, insisting she visit the chamber of horrors.

'I'm not sure that I like this,' she said looking at the life-like images of the Kray twins and turning away in disgust. 'Even the smell puts me off.'

'Right. Then I'll take you to the Tower of London where they chopped off heads.'

'Daddy, it's David you should be taking to these places. I haven't the stomach for them.'

He would not listen. They took a taxi to the Tower and later strolled around Hyde Park, because Hannah was exhausted from parading around dark, historical rooms, taking in details of Henry the Eighth, and his successive wives, doled out liberally by the Beefeater, as he guided them from room to room.

'I've only got tomorrow. Then I'm going home.' They were sitting on a bench in Hyde Park overlooking the Serpentine.

'That's not long considering the journey it took to get here. Why the rush?'

'I've things to sort out. Like my future.'

'When are the results out?'

'Anytime now.'

'Does your mother still want you to go to university?'

Hannah hesitated. 'Yes, I suppose she does, eventually.'

'What do you mean, eventually?'

'Sometime, I suppose.' Hannah turned away from her father's piercing eyes, her cheeks burning.

'What is it, Hannah? Obviously you're not just here for a bit of a break. There's something you have to tell me, isn't there?'

She moved along the bench away from him, as though his touch scorched her. He shifted uneasily as he waited for her to speak.

'You're not going to like what I have to tell you,' she said, her eyes glazed with tears.

'Try me.' His voice was patient.

'I want to enter the convent.' She turned to face him.

He was looking ahead, the contours of his face granite-like. Then he fumbled for his cigarettes before he spoke.

'Are you telling me that you want to be a nun?' he asked abruptly.

'Yes.' This time Hannah focused her full attention on him. 'Is that so amazing?' She hoped she would not have to talk about the events that led to her decision. Events she felt she could not share with him.

He cleared his throat. 'No, I suppose it's not so amazing. Not considering the mother you have. I bet she's delighted with your news.'

'Yes, Daddy, she is. I want you to be delighted too.'

His voice tightened. 'Well, that's not possible. How can a devoted father be delighted when his little girl tells him she's off to be locked up with a crowd of weirdo's for the rest of her life?'

Hannah rose and swung nervously away from him. Then she turned on him. 'Nuns are not weirdo's. Besides it's my choice and I was hoping you'd try and be happy for my sake. There's no point in getting angry.'

'If it was your choice I'd accept it, though God knows I can't say I'd be delighted. I'd be a hypocrite if I did. What worries me is that I feel your mother badgered you into this.'

'She did not. I only told her a couple of days ago.'

'Maybe so. Nevertheless she spent your whole life gearing you for the religious life. Anything to escape marriage and the bitterness her own marriage brought her.'

Hannah did not answer. She tossed back her hair and stared ahead at the swans quietly rippling along the water.

'Hannah, I'm sorry. I shouldn't have said that. But it's what I feel.' He was beside her, throwing out his hands in despair.

'I know what you're trying to get me to say, Daddy. I won't say it. I don't want to be part of your problems with Mammy. It isn't fair. I've suffered enough over the two of you.'

'You're so beautiful, so grave and beautiful. I'm only thinking what a terrible waste it would be to hide yourself away in a damn cloister for the rest of your life.'

'You're only thinking of yourself as usual. When did you ever consider me? Certainly not when you ran away, leaving me to take care of Mammy and David. Did it occur to you how heartbroken we were? No. You couldn't stand it, so off you went. And, before that when it didn't suit you, you just went out and drank with your cronies. All my life you seemed to have escaped me.' Hannah sighed a shuddering sigh and forced herself to continue through her tears. 'You knew I was waiting for you all those times you stayed out late.'

'Why do you think I came home at all? Only because of you.' His voice was just above a whisper, as he reached out and touched her mass of hair, glinting gold in the sun.

'What went so wrong with you and Mammy? Why are you here in his strange country when you should be at home with us?'

He bowed his head and rubbed his eyes, as if her words were assaults on his person, forcing him to look at something he did not want to see. He reached into his pockets and took out his cigarettes. Slowly and deliberately he lit one, scorching the tips of his fingers with the match before he absently blew it out.

'I miss you, Hannah. I miss you all. You're right. I haven't thought about you enough. Seeing you makes me sad because I realise what I'm missing. Your growing up years.' Shame prevented him from continuing.

'You don't have to live here. You can come home.' Hannah's face brightened. 'Come home with me. Please, Daddy.'

There was silence as he looked away and Hannah studied his face. It seemed as if he was frozen in time. He flicked his ash and drew deeply on his cigarette. Then he said, 'I can't.'

'Why?' She began weeping, making him feel tense, and unable to comfort her.

'I don't know. I'm sorry about it all. I only know I was greatly relieved to get away. It was a living hell for years. Your mother sentenced me to death after she lost the baby. Our lives were miserable and then when things started to go well after David was born, she didn't seem to need me anymore. Not even to persecute me with her wailing and moaning.'

'It couldn't have been all her fault.' Hannah's voice was cold, defensive, her face sorrowful from her father's rejection of her mother, and herself. 'I'm sorry if all this hurts you but I'm hurt too. We all are.'

'Let's go and get something to eat. The sun's gone in.'

He took her to the pub he worked in near Pimlico, and proudly introduced her to the staff.

'She's beautiful, Tom, the image of yourself.' Joe, a small, rotund man with a bald head, told him.

'That's the first time anyone told me I'm beautiful,' Tom joked, his old self now that he had given himself a reprieve from Hannah's intense probing. He felt safe among his friends in the pub, for the moment anyway.

'What'll you have, Hannah? It is Hannah, isn't it?'

'Yes,' Hannah said to the friendly barman who eyed her from head to foot. 'I'll have a glass of lemonade please.'

Someone laughed. 'Nothing stronger? Gin and tonic? Drop of scotch in the lemonade?'

'No, thank you. I don't drink.'

'No vices either. Where did you get this perfection of a girl, Tom?'

'She was always a good girl,' Tom smiled and Hannah saw the pride shining in his eyes.

Later when they were alone in his bedsitter he said to her, 'I suppose I haven't been the world's best father to you. Or the husband your mother had hoped for. I tried, Hannah. You see I never was able for scenes. I suppose we had enough of them when I was young.'

'Tell me about when you were young. You never talk about it.'

'I grew up on a small farm. I worked with the rest of the family during the holidays. Sometimes my father kept me home from school when they were busy. I resented that because I wanted an education. If I didn't stay my mother would have had to do the work and she wasn't strong. I couldn't bear to see the way she slaved in the house, and on the farm as well. Her health was destroyed from trying to take care of seven of us with very little help from my father. He certainly didn't give her many luxuries.'

'He probably didn't have much to give.'

Her father gave a bitter laugh. 'He'd have had more if he drank less. He drank too much and that was the problem. He shut himself away in the shed for hours in the evening, and if the lads didn't have all their jobs done about the place when he came out, he beat them. He even beat my mother for not making them do the chores. When he went to the market to sell the pigs, or the calves we'd all help to fatten, he was gone for a couple of days. My mother never spoke while he was away. She didn't eat anything either. We all knew she was terrified of his coming back, or not coming back. One fear was as bad as the other. She would tremble when she heard the clop of the horses hooves coming into the yard, and the jolt of the cart as he swung himself down from it.'

"I had business to attend to," he'd say, throwing the parcels of food in the door ahead of him, a sort of peace offering. My mother wouldn't answer, she'd just bend down painfully in gratitude, to pick up whatever he gave her.'

'That's shocking.' Hannah's face had whitened while her father spoke.

'It wasn't all bad. Christmas time was wonderful.' Tom's face lit up at the memory. 'He'd bring us balloons, and a whole jar of sweets, a side of beef, salted fish, candles, enough food for weeks. Little trinkets from Mad Kate's.'

'Who was Mad Kate?'

'She owned the only toy shop in the village. God knows where she got her stock from but she sold the best guns and holsters, and the prettiest dolls. I think she made the rag dolls herself. They all looked floppy and had wild raggy hair like her own.'

Hannah laughed.

'He'd have a special present for my mother like scented soap, or a lavender bag for her sheet drawer. If he was feeling really generous he'd buy her material to make herself a nice lace blouse, or a length of cloth for a skirt. She'd smile at him while she cooked his tea, letting go of her long-suffering silence for once. She'd ask him about the people he met. Friends, relations, anyone who bought and sold in the market. She'd even forget how he had her trapped into a life of drudgery, so grateful was she for the little she got. That was during the good times.'

'Don't tell me any more if it's going to upset you, Daddy.'

'All I wanted was a bit of an education so I wouldn't get trapped like her. I hated her for her calm acceptance. I blamed her for letting him bully her, and I pitied her. To tell you the truth I couldn't get away from them quick enough. Father Brophy spoke up for me, begging my father to let me go to the vocational college because I was so keen on electronics.' He shrugged.

'Come home with me Daddy, please.' Hannah extended her hand to him.

'You know when you were born I was terrified of you. You were so quiet, so placid, that I thought there might be something wrong with you. I was afraid to hold you in case I'd hurt you. Most of the time I kept away from you, and your mother complained about my coldness, my removal from her and you. So I lifted you up when you cried, until I found myself looking forward to holding you. Sometimes I held you until my arms were stiff, and then I'd go for a few pints with the lads and she would be resentful and bitter when I returned. She expected too much because she had invested so much in our marriage. That's what she said anyway.'

He moved to the window and looked out at the bleak houses across the street, their shadows lengthening in the evening sun. He looked lonely standing there in the quietness.

'Maybe if you stopped living in the past and joined us in the real world, Daddy.' Hannah crossed the room and stood in front of him. 'Everything is changing. Since you left David has grown so much. He's playing football and he's really good at it. Mammy has to go to all the matches because you're not there. She really misses you. And I'm finished school ...'

'And about to enter a bloody convent.' He slammed his fist down on the table.

'You're still married. You're not free to walk around London doing what you like, and feeling sorry for yourself. You are my father and I need you at home with me. We all need you.'

'I can work here, send you money. You need that more.'

'Rubbish.' Hannah leaned forward and thrust her face into his. 'That's an excuse. You could easily get a job at home. One more suitable than working in that dingy pub.'

Suddenly she was crying and a desperate feeling for him to comfort her like he did when she was a child came over her. She moved away. He heard her as though from a great distance offering to make tea or coffee for him. He went to the sink where she was filling the kettle and put his arms around her. Her cheeks were flushed from crying, her hair damp from the tears. 'Hannah, lovey, we need to talk.'

'More?'

'Yes, my darling.' He turned her face to his. 'We need to talk about sending my beautiful daughter to become a nun.' His voice was full of tenderness. 'I suppose I need to be there to make sure you mother doesn't have the last say in everything. To satisfy myself that what you are doing is what you really want to do.'

'Oh, Daddy,' Hannah threw herself into his arms and sobbed and sobbed.

'I'll come home with you.' He held her, rocking her gently and lovingly as if she were a baby again, whispering tender words of comfort to her.

Chapter 12

The city centre was a flurry of activity, people dodging and weaving in and out of heavy traffic, queues lengthening for buses. Hannah, ignoring the rush-hour commuters, moved swiftly through the crowd with self-assurance and confidence. She made her way to the Community Centre where she worked every day now. Here a group of teenagers awaited her.

'Hi, Sister,' they chorused, their greeting friendly.

Adjusting the short skirt of her blue suit, and straightening her shoulders, she stood before them, scanning the familiar faces.

'How's everyone since our last meeting?' she asked.

A mixture of expletives reverberated around the room. 'Not bad' was the one Hannah picked up on.

'You're not bad, Fiona. Tell me about your week?'

'I managed to stay off the sauce for four whole days. Mainly because I was stone broke.'

'Stoned, you mean,' someone said and everyone laughed.

'You did well. How about you, Philip?'

A lean-faced boy with a crew cut shrugged his shoulders. 'I'm clean, for the time being anyway. It's not easy though.'

The smile that hovered around Hannah's mouth widened.

'Great news. As I said to you before, Philip, if you want to talk about it, phone me. We all need a prop.'

'What's yours?'

'God, and believe me I need him.'

'How do you phone him?'

'I dial direct.' There was a hoot of laughter.

'What do you say?'

'I tell him that my life is in his hands, because I have a commitment to him and that I know he will honour our contract. Then I listen to his voice.'

There was silence.

'He's my crutch, like drink and drugs are yours. The difference is he's good for the health. Drink and drugs aren't.'

'Look what you had to give up though!'

'Yes. I gave up a lot, if you consider wordly pleasures, independence, freedom. Then there are the compensations.'

'Like what?' Philip's voice was edgy.

'I have his protection, his undying love. He's not going to drop me for someone else, no matter how old or ugly I become.'

'You'll always be beautiful, Sister,' Maureen in the front row said, and a voice added, 'Lucky God.'

Hannah blushed and said, 'You are all special too. Just because you're not in touch with him doesn't mean he cares any less. Don't lock yourselves away in your depression, saying no one cares. He cares. I care through him.' Some had a fixed stare that denoted their dependence on drugs, others listened intently.

'Do you mind being broke all the time, Sister?'

'No. Do you?'

'Yes. I hate it.'

'Well then, we'll have to talk about getting you something to do that will earn you some money.'

'You don't look poor, Sister,' one teenager said.

'I'm supplied with everything I require. Since the Second Vatican Council we have more access to pocket money because we have more freedom. I have no possessions though and that suits me fine. They're cumbersome when one is on the go all the time like I am.'

'No fixed abode like me?'

'Well, I have shelter in whatever convent I'm asked to work in.'

'You've no responsibilities either.'

'That's why I can give you my full concentration. I don't have to rush home to get the husband's dinner.'

Hannah had taken these group meetings for several weeks now, yet the young people's fascination with her never seemed to diminish. 'By the way, where's Sandra?' Sandra was a young woman about whom Hannah was especially concerned.

'She said to tell you she couldn't make it. She'll probably be at the disco tonight.'

'I see. Now who had a bad time during the week and would like to talk about it?'

Hannah sat among them, coaxing their problems into the open, so that they could be identified and worked at.

Later she went with some of them to Blinks, the trendiest disco in town. The ear-splitting noise of music and laughter assaulted her ears.

'I'll never get used to this,' she said to Father Paul, who came to meet her.

He nodded. 'What'll you have to drink? The usual, or could I tempt you to something stronger?'

'Lime juice, please.'

While the place hummed with voices and explosive laughter, Hannah searched for Sandra. Sitting among the youngsters she realised the enormous task she faced. The discipline from a recent rigorous training course in drug addiction hadn't prepared her fully for the difficulties of this depressing mission. Her brief was to save the youngsters from the pitfalls of city life.

Hannah had moved back into Waterloo Road to work with the Drug Squad. Each day she tackled the pitfalls facing the youth in the city. She worked with two Jesuits, who lived among the youngsters and worked on the streets, while following the austere Rule laid down by Saint Ignatius Loyola. Life for the religious had changed since the Second Vatican Council. Hannah had effortlessly shed the image of the self-effacing, obedient nun, to emerge from the restriction of her cloister and habit, a beautiful woman, with red-gold hair that fell in natural curls around her face.

The older nuns found the heavy habits and plain chant difficult to discard. Only occasionally did Hannah fumble for the vast non-existent sleeves of her habit, where she used to hide her hands.

As the noise of the disco, rent the air she watched the kids who ran wild by day, and experimented with drugs, often driving themselves to madness. When the bishop had approached her and asked her to spend a year among the deprived street kids she had agreed happily.

'There you are, Sister.' Janet, a student with a mass of aggressive hair, joined her, her earrings swinging as she placed her wide bottom, tightly encased in jeans, beside Hannah.

Maureen, her friend, was waiting for Father Tim.

'Are you going to ask me to dance, Father?' she grinned.

Janet whispered to Hannah, 'She's obscene, chasing that poor priest. He has to mortify his flesh.'

Hannah laughed. 'I wonder what you'd think of the mortifications of the flesh that used to take place in our convents.'

'Such as?'

'The kissing of the feet in penance, for instance.'

Janet made a face. 'Obscene,' she repeated. 'You were lucky to get away from all that.' Her big soft eyes were trained on Hannah in sympathy.

'I still have my Rule to follow,' Hannah said, suddenly missing the quiet ordered existence of her convent.

It was in silence she could hear God. In the shadow of the cloister she could communicate with him. Yet it was in the clamouring of the disco that she fulfilled her vocation.

She excused herself and moved among the twisting limbs of the dancers, their eyes glazed, their bodies free of physical constraint. Combing the expressionless faces, she found Sandra wrapped around a tall young man with a shaved head.

'Ah, there you are.' The music stopped.

Sandra unwound herself and came towards her.

'Hello, Sister.' She smiled at Hannah.

'I have a place for you to stay, Sandra. You can move in tomorrow.'

The girl's face brightened. 'Oh, Sister, I can't wait. Last night was the worst. Luckily Mum came into the room or he'd have ...' She cast her jaded eyes downwards. 'If he knew I was leaving he'd have a fit. He expects me to stay to mind my mother.'

Hannah noticed the exhaustion creased into her features, as she recalled the roughness of Sandra's father, the sour smell of his breath. Inwardly recoiling, she said calmly, 'You'll have to leave before something terrible happens. Call in to me tomorrow.'

Next morning Hannah answered the knock on her apartment door to Sandra, she stood bleary-eyed, her hair untidy around her head.

'Come in,' she smiled. 'I was just making coffee.' She led the way to her tiny kitchen.

'I'm glad to see you,' she added.

Sandra took a seat, her dark eyes glinting under the sweep of her long lashes, as she eyed the poster on the door, 'Come to me all ye who laboured and are heavily burdened, and I will give you rest.'

Hannah placed a cup of coffee in front of her.

'He came home last night. He had a fit when he saw my bag half-packed. Got mad as hell.' Her voice roughened as she recalled her father's tantrums.

'I thought that might happen.' Hannah was full of sympathy as she looked Sandra sitting there in a man's outsize shirt over frayed, slitted jeans, that made her curvaceous figure look bulky.

'What about your training course? Isn't the interview today?'

'I'm not really dressed to go.' She looked half-apologetic, half-defiant. 'Anyway I've got a job.'

'Oh?' Hannah waited.

'Not bad money, fewer hours.' Sandra was evasive.

'Doing what?'

Sandra's eyes slid away from Hannah's direct gaze and settled on the far wall. 'Singing,' she said finally and then added, 'in a nightclub.'

Hannah looked at her sharply.

'It's decent enough.' Sandra was defensive. 'And I've always wanted to sing.'

'How did you get it?'

'Dave. That's the fella I was dancing with last night. He knows a lot of people in the show business world.' Her eyes shone proudly as Hannah recalled the lanky lad with the earring and shaved head.

'You could still do that training course, seeing as you're working nights. Have some sort of training for the future.'

Hannah was mentally picturing Sandra, semi-nude, in front of leering men who ran sweatshops and exploited women.

The plight of young girls like Sandra, exploited and oppressed, sent waves of nausea and outrage through her. As she looked at this lovely young creature of God who sat before her, her heart felt heavy, knowing that the next step for Sandra was the streets.

'You can stay here for a couple of nights if you like, Sandra. Until it's safe to move out permanently. Your father would never think of searching for you here.'

Sandra's eyes returned to the poster on the wall and then took in the neat, sparse apartment in a sweeping glance.

'No, thanks all the same. It's a bit inconvenient for work.' Her face was a mixture of sullen resentment and apathy. 'I'll be alright. I'll think about the course in a couple of weeks when I'm settled into this job.' Sandra sipped the fresh coffee Hannah place in front of her.

What she didn't want Hannah to know was just how much she was looking forward to singing in the different venues Dave had lined up for her.

'Keep in touch, Sandra. Let me know how you're getting on.'

'I will,' Sandra assured her and continued to sip her coffee as if she had all the time in the world.

Hannah gave her a ten pound note before she left, to tide her over until she got paid.

Hannah discovered what happened to Sandra subsequently by piecing together the young woman's disjointed descriptions when she visited her in hospital the following day.

Sandra had sallied forth to her new job, pressed the button in the lift of The Sundown Hotel marked Penthouse Suite, and shot up to the top floor, a long trench-coat covering her scantily-clad body. She walked down a long corridor, her spikey heels catching in the pile of the thick carpet, to a door marked Private. There in a bedroom designated for 'the artiste' she removed her coat and began her preparation for the night's entertainment. From a carrier bag she removed the black fishnet stockings, the red and black silk and lace bra, matching suspender belt and tiny matching panties. She fumbled with the fasteners, then levered her generous breasts into the cone-shaped cups, the lacey edges resting seductively against the solid flesh of her breasts.

She applied her make-up thickly and put lashings of mascara on her long lashes. Squalor and exploitation were the last things on her mind as she sprayed herself with her favourite body shop fragrance.

From outside the door marked 'Strictly Private,' she could hear the laughter, the clink of glasses, and the popping of champagne corks. As she opened the door she peered cautiously in, trying to pick out Dave in the intimate gathering of men

through a cigar smoke screen and semi-darkness.
She couldn't see him so she entered the noisy
room in nervous anticipation, and as she made for
the stage a spotlight found her and picked her
out. A cheer went up and then as the three-piece
band started to play the room fell silent. She
nodded to the band and smiled as they gave her a
thumbs-up sign; then she turned to her audience
and looked directly ahead into the darkness as
she began to sing.

'The first time ever I saw your face,
I felt the earth move beneath my feet and
I thought that the stars...'

Her pure voice came from the heart and as she
sang everyone stared at her. The power and
vitality she exuded took them by surprise. The
tempo changed to the beat of 'When am I goin' to
make a living?' Then she sang requests, bopping
around for the fast numbers and finally strutting
in a new-found confidence, inviting her audience
to join in with their stomping and clapping.

The applause was deafening and brought tears
to her eyes as she reluctantly left the stage. A
hand reached out and twanged her suspender belt
and, tingling with pleasure, she ran from the
room. At last she was going to make something of
herself. She was a singer. She could entertain. Her
father couldn't abuse and debase her any more.
She was somebody now. Somebody who could
stand on her own two feet. With the applause still
ringing in her ears she began to change. She

wished Dave would hurry up to share this wonderful happiness with her. After all, he'd made it possible for her. She was so preoccupied she didn't hear the noise until he was right behind her. She turned.

'Dave ...' The name died on her lips as she saw the big strange man from the front row leering at her, a bottle in one hand, a cigar in the other.

'Not thrilled to see me, Lolita?' he jeered, in a voice that was roughened by drink.

There was an ugly look in his eyes and she turned away from him.

He grabbed her arm and forced her to face him again.

'You'd turn your back on me, would you?' He staggered.

She met his bloodshot eyes defiantly. 'Will you excuse me, I'm expecting someone.' She managed to keep her voice steady though she was trembling inside. 'I must get dressed.'

'I want to see you completely naked. That's why I'm here,' he laughed, and she shivered visibly.

'Go away, please.' Her eyes were directly on his face, now red and perspiring.

'Oh, nice and polite aren't we all of a sudden. You weren't so polite in there wriggling your bum, enticing the men. So don't get all snotty with me. You're not just asking for it, baby, you're begging for it. Now take your clothes off.' He waited, taking a swig from the bottle in his hand.

'Please go. I'll call security.' She made a dash for the door, but suddenly he was ahead of her, turning the key, his agility astounding her.

He grabbed her. His breath fanned her face as he panted into her mouth.

'Now you listen to me. You're going nowhere.'

She stumbled, trying to keep her balance.

'I've got plenty of time and so have you. But I don't intend wasting it.'

He reminded her of a bull as he held her in a vice grip.

'If you won't remove your clothes, I'll oblige.' He tore off her bra.

Shaking with fear, tears blurring her vision, she kicked out, aiming at his genitals. She missed and he struck her across the face, 'You little slut.'

'Please,' she begged, 'let me go.'

So strong was the pressure on her arms as he held her that she slid to her knees without realising it.

'You'd prefer it like that, would you? Thought you might.' He started unbuttoning his fly.

She tried to get up and stumbled as he clamped his hand over her mouth to stifle a scream. Fighting for her life, she hit out at him but he retaliated by hitting her so hard she fell back into a heap on the floor.

'You bitch. If you just did what I told you ...' He crouched over her, grinding his huge body against her, while she sobbed and pleaded, 'Please, no ... please ...'

'I knew you'd be begging for it.'

Oblivious to her helpless cries, he straddled her and effortlessly pulling off the last vestiges of her underwear, he pulled down his trousers and pushed his throbbing penis into her. Groaning and lurching with each thrust he threw her into a paroxysm of agony, blinding her senses so that by the time he'd finished she lay in a crumpled heap on the floor. Sated, he lay beside her, oblivious to the fact that he was lying in a pool of her blood.

She must have passed out because when she came to she was alone and in terrible pain. Struggling to her hands and knees, she crawled to the door and tried to open it, only to find it locked from the outside. She cried out but knew that her voice was too feeble to be heard. She crawled to the bed but couldn't make it...

'Dave, where are you?' She wasn't sure if she was even making a sound.

She remembered the ambulance, the blurred faces, the hospital. She remembered the nurses bathing her gently, her cries as they tended the swellings and bruises between her legs and the scratches on her face. Unable to move and half dazed, she realised she was lucky to be alive. Then there was the gentle probing of the doctor and the questions she couldn't assimilate.

Dave found her there in the snow-white sheets, her face distorted with the swelling of the purplish bruises, the tears and the pain.

'He'll have to be punished for this,' she whispered.

'We don't want any trouble, Sandra.'

Her father stormed into her hospital room. His hysterical ranting and raving more than compensated for Dave's passivity.

'I'll kill the bastard,' he roared, clenching and unclenching his fists, and flexing his muscles.

Silent and ashamed, Sandra lay there, broken in body and spirit.

'Of course it's your own fault,' he declared. 'Dressing up like a tart. Enticement, that's what they'll call it in court. You led the bastards on and you knew it. Wait 'till I get you home. I'll make sure you don't run around half-naked again. As for that bastard who did this, he'll be singing soprano when I'm finished with him.' He laughed, a rough, ignorant laugh.

'I won't be coming home.' Sandra trained her eyes somewhere above his head so she wouldn't have to look at his murderous face.

'None of your cheek. Of course you'll be coming home.'

'Stay away from me. Do you hear? I want nothing more to do with you.' She spat out the words, her eyes blazing.

He wasn't prepared for the venom in her voice, or the savage hatred in her eyes as she looked at him squarely for the first time in her life.

'How dare you, you little tramp! That's my line. I should have disowned you, instead of which I'm here seeing to your welfare.'

'I hate you. I'm not taking any more of your crap. Do you hear? What have you ever done for me apart from ...' Her voice died but her eyes blazed as she remembered his horrific abuse, starting when she was only seven years old.

She remembered the pain he had repeatedly inflicted in the night when he came to her room and, without preamble, slid into her bed and lifting her nightie, tried to shove his enormous penis into her. She'd shut her eyes and when she cried out for her mother he had clamped a hand over her mouth.

'Mention this to your Mammy and she'll drop dead because her heart is bad,' he'd say. Or 'Do you want to kill your mother? Do what I say and your Mammy will be there for you forever.'

The pain of penetration would sear through her, knocking her senseless. She never knew when it would happen. Weeks would pass by, even a month and just when she thought it was all over and he'd forgotten, she'd see the shadowy figure lurching towards her, close her eyes and wait for the heaving and shoving to come to an end quickly.

If only her mother had intervened, taken her part, even taken more of an interest in her. Was it her declining health that caused her vagueness in regard to everything around her? Or did she really not know, or care?

It made no difference any more.

'You lay one finger on me,' she said to her irate father, then stopped as her mother entered the room.

The frail women in a black coat stood and stared from one to the other in amazement. When she saw the expression of hatred in her daughter's eyes she suddenly looked very old and very, very sad.

It was when Hannah came to visit that Sandra felt confused and frightened. Hadn't Hannah tried to warn her? Tried to steer her away from the gang she was mixing with, and direct her into a routine and towards a better future? She wouldn't listen.

There were no recriminations. No 'I told you so.' Just her sweet, reassuring smile.

'I've brought you a few things you might need.' Hannah took out the neatly pressed nightdress and underwear.

'Some chocolates to cheer you up from Father Tim.' She placed them with the latest women's magazines on the locker.

Sandra began to cry quietly, riddled with shame and guilt.

'That invitation still holds if you'd like to stay for a while. Just until you find your feet.'

Sandra nodded, unable to look at her, thinking of her slogan, 'Come to me all ye who labour and are heavily burdened ...'

'I should'a listened to you,' Sandra sobbed.

'You did what you felt was right. Who could blame you for wanting a career? Especially when your voice is so good. It's just unfortunate that the venue was the wrong one.'

No accusation, only compassion in her voice.

'Come home with me for a while, Sandra. At least until you feel better.'

Sandra finally agreed. Hannah accompanied her to her home to pack. Her mother didn't seem to care. Her father was away.

'Well, I hope you make a better fist of your life from now on. God knows, Sister, I did my best for her.' Her mother seemed stricken.

Sandra looked at her in amazement. Maybe she'd never really cared. Tears trickled down her cheeks as she recalled her mother's lack of interest in her welfare over the years. There was always the sickness, heart trouble, reasons why she couldn't be upset.

As her mother said goodbye Sandra seemed relieved. She was suddenly resentful of the lack of interest, the love withheld, the pain inflicted repeatedly on her by her father. Had they ever really wanted her?

Hannah tapped gently on the bedroom door.

'Come in,' a bleary voice called.

'Sandra, how are you?' Hannah asked, placing a tray of coffee and toast on the bedside table.

Sandra struggled up from beneath the duvet and tried to smile. Her mass of hair was caught up in an untidy knot. A film of perspiration made her skin glisten. Her worried eyes hovered on Hannah's.

'Feel any better?' Hannah poured out two cups of coffee and sat at the edge of the bed.

'A bit.' A weak smile flittered across Sandra's face and died.

'Eat some toast. You'll feel better.'

Sandra shook her head and leaned back on the pillows.

'I'm alright. I'm not sick or anything.' She began to nibble a piece of toast as if to prove her point.

'I know. But you've had a traumatic experience and it'll take a while to get over it. ' Hannah's hand reached for hers and held it gently. 'When you feel strong enough I want you to come with me to see Doctor O'Reilly at the Rape Crisis Centre.'

Sandra sat bolt upright, shocked.

'Rape Crisis Centre. What's that, for God's sake?'

'It's a centre for the victims of rape. You'll get counselling and a doctor will check you out thoroughly.'

'Counselling?'

'They'll talk to you to help you deal with the trauma. That's all. Don't be afraid.'

'I suppose you think I might be pregnant.' Sandra turned away.

'No, I don't. But there's always a possibility. What we have to do is make sure you're not. Ease your mind. Believe me, Sandra. These people are experts and can help you. You need to see them.'

Sandra's lip trembled. 'Will you stay with me, Sister? I mean for the examination ... with the doctor.' Her face was crimson now with distress.

'Of course I will. That's the whole idea. Now eat up and have a nice hot bath when you're ready.'

'Thanks. Thanks a lot. I'm sorry to be such a nuisance.'

'You're not a nuisance. That's what I'm here for. And don't worry. They won't bite you. They know what being a woman in today's world involves. Believe me, they're shock proof. Anything you tell them will be treated confidentially.'

Sandra smiled wanly.

'I won't be long getting ready,' she said.

As Hannah drove Sandra to the Rape Crises Centre she secretly hoped that the seeds of her downfall had not already been sown. Casting a glance at the girl beside her, her eyes hidden behind a mask of eyeliner, cheeks gaudy with blusher, lips enlarged with bright pink lipstick, all disguising her pretty, girlish innocence, Hannah wondered what chance she had in this competitive world where a young innocent girl was encouraged into a life of sin. Because it was fashionable. And because she was poor.

* * * * * *

Sandra reminded Hannah of Katie. Her school pal had done well in London in the beginning. Her outraged defence of her actions in a letter to Hannah, bore out her love for Patrick. She wrote, explaining her silent battle of wills with her mother, adding passion to her brave deed.

'I didn't mean to fall in love with Patrick,' she explained. 'It just happened. I didn't want to disgrace my mother by having an illegitimate baby in Kilgarragh. Patrick is standing by me. We had the good fortune to get jobs. I'm a receptionist in the Regent Palace Hotel, in Picadilly, and he's working there as an electrician.'

Hannah kept writing to Katie and, from Katie's replies, she was able to piece together the ups and downs of her pal's first months in London.

Soon after arriving in London, Katie had discovered she was pregnant. One morning, on her day off, in fact, she lay in bed, musing. Reluctantly she opened her eyes and watched the dust motes dance in the light as she tossed back the quilt. She swayed on her feet, full reality dawning on her. Today she was going to tell Patrick.

She padded along the thick peach carpet to the pine kitchen and sipped reheated coffee, her silky shoulders hunched. While the toast burned she stuffed her slim black briefcase with files and gave herself a little time to think.

She'd done well since she came to London. Running off with Patrick had charged her with a feeling of dramatic romance. The conspiracy and silent battle of wills with her mother excited her. When the euphoria wore off she wrote at speed to her mother telling her of her good fortune in landing a job. She and Patrick were saving to get married the following spring. She hoped her mother and father would understand and be happy for them both. She read over the letter and realised that her mother would see that it was a small offering to pacify her and wouldn't consider it good enough. She decided to keep silent rather than face the criticism and abuse her mother would hurdle at her. She'd drop into oblivion. Given time, her mother she hoped would accept the situation, even if only with quiet endurance.

Back in her bedroom she wriggled into a mini business suit, coaxing the zip over the bulge of her tummy and the swell of her breasts. Carefully she pulled sheer black stockings over perfectly shaped legs and tamed her sleek dark hair.

At the reception desk she crushed her baby-filled body behind her large desk, and waited for

Patrick. He eventually strode in cool and confident, his smooth high cheek bones pale beneath shadowed eyes.

'God, I'm tired,' he said, squeezing her shoulders when no one was looking, and checking his watch at the same time.

'Another stressful day begins. I have to rewire the sixth floor. Get's a cuppa coffee, love. There's a good girl.' He sighed and flicked through the post lying on the desk.

'Confidential,' she snapped and moved the letters out of his reach.

Suddenly she felt primitive and defensive about her condition.

'I've planned dinner tonight in the staff quarters. Would eight o'clock suit you?'

'Great. I love your cooking.' He kissed the top of her head. 'Filet mignon or tripe and onions?' He raised his eyebrows. 'Tell you what! Surprise me!'

'That I'll do,' Katie murmured while making a grand gesture out of tidying her desk.

'What's the occasion?' He raised a quizzical eyebrow.

'Nothing special,' Katie lied.

He gave her one of his heart-stopping smiles, blew her a kiss and sauntered off in the direction of the lifts.

She left slightly early in the evening. Her popularity among the staff would ensure that someone would cover for her. Over the glint of silver, the chink of china and cut glass, borrowed from the kitchens, the table between them giving her false confidence, Katie told Patrick she was pregnant.

'I was waiting for the curse and it never came. The test proved positive.' Her voice trailed away, and with brimming eyes she gazed at the window where outside branches made shadowed patterns that swayed in the evening breeze.

Patrick jumped to his feet.

'For Christ's sake, Katie,' he shouted, banging his fist on the table, shattering one of the glasses, 'What the hell were you thinking of? You're on the pill, aren't you?'

'I forgot to take it a couple of times.'

'You're stupid,' he roared.

'Patrick.' Katie was horrified.

He didn't hear her. 'I always knew that behind that veneer of quick-witted intelligence you were dumb.'

Stuffing his hands into his pockets he moved to the window and gazed out, seeing nothing.

Katie's chair crashed to the ground as she jumped to her feet. 'How dare you!' she exploded.

'Do you realise what this means?' he continued, ignoring her. 'It means,' he repeated for emphasis, twirling around to face her, 'that we won't have a penny starting off. You'll have to give up work. We'll have to get married sooner. Plus there's the burden of carrying the child for nine months and the ordeal of giving birth. Of course the decision of whether to have it or not is ultimately yours.'

She saw for the first time an expression of dislike on his face.

'You make me feel like a traitor,' she said, at the same time recognising that his point of view was valid.

'What choice do I have?'

'Get rid of it.' His response gave the whole mess a tragic dimension.

She was appalled.

'I may have been dumb enough to get myself into this fix but I'm not stupid enough to expect or want anything from you.' As she spoke the brave words Katie searched her heart and realised she couldn't manage without him.

Patrick perched himself on the edge of the sofa and contemplated his fingernails as if seeing them for the first time.

'I'll get another job so I won't be an embarrassment to you.'

'Don't be stupid. You wouldn't get another job. Not for long anyway.'

'So you want me to murder my baby. You'll probably be glad to see me dead too. You don't want to marry me at all. You're a thief. You've taken everything I had to give you and now that I served my purpose ...'

She raged. Her eyes blazed. She raised an empty glass and smashed it against the wall. She lifted another one and flung it across the room. He wrenched a crystal decanter from her and she grabbed a jagged piece of glass as she backed away from him, her eyes blazing, her mouth working but no words coming out.

As he watched she slashed one of her wrists with the glass. Blood pumped out of her as she screamed a demented scream, moving around, trailing blood in her wake.

'Get out of here. Leave me alone,' she screamed.

'I just said I'll stand by you.' He was frightened.

'Thanks, but no thanks. Now get out'. She spat at him, then cowered in a corner while he phoned for an ambulance.

In the hospital he tried to talk to her. She just kept screaming.

Grief and guilt overwhelmed him when he saw the dreadful state she was in.

'Katie, I'm sorry. We'll get married. Everything will be alright.'

The doctor asked him to leave.

'I'll be in touch when you're more reasonable,' he said to her.

'I'm as reasonable as I'll ever be,' Katie shouted.

As the door closed she found herself already feeling the pain of his departure. She clutched her body instinctively in a protective gesture.

Plans and cold hard facts were nothing new to Katie. Her life had been planned by her mother every inch of the way. Targets and deadlines were set until the day she left home for London to take charge of her own life and destiny. She'd take the first job she was offered outside London to get away from Patrick. She thought suddenly and longingly of the career in dress designing she always craved. That dream will have to die now. She'd write to every hotel in England if necessary. She'd get a job now, no problem. She wouldn't tell them she was pregnant.

While she planned she used her anger as a weapon to keep the pain under control. When she was discharged from the hospital she went back to the hotel alone, the gash in her wrist concealed by thick wadded plaster. She attacked her work with ferocity and arranged her departure without speaking one word to Patrick. It was difficult to avoid him. She met him in corridors and in the canteen. Each time he tried to speak to her she ignored him until he too fell into a sullen silence.

The day she left she did her full quota of work as usual, and flung her diary in the wastepaper basket along with a bunch of memos from Patrick that began with 'I'm sorry, please forgive me. Can you ever forgive me?' That's as far as she read, then began clearing out her desk.

In the evening she watched homeward-bound pedestrians making slow-moving shadows on the littered street below. If only she could freeze everything in a time-warp and progress with her life just as before. But one thing was certain. Life would never be the same again. Not since her biological clock went wrong by a couple of months and won over her cleverness.

She sighed deeply and on second thoughts wrote a cryptic goodbye to Patrick. She left no forwarding address. By this time tomorrow she'd be dispossessed of everything familiar and dear to her.

A week later she unpacked her few possessions in her comfortable room in the Grand Hotel in Leeds. Receptionist in the Grand Hotel meant little travelling and more office work. She was too tired to socialise so most nights she lay in bed in semi-darkness, listening to the noise of the night traffic below and thinking of Patrick.

She missed him. Missed his dark, manic intensity. His passion. But passion was a cold and lonely companion that swept you up and carried you along only to leave you high and dry. Her loneliness cast a shadow over her life, a shadow upon which to focus her unease about her future. She had to admit that the life she had shared with Patrick was good, if volatile. They nurtured each other's ambitions with their separate enthusiasm. They planned their future together until she reneged on him and upset the fine balance of their relationship by getting pregnant and ruining their future prospects. She missed him.

Early one afternoon he phoned.

'I'll be in Leeds on business tomorrow. How about lunch?' he said, disguising his nervousness behind a laconic familiarity.

The shock of hearing his voice again reverberated through Katie.

'I don't think so,' she began.

'I need to see you, Katie. Talk things over. No, don't hang up on me.'

The yearning for him returned and she succumbed. The hairdresser sighed condescendingly to convey the enormous favour he was doing her by fitting her into his lunchtime break at short notice, so she tipped him handsomely. She bought a ridiculously expensive baggy shapeless dress but still managed to look fat. Would he notice how dull and prosaic she'd become? The hormonal changes in her body were her undoing.

'I miss you,' he told her, sitting there glowing with good health and humour.

The smell of his cigarette smoke made her feel nauseous and lonely.

He ordered drinks.

'To us,' he said. 'How's the job?'

They raised their glasses in unison and Katie watched the tiny beaded bubbles surface and burst.

'I like it. I like the freedom.' Her look was defiant.

He wasn't listening.

'We'll make up for everything,' he said, attacking his steak while she remembered everything she'd ever loved about him.

'You're coming home with me.' Though he kept his voice casual it was delivered in the form of an instruction.

'No.'

His eyes were disbelieving.

'You have to come home. You have to let me take care of you.'

'I can take care of myself, thanks. I've proved that. Now if you'll excuse me I've a lot of work to catch up on. Thanks for the lunch. It was nice seeing you.' She scraped back her chair and called goodbye over her shoulder to a dumb-struck Patrick.

She left quickly, winding her way through the tables. She'd have to work out her leave of absence to coincide with the baby's birth. She could work after the baby was born, when her social welfare allowance was finished. She would write to Hannah today and tell her. Hannah would understand. She could rely on her for sound advice. She felt guilty about Hannah. She owed her an explanation if nothing else.

While she moved through the lunchtime shoppers she checked her watch. She walked faster and then remembered that the hotel was only around the corner.

Hannah replied to her letter by return.

'I'm glad you decided to keep the baby. You must come home at once and let me take care of you. You can't be on your own at a time like this. You need help. Come home. I'll help you.

Best love, Hannah.'

Katie wrote again and told her she had decided to have the baby in England and would make a decision then about the future.

'Have you ever heard of an unmarried mother returning to have a baby? I'm well organised here with my insurance to cover the end of my confinement.'

But Katie didn't take the loneliness into consideration. She attended her anti-natal classes and chatted to the others, all the time keeping her distance. Two weeks before her baby was due she went into labour. She took a taxi to the hospital and quietly signed herself in. When her beautiful baby daughter was born it never occurred to her to tell anyone. She lay with her baby wrapped in her arms gazing at the rosebud mouth and downy hair.'

'I'll look after you. I promise.' She kissed the tiny head. 'I'll make sure you have a good life. I promise,' she whispered, unconvinced.

The door opened and Patrick stood there, smiling, an enormous bunch of flowers in his arms.

'Who told you?' Katie asked.

'I have my contacts. I came as soon as I got word.'

'You needn't have bothered.'

'You didn't think I'd desert you. I came to take you both back to London with me. I found a flat.'

He beamed with pleasure at his little daughter.

Katie didn't have the strength to resist. Secretly she was glad.

Chapter 13

Just before Easter Hannah returned to her convent in Wicklow for her annual retreat. Each evening after Compline, during meditation, she re-dedicated herself to God. Repeating her vows before the blessed sacrament, she meditated on them. Poverty, chastity and obedience. Recalling the day she decided to tell her mother she wanted to be a nun, she remembered sitting in the garden, the sun on her face, the blare of the Beatles singing, 'Are you going to Strawberry Fair' on the radio next door. Her first mini-skirt was hanging in the wardrobe, bought out of the meagre wage packet from Mrs Cunningham. It never occurred then that she would miss The Rollings Stones, the Beatles, her long hair or the occasional dance in the local club on a Saturday night. Deep down she always wanted to be a nun, from the day of her First Holy Communion, when, without realising what she was doing, she promised herself to God, because her mother whispered in her ear to do so. Her religion was her birthright, her mother said, and it was her mother's reliance on her faith that nurtured it. As a child she accompanied her to daily mass.

Reflecting on her vows she felt comfortable with them, believing that her life was the way that God had ordained it. She was content to devote her affection to God, and through him, to love others. Stephen was conveniently grouped in her 'love other' category because she could deal with her feelings towards him in that way. The gnawing guilt of their love for one another bothered her conscience.

In his letters he openly expressed his love, distance giving him the security to do so. She blended the solace and strength they gave her into her solitary life. Dealing with the youngsters in her care gave her new insights into the purpose of her existence, and how she related it to others. She meditated on God's divine plan for her, as it unfolded, and felt satisfied.

'The followers of Jesus must love their neighbours,' she read from her *Imitation of Christ*. She worried about her charges, particularly those who were sleeping rough. She prayed for them and for her parents. Were they happier now? They always seemed cheerful when they came to see her. David was a law student in UCD and called to see her frequently. Could she have served them better if she had stayed at home and got a job after university? There had always been a shortage of money. Her mother would be outraged if she knew Hannah even harboured such thoughts. She had done the right thing by her mother. Early in the Novitiate she had found the silence, the lack of communication, a trial. Now she sought out silence, so that she could listen to God. Mother Clement was dead now but her simple message lived on in the spiritual readings, 'Strive for perfection in all that you do, whether sweeping the floor, or counselling the needy.' Hannah could still hear Mother Clement's voice in the recesses of her mind, 'Keep yourselves tidy, keep your sewing perfect. A tidy body is a tidy mind.' As the retreat progressed her active world receded and she prayed.

This was a time of quiet. No laughter, no voices, no scented bath, a luxury she occasionally allowed herself. During the rosary she prayed for her young people, remembering each one's individual needs. Sometimes during divine office she could feel God's love. At other times he was so remote to her that she questioned his existence.

'Unless you be like little children,

You shall not enter the Kingdom of Heaven.'

She listened to the words, was consoled by them. After the silence, she knew she would find the enthusiastic conversation of her friends in the inner city tiring.

'My soul glorifies the Lord and my spirit rejoices in God my Saviour, because he has looked down on the lowliness of his handmaiden and behold, all generations shall call me blessed.' Changes had taken place in the convent over the years. The gregorian chant had disappeared, along with the black habits. The old nuns who had died had not been replaced. Vocations had dwindled. How long would her community survive without new blood? Hannah began to pray.

'How about it?'

'How about what? Hannah met Billy's gaze, her lips curved in a slight smile of encouragement.

'How about a quick fuck?'

'Billy!' Astounded, Hannah lowered her eyes and concentrated on the notes she balanced in her lap.

Billy grinned at her embarrassment, his face level with hers, his dark eyes studying her disapproval. His cheeks were hollow, his hair tousled. But the blue shirt and faded jeans were neat and clean. He had made himself presentable for her.

'Well, you can't blame me. I haven't seen you for a whole week. Missed you the last day you were here. Were you avoiding me?'

'Goodness, no. The last time I called you were gone for assessment. Then I went on retreat. Didn't the warden tell you?'

'Typical.'

Hannah's eyes roamed the narrow, airless cell where Billy was incarcerated for the last six months for drug offences. A shaft of sunlight glanced off the side of the high window, making the cell unbearably claustrophobic. He stood up, his long legs encumbered by the lack of space, frustration obvious in his jittery movements.

'They won't believe I didn't do it.'

'Don't resist them, Billy. Try to relax and answer the questions.'

'You mean stop fucking and blinding at them.'

'It would make it easier on yourself in the long run. Have you seen any of your family?'

'No and I don't want to. Solitude suits me fine for the moment. I don't trust anyone, apart from you of course.'

'Right. Let's go through this again. You couldn't have put the drugs in the teddy bear because you were in Galway at the time.' She took notes, earnestly writing while he talked, translating his frustrations to paper.

'I hate to admit it, Hannah, but I can't cope.'

She looked at him. 'You look well. A bit thin but all things considered you're coping in spite of yourself. Would you like a cup of coffee?'

'Well, I suppose if I can't have a fuck I might as well settle for the coffee. The only time I get a decent cup is when you're here.'

'You never give up,' she said, shaking her head as she went to the door.

'Hannah, I didn't plant those drugs in the teddy bear. I didn't have any drugs at the time.'

'I know that, Billy. You'll have to be patient. The appeal will clear you. Are you eating?'

He nodded.

'Exercise?'

'Yes.'

'Have you decided what you'll do when you get out?'

A shaft of light lit up his face as he turned towards the window. 'I'm going to take your advice and go back to college. Unless the folks have written me off.'

'I'll go and see them. Convince them that this time you're determined. If you are serious about college, Billy, it would be wonderful.' Hannah's face was radiant with enthusiasm as she spoke.

'Will you come to Australia with me, Hannah, when I'm qualified. I'll have something to offer you then.'

Hannah looked at his earnest face. 'I'm not free' Billy. You know that.'

'Would you come if you were free?'

She blushed. 'Who knows? The fact that I'm not free denies me the right to answer it.'

'You nuns are all the same. Evasive. Or else you talk in riddles.'

The warden came into the cell. 'Your coffee, Sister,' he said, without a glance at Billy.

'Thank you, Tom,' Hannah began pouring the coffee into the disposable cups.

'No trouble at all, Sister. Anything else you'd like?'

'A couple of chocolate biscuits,' Billy said.

The warden ignored him.

'No, thank you.' Hannah shot Billy a silencing glance.

When the warden left Hannah said, 'I'll be in the court, Billy, to hold your hand.'

'When do you think it'll come up?'

'Anytime now.' She finished her coffee and prepared to leave.

Billy's eyes never left her face.

'Take care of yourself. Soon as you're out of here you'll begin to feel like a whole person again.' She rumpled his hair affectionately and he caught her hand in his.

'I never want to live through anything like this again. I'm frightened, Hannah.' Tears shone in his eyes. 'I wouldn't have survived without your visits, only they end too quickly.'

'You'll make it. You'll see.' Honest belief was in her eyes.

'Just my luck that you're a nun.' His smile was bitter.

'If I weren't a nun I wouldn't be here. We'd never have met.'

'Yes, I suppose,' he said grudgingly. 'See you on Monday and thanks.'

Hannah arranged civil aid for him and kept his family informed of his progress. She encouraged him to write down the reason why he got hooked on drugs, and as much as he could about his dependence on his habit.

'Writing it down will force you to look inside yourself. You might find your own solution,' she told him.

Leaving him alone now, she felt the disturbed

silence.

One month later she stood outside the courtroom with a jubilant Billy, his freedom regained. He had to face the reality of returning to his temporary home, a cardboard box in the shelter of a doorway near the rank-poisoned Liffey. He'd lent his pitch and box to his friend Johnny for the duration of his stay in the Joy.

'I hope Johnny hasn't scarpered, leaving my well-insulated double duvet home to the mercy of the others.'

Hannah laughed. 'We'll get you another one.'

'I'm attached to my patch. I like the neighbours. Nobody asks questions because they don't care. Too busy surviving themselves to bother about other people.'

They found Johnny in Billy's doorway, the box covered with newspapers and plastic sheeting, to keep out the cold.

'You're back.' Johnny was unenthusiastic.

'What's she doing here?' He eyed Hannah suspiciously.

'She's a friend.'

Johnny threw his eyes heavenwards. 'Weirdo,' he said under his breath.

'Make a cup of tea and shutup.' Billy lit the primus and put a dingy saucepan on to boil.'

'You weren't in too long.' Johnny rubbed his hands together before the primus stove.

'Sorry to disappoint you.'

Hannah had bought groceries and rummaged

among them now for the tea bags.

'Anyway,' Billy continued, 'I was innocent. They got the guy who stuffed the teddy bear. When I get him I'll knock the stuffing out of him.'

'Billy, get the cups,' Hannah said.

'What did he get?'

'His case hasn't come up yet. It'll be nothing to what he'll get when I get my hands on him for planting me.'

'Billy.' Hannah looked exasperated. 'You have more important things to do with your life.'

'Such as?' Johnny said.

'Such as mind your own business and have a cup of scald. How are things with you?' She asked Johnny.

'Not bad. Got a few spots from Red. Kept me going. You'll miss the Joy, Billy. Warm food, warm bed, snooker.'

'Great welcome home. I can see I'm wanted. I'll never miss jail.' Billy looked at Hannah. 'At least here I can think. Do what I like without the noise of those bloody ping-pong balls ringing in my ears.'

'You're not staying here.' Hannah said.

'Planning another trip abroad? Turkey maybe?' Johnny guffawed.

'Shut your foul mouth in the presence of a lady. I'm going straight from now on.'

'I won't be here much longer either.' Johnny looked sad.

'Where are you off to?' Hannah asked.

'James's before long. Those bloody sores have festered again,' Johnny pulled up the sleeve of his jumper to expose the pocked-marked arm, the blood already oozing.

'Let me look at that.' Hannah lifted his arm and studied it.

'You'd better get down there quickly and get yourself seen to.'

'Yea. Get yourself tested for everything. God knows what you might have picked up.'

'I'm a virgin,' Johnny protested. 'No woman has ever touched me.'

'I'm not surprised,' Billy turned away in disgust.

'You're using dirty needles, Johnny. I'll drop you down to the hospital when you've finished your tea.'

'I'm not ready to go yet,' Johnny protested.

'Do what the lady says.' Billy commanded.

There was a letter from Stephen waiting for Hannah on her return to Waterloo Road.

'I'm coming home for a holiday and I don't want to go back without seeing you. So much has happened since we parted. I have come to love my work here, and grown spiritually among these people. My love for you has grown too. In spite of everything, I have to see you, because I think you feel the same about me. It frightens me, yet I know I love you, and to say otherwise is not true. I can't continue my work until I resolve this conflict which is at the centre of my being. I know you are happy in your vocation and I will understand if you refuse my request. If you could arrange somewhere for us to be together...'

Her mind was pitched into a turmoil. Over and over again she read the letter, excitement at the thought of seeing him again, and dread of what might happen, filling her with panic. How would she arrange their meeting? How would she respond to the letter? His words forced her to examine her conscience and reveal to herself fully that she loved him. They loved each other, and as she made plans for their reunion she knew it could only bring heartbreak to their lives. The draw to him was stronger than the warning voice in her head. All the years they were apart they seemed to need the love they shared to sustain them. She was unable to express her love in words, so her expression was a caring, devoted one of communication through letters, itself a commitment.

Next day she asked Father Tim if the summer-house in Carrigeen, County Kerry, which the Jesuits used for holidays for deprived children, would be available to rent in August for a few weeks. She explained that her mother wasn't well and she wanted to give her a holiday.

Chapter 14

Hannah walked slowly towards the low white bungalow in Carrigeen, unremarkable except for the dull brass nameplate that read The Sanctuary. Blooms of neglected roses leaned against a stiff hedge, giving the place an austere look. It was a summer residence that stayed abandoned all winter. The stiff windows creaked as she opened them wide to the sea air. Gulls cried in the distance, and the smell of the sea crept into the sunlit rooms. She made up the beds with fresh white sheets, deciding as she did so to let Stephen have the room with the double bed. She put towels in the bathroom. When she had dusted the furniture in all the rooms she inspected her work. Pleased that the house looked habitable she took a shower, dressed, then made herself a tuna fish salad. Sitting out on the veranda, facing the sea, she planned each day's menu and wrote a shopping list.

Later she went for a walk along the cliff path. She noticed a heightening of her visual senses. Everywhere was alive and more intense than before. The blue of the sea, the green grass verge.

Fresh air seeped into her skin, warming it with a breath of sunshine. That night she lay in her bed, the anticipation of seeing him again making it impossible for her to sleep. She rose early next morning and walked for miles along the winding cliff path bordered by the sea. Dressed in a pale blue summer dress, hair wild, body lean, she walked fast. The salty tang in the air made her skin smart as the sea breeze assaulted it. She strode across the mud flats and, taking her shoes off, waded into the icy water, to the calling cries of the curlews. Barefoot, she made her way back up the steep cliff path. As she reached the top she heard someone calling her name. She stood at the edge, looking down on the beach, where the voice had come from. The silhouette of a man against the July coloured sky came towards her, a small dot in the distance, growing larger and larger, disappearing and reappearing around winding corners, until they finally came face to face.

'Hannah,' breathless he stopped and gazed at her, his eyes intense, his hair streaming in the wind.

His face was alive and joyous as he said, 'I can't believe it.'

The strong handsome features were more lined than she had remembered. How had she ever thought she had forgotten him? There was no one on earth like him and there never would be. He stood remote and magnificent. His hands reached out for hers and gripped them. Her eyes closed as he lifted her hand to his cheek and kissed it gently.

'Stephen.' Her voice was barely a whisper as he wrapped her in his arms, pressing the cold skin of his face against hers. She felt the warmth of his breath, the thrill of his body, as his exuberance carried her along in the wind.

He stopped and stood back, staring at her.

'I'd recognise that hair anywhere.' He lifted a strand to his lips. 'I've never stopped thinking of you.'

'I know.' Hannah felt intense and happy all at once. He touched the sprinkling of dusky freckles across her nose and ran his fingers down her tanned arms.

'Hannah.' His voice had the same rich vibrancy and he spoke her name as if he could not believe he was saying it. 'Hello, Hannah,' he repeated and she laughed.

Then suddenly she was in his arms, being hugged and held. She felt fragile to his touch as he gently let her go.

'How are you?' Her eyes were anxious.

'Much better now,' he smiled.

Suddenly he looked youthful and happy and Hannah's heart lurched with the pain of remembering.

'And you? I don't have to ask. You look beautiful.'

She breathed in the pure air, trying to stop herself from trembling.

'When you weren't at the house I came looking for you.'

'It's beautiful, isn't it?'

He nodded, gazing at the outstretched sea.

'It's best at the crack of dawn.'

He grabbed her hand. 'Let's cross the fields. If you'd risk climbing a few fences we're there.'

He lifted her over the first fence and held her. 'You're as light as a feather.'

She laughed, defusing the intensity between them.

The summer house sprawled on the side of a hill, with seaviews everywhere. The rooms were already sun-filled.

'I bet you'll feel at home here.' Hannah led the way into the kitchen.

'I love it already.'

She smiled into his earnest face.

'I'll put the kettle on. You sit down.'

Hannah stood watching the cliffs all around drop to the frill of foam that edged the sea and the empty beach.

'It looks treacherously steep at this end.' Stephen handed her a cup of tea.

'I'll stick to the gentler slopes. I find them exhilarating enough.'

Together they watched the cliffs stretching for miles, bleakly beautiful. She turned and looked at him. Their eyes met.

'You're as lovely as ever. You haven't changed.'

'Make no mistake I've changed.'

'All those years ago I loved you, Hannah, and wanted you. It nearly ruined my life. I was glad to get away. I don't think I'd have survived the priesthood if I hadn't.'

She saw the ferocity of his pain and was speechless. Watched him gather all his emotions and marshal them into rigid control. Love, desire, duty, will-power. She saw them all, separated them in her mind and wasn't deceived. It was he she had dreamed about and tried to forget, he she had loved and longed for. She turned her attention to the cliffs again so that she would not have to look at him. Nothing in her life had prepared her for this meeting. She stood still. He was here and nothing else mattered. Why didn't she run into his arms. She could not move, and prayed that her longing would not be revealed in her face.

They stood in silence and the silence grew. She kept her eyes ahead, taking in the small neat garden, the summer flowers.

'Hannah, what's the matter?'

She tried to study him objectively. A priest first, a man of God. An invisible God, timeless and remote. He was watching her, his vulnerability weakening his features to an almost liquid quality. Loneliness, lost opportunity and pain. Always pain. Did he still love her? He'd spent so many years controlling, dominating, subjugating his sexual desires that she wondered if his vow of celibacy had crushed them. He was first and foremost a priest.

'Hannah?'

She turned her eyes to him and before she realised what was happening she was in his arms. She left him in no doubt that she wanted what he wanted from the time of that first kiss. She was plagued by the wanting, never free of the draw to him. Her fascination for him went far beyond the acceptable boundaries of decency.

The image of her mother, when they visited the home farm in Tipperary, flashed through her mind. Her mother and John. Alive and radiant. Had she felt on the brink, as Hannah felt now?

'I'll have to go.' She moved away but he caught her arm and held her.

'Don't disappear on me, Hannah. Now that I've found you I couldn't bear to lose you again.'

'I won't,' she promised.

They went for walks along the deserted beach in the afternoons, walking close together, sometimes bumping into one another, occasionally apologising and moving rapidly away. They talked about their lives, absurdities, anything but their shared past.

'You look wonderful,' he told her over and over again.

He brought her chocolates, icecream, little gifts. They lazed in the afternoon sun, eating, talking. She never seemed to be able to part from him.

Then it happened.

He took her in his arms and kissed her, bringing back the longing, the pain, the love that had endured in her all those years.

'Come,' he said, taking her hand and leading her upstairs to the bedroom.

He locked the door and drew the flimsy curtains. She felt the fire in his body as he held her. Slowly he undid the buttons of her blouse, watching her body reveal itself to him. Her skirt fell to the floor. She helped him undress, removing his shirt, his pants. Naked, they lay in each other's arms. The strong afternoon sun exposed their nakedness to one another through the curtains. She was selfconscious, watching his intent expression as he knelt over her in a position of worship. The posture he adopted was reminiscent of the times he had knelt before the tabernacle in rapt adoration of his God. She said it to him.

'You're the temple of my soul,' he said simply. 'Your body is my tabernacle.'

Yet his adoration of her body made her uneasy. She felt exposed. He took her hand and guided it across his chest, slowly down his legs, familiarising her with the feel of him. Then he took her breast in his cupped hand and kissed it. She moved closer. As her excitement grew her inhibitions fell away and she was able to look at his naked body. She was careless and selfish all at once, gathering him closer to her. He came in her hand.

'I'm sorry,' he said

'It's alright. I'm happy to be in your arms.'

They made love in the growing darkness. This time he lay between her legs, gently coaxing her with butterfly kisses down her body, until he reached her stomach and thighs. When he found that most secret of places, her body exploded with longing, the depth of her feeling a revelation to her. She wanted to do the same for him. In her eagerness she grew desperate.

'What would you like me to do for you?' she asked him. 'Show me.'

'You don't have to do anything. Being here with you is all I want.'

He entered her gently, coaxing her with loving kisses. And after that, they could not get enough of each other. Making love was all they cared about. He looked magnificent and startled by it all. He was as much caught up in this labyrinth of ecstasy and deceit as she was, and as unwilling to do anything about it.

'I'm only happy when I'm with you,' he told her.

She never objected when he tried out new things with her. She knew his love was total. He was happy and well again, exhilarated by the sea and fresh air and Hannah's love for him. They drove into the countryside, cooked meals together, drank wine. They basked in the sun during the day and in the evenings watched the luminous sea stretch in a straight unbroken line along the horizon, its gentle ripples the only visible movement.

Hannah knew she was adrift. The reasoning side of her wanted to run back to the convent and hide before it was too late; the recklessness in her wanted to be carried along in the tide of passion that was dangerously out of control.

They were often caught out in the rain, but Stephen walked along uncaring. Hannah was concerned for his health. Some days he was tired, others vigorous and refreshed. Sometimes he woke damp with sweat and shivering uncontrollably. She sponged him down, all the time whispering words of love. Her tending calmed him. He got well again.

Days flew by, nights even quicker. They never talked about his imminent departure. As she watched him, when he was reading or listening to music, and saw the haunted look in his eyes, she knew he was being hunted down. God sat on his shoulders. Waiting. More than anyone she understood that he would be reclaimed by his God. She knew she did not stand a chance even if she were prepared to give up her own life as a nun.

He went for walks alone. She spent that time praying, trying to prepare herself for when she would be without him. How would she quell her passion? How would she live with herself after he had gone? The loneliness reared up at her as she admitted to herself her need of his love.

'We have to talk,' he said one evening as they lay in bed after making love.

She looked at him with dread.

'I love you, he said. 'I miss you already. I don't want to think of the rest of my life without you.'

'I love you too ...'

He raised his hand. 'Hannah, this isn't easy. Let me finish. I'm torn between my longing for you and my vocation. My love for you has got the better of me. I let it. We played a game, broke all the rules. Now we're going to suffer.'

They looked at each other. She felt the sensuous contact of his body as he brushed her lips with his.

'I love your laughter, your voice, your love for me. It's there in every movement of your body. It makes me helpless with love. I'm also scared of what our love has done to us.'

'Don't say anymore.' Hannah leaned forward, tears in her eyes. 'Please let's not talk about it.'

'We have to face facts, my darling. That means talking about the future, and that includes the Church. It's so much part of us. The liturgy, the ritual, its power. The working for a life hereafter. The vows we took. I saw my vow to remain celibate as the closest possible way to live in Christ and do his work. Now it's a nightmare.' His eyes filled with tears.

'Do you regret what we've done?'

'No. To regret it would be to deny our love. It's a dream that I never want to wake up from. A beautiful, erotic dream. Now we have to make choices. Leaving each other is an impossible demand to make.'

Hannah was thinking of him holding her in bed. Of tossing and turning, unable to sleep when he was downstairs reading, wanting him, yet knowing and accepting his greater commitment.

'I've prayed but there's no consolation from my prayers. It's as if God isn't listening,' she told him. 'If I were honest with myself I would admit I knew from the very beginning that you are essentially a priest.' She began to cry.

'Don't cry, darling. It will break my heart.' He reached for her but she pulled away.

'I justified my love for you by convincing myself that God wouldn't be angry. I deluded myself into thinking there was nothing wrong in loving you all these years. I have lived a lie.' Her voice broke.

'Yours was the sweetest face I'd ever seen. How could I resist those wide hazel eyes, reflecting the purity of your soul, the innocence in your quiet expressive features? God forgive me, but I couldn't help falling in love with you.'

Now he was crying too, racking sobs that convulsed his body.

'What have I done to you? To me? Will we ever be able to perform our religious obligations again?'

They held each other as they cried together ...

In the end their parting happened casually. Although she had warned herself to be prepared, Hannah was startled when he turned to her and said late one evening, 'I'm leaving tomorrow.'

They were walking along the beach. She did not answer, just moved away, picked up a few stones and began throwing them into the sea.

'Hannah, I have to.' A note of pleading for understanding had crept into his voice.

She did not turn around, just aimed and flung the stones with such ferocity that the plonking sound they made as they hit the water was like thunder in the silence.

'Stop throwing those blasted stones,' he shouted.

Startled, she let her hands drop to her sides.

'I'll write to you.' There was anguish in his face as he took her in his arms and buried her head in his shoulder.

'Of course you have to go.' She smiled encouragingly up at him, her heart breaking. 'You have lots of work to do. Come to think of it, so have I.'

Next morning when she woke up his space beside her was empty. She ran downstairs to the kitchen. The note propped against the kettle read 'Goodbye, my darling. Forgive me for not waking you. I couldn't have left you if I had had to say goodbye to your face. I love you. I'll write when I get to Nigeria. All my love. Stephen.'

She walked for miles and miles alone, breathing in the clear air, surveying the tiny frills of foam that edged the sea. She climbed the bare and treacherous cliffs he had warned her against, remembering him, re-living every intimate detail of their lovemaking. She stood looking over the stretches of sand bleakly beautiful, the tears rolling down her cheeks. She was desperately sad.

Chapter 15

The cold air whipped around Hannah as she hurried up the drive to the convent. She entered silently and made her way to her cell with only the bulb from the hall to guide her.

'Sister Marie Claire, you're back.' A light flooded her face and she blinked in the direction of Reverend Mother.

'Yes, Mother.' Hannah bowed her head to receive Reverend Mother's blessing.

'Did you enjoy your holiday? Are your family well?'

'Yes thank you, Mother. Everyone is fine. The weather was glorious.'

'Good. You needed that break. Sister Mary left your supper on a tray. You look as if you could do with it.'

'Thank you, Mother.' Hannah retraced her steps to the kitchen and sat down in its warmth to eat.

Everywhere felt strange and different. The familiar smell of the convent gave her no comfort. Her chicken salad nauseated her. That night she could not sleep. Next morning in the chapel she found it impossible to concentrate on the mass.

She returned to work with eagerness, gathering as many people around as she could, but lethargy overtook her and she found herself dozing off in her office in the afternoons. Then she began to feel sick.

When it finally dawned on her that she had missed a period she was terrified. Her religious training in obedience had taught her mind to die, so that she could subjugate her will to the authority of her superiors. To think for herself now and make decisions was almost impossible. She would have to leave the convent and her work among her deprived friends. Her heart was torn, knowing that the decision she was about to make would take her away from her convent, her sisters, and possibly her God, forever.

Sister Mary said to her, 'You're not eating. You look pale, Sister. Perhaps you need a medical check-up.'

Hannah looked at her in astonishment. Suddenly she was desperate to confide in her but all she said was, 'I'm probably getting the 'flu. I'll be alright, thank you, Sister.'

Had she imagined the strange looks of her sisters? She would have to leave before her condition became obvious, find herself a job, rear her child, and eventually seek a dispensation from Rome. More and more she turned from her sisters while she plotted and planned. Finally she made an appointment to see Reverend Mother.

'There's a course in London I'd like to attend, Mother.'

Reverend Mother's eyes shone in the lamplight as she gazed intently at Hannah.

'New information about drug addiction has come to light. Father Tim ...'

'Are you up to it?' Reverend Mother pursed her lips, her eyes never leaving Hannah's face. 'You don't look well. You work very hard as it is.'

Hannah felt the gloom gather around her heart. Katie had not answered her recent letters, but she would find her. At least she could rely on Katie.

'Is it absolutely necessary? Have you any idea of the cost?'

She would not tell Stephen. They had agreed that he would stay in the priesthood. One ruined life was enough. She would manage.

'Sister Marie Claire, you're not listening.'

'Sorry Mother ... I really do need this course to keep up to date with what's going on ....'

Reverend Mother lowered her head to train her eyes on Hannah's. Hannah felt as if she were drowning in their depths.

'Leave it with me. Let me review the situation and talk to Father Tim. Let us pray together about it, Sister.' Reverend Mother blessed herself. Hannah bowed her head. The room began to spin and she gripped the chair, willing herself not to faint.

She packed a small suitcase and collected her allowance and ticket from Mother Bursar.

'I'll see you soon.' She smiled casually, the lie on her lips almost choking her.

Leaving was easy compared to the realisation that she would never see Reverend Mother or her community again. She took the train to Dublin and the boat to Holyhead. As the train to London raced through the darkness she closed her eyes and tried to sleep. The swaying movement made her feel sick. Finally she slept and awoke to see wide fields darkening under a dull sky. She felt their solitude inside her. Everything seemed to move in slow motion, as if she were a spectator in her own life, with no control over it.

By the time she reached London she was frightened. At Euston station she bought a cup of tea and a sandwich. Sitting quietly in a corner of the station, she watched the milling crowds while she ate. As soon as she finished she had to rush to the toilet to be sick. The wind whipped her face as it blew cold and harsh at the bus terminal. She queued for the city centre bus, huddled into her coat, lonely and anonymous in the semi-darkness. Here she was, homeless, helpless and pregnant. The important aspects of her life came up before her in sharp relief. Her baby brother's death, her mother's grief, the joy of David's birth, her father's departure. Only now did she understand her mother's neurosis throughout it all.

She remembered how her mother wore her sadness like a badge of honour after she recovered from her love affair with John. Or did she recover? Did she endure? Hannah reminded herself that she was no stranger to personal sadness. She would handle this situation too.

The middle-aged woman in the YMCA wore her hair in a bun, which gave her a business-like appearance. She eyed Hannah with the same suspicion she probably accorded every stranger who walked through the swing doors.

'Do you have a room for the night?' Hannah asked.

Without answering, the woman took a bunch of keys down from the hook behind the door and looked around.

'Just for yourself?' Cockney overtones disguised an Irish accent.

'Yes.'

'You'll have to share. We're crammed.'

She led the way through a dingy passageway to an antiquated lift-shaft, which clanged to the third floor. The room she showed Hannah was furnished with two single beds and a wardrobe. Clothes lay scattered on the bed next to the wall.

'Your roommate might be away for a day or two, come to think of it,' she said absentmindedly.

Hannah washed and fell into bed exhausted. Staring at the web of plastercracks on the ceiling, she thought about Stephen. The way his smell lingered after he had left her bed. The comfort it gave her. Loneliness engulfed her and she began to cry to herself. How soon would it be before they began to wonder at the convent why she was not returning?

Thinking of her convent increased her loneliness. Reverend Mother's stern yet understanding face, her sisters who had been her companions for so long. It had been a safe haven. Now she could never return. Who had ever heard of a nun with a baby? Holding her stomach, she cried herself into an exhausted sleep.

Street noises woke her. Children shouting on their way to school, cars screeching in the distance, dogs barking, taxis disgorging passengers to their busy offices. She dragged herself out of bed and washed in the communal bathroom. In the dining-room she was too preoccupied to take much notice of the assortment of guests who came to eat before joining the hubbub that was London, in search of their futures.

Wrapped up warm she went to look for somewhere to live. She took a bus to Cricklewood and walked further past a group of shops. As the shops thinned out she saw the endless rows of georgian houses, all converted into flats. Reading the To Let signs, she picked out one at random. A man who looked like a caretaker answered the door and looked her up and down while she inquired about the room.

'You'd better have a look at it. It mightn't be what you have in mind.'

Several flights up a dingy staircase, past peeling paint and plasterwork, he stopped and opened a door on the landing. Hannah was surprised to find that the room he showed her was large and bright. The early afternoon sun was trickling in, making muted patterns on the worn turkish carpet.

'It's nice,' she said.

'South-facing,' he replied. 'There's a kitchenette here.'

He opened a wardrobe to reveal a sink and tiny cooker. 'Bathroom down the hall.'

'How much?'

'Three hundred a month, payable in advance.' He didn't take any notice of her sharp intake of breath.

'It'll be let before this evening,' he said.

Sensing his disinterest, Hannah handed him the deposit in cash.

'Hope it suits.' He wrote out a receipt and left.

Dust motes danced in the rays of the sun as Hannah opened the window. The fresh cold air invaded the musty room. She lay on the lumpy bed and wrote out a list of requirements. Tea, sugar, bread, butter. In her confusion she had forgotten to bring towels with her. She added them to her grocery list. Tomorrow she would begin job-hunting. Take the first job that came her way. She remembered her mother when she was pregnant, lying in a bedroom not unlike this one, awkward, lonely and sick. Her father's lack of interest in her. What would she say if she saw her here, alone in this room, in the same hopeless situation as any other pregnant Irish girl who sought out London as a refuge or a means to an end?

Eventually she slept and woke up hungry. She walked to the nearest shopping precinct and bought a bag of chips which she ate while she shopped. Tomorrow she would visit Katie.

Katie had changed. Her pretty face had coarsened. Her eyes were hollow, her nose more prominent because of her thinness. Her once glossy hair was straggly and unwashed. There were bruises on her face and arms.

'He beats me up,' she said matter-of-factly, sending shock waves through Hannah.

Hannah hugged her, almost afraid to let her go. 'Why does he beat you?' She held her at arms length to study the purple marks.

'It's not that shocking. You must come across it often enough in your line of work. You should hear the names he calls me. Whore, slut ...' Her voice faltered. 'And when the baby cries there's murder.'

Hannah went to the pram and lifted out the tiny undernourished baby. Its red-rimmed eyes looked ready to burst into tears at the sight of her. 'What's your name, my little darling?' she said softly, holding him close in spite of his wet clothes.

'That's Patrick too. Another Paddy for the building sites,' Katie said bitterly.

A little girl entered the room and stood gazing at Hannah with big, anxious eyes.

'Who are you?' Hannah smiled encouragingly.

A look of concerned effort crossed the small nervous face before she answered almost in a whisper, 'I'm Lucy.'

'What a lovely name.'

'I fought for that one. The fight had left me by the time I had Paddy,' Katie said.

Hannah sat the baby down on her knee and called Lucy to come and sit beside them.

'Why didn't you keep in touch, Katie? I could have helped.'

'How could you? A nun stowed away in a convent. Anyway, I wasn't exactly proud of the way I ended up. Nothing to write home about.'

'But these children are beautiful. Aren't you?' Hannah hugged them close. 'I'm your mammy's best friend,' she explained slowly. 'Do you know what a best friend is?'

Anxiety made Lucy dull and unresponsive. It was as if she knew inherently that to make any kind of scene would anger her mother.

'I was always rebellious. I had nothing but contempt for my mother, and as for my father,' Katie took a deep breath, 'he couldn't care less. As long as he has his booze and a woman occasionally, he'd condone anything. If only to annoy my mother.'

Hannah was remembering the reaction of the local gossips in Kilgarragh when Katie and Patrick left. 'She had it coming to her. Isn't she lucky he stuck by her? He'll have no respect for her.' A shaft of sunlight sought out Katie's face like a spotlight. Hannah's own nightmare was forgotten for a minute as a surge of love, mingled with pity, for her and her helpless children, rose up in her. Their flat, in an old tenement house, had the same feeling of clutter Hannah recalled from childhood. The two rooms were damp and musty, the air rank with the sour smell of cooking. Nappies draped around the fire held back the heat. Hannah recognised the spongy spots on the wall as the same dampness that plagued her childhood home in County Cork.

Katie put the kettle on.

'Where's Patrick?' Hannah asked.

'God knows.' Katie turned bloodshot eyes up to heaven.

Hannah felt a rush of sadness, remembering her own mother in similar circumstances, not knowing where her father was. She had secretly blamed her mother for being cross with her father. Now the weight of her memories hung coldly in the pit of her stomach. It was obvious in retrospect that her mother was desperate like Katie was now. It was also obvious that Katie was frightened of Patrick, her fear of him blowing her helplessly along in a permanent state of shock that estranged her from the raw wounds life inflicted on her daily. She lived in a trance, deprivation and depression her constant companions.

'Have you any neighbours? Friends?' Hannah asked her.

Katie shrugged. 'I don't bother. I don't even care what people think anymore. Guilt is an emotion I can't luxuriate in.'

It was obvious that Patrick had pushed her over the edge of reality. 'You're living in a vacuum, Katie.'

'You don't call this living, do you? Do you remember the frocks we bought for the dances? The way we used to button our cardigans down the back, and comb our hair up into a beehive?' There was genuine mirth in her face as she recalled her brief happiness. 'And you did everything right while I did everything wrong. How we were such good friends I'll never know. Miss goody-two-shoes went off to become a nun, no less, after I stole her boyfriend.'

'I didn't mind you stealing Patrick. I told you that often enough.'

'You had more sense than I had. A perfect daughter, doing everything your mother ever wanted. Even becoming a nun, her ultimate dream. She must be very proud.' Katie began to cry, wiping her eyes with the back of her hand.

'Katie, stop it.'

'Do you remember the first bras we bought in Cullen's? They were pointed and we had to stuff them with cotton wool.'

'I remember the coffee shop. What was it called? Bimbo's after the song 'Bimbo, Bimbo where you going to-goiy-oh?' Hannah sang and they burst out laughing together. 'And the first cup of expresso.'

'We felt so grown-up and rich with a shilling,' Katie laughed.

'And if we could afford a club milk with it, we thought ...'

'We'd died and gone to heaven.' Katie was laughing and crying all at once. 'Bugger it, Hannah. Look at the mess I've made of my life. Now you know why I lost touch. I'm sorry, but I lost heart.'

The baby made sucking noises as he tried to shove his fist into his mouth. Katie heated his bottle and settled him into her lap, while Lucy watched dolefully, never moving from her position beside Hannah.

'I usually take them to the park in the afternoon, if it's fine. They like that. Don't you, Lucy?'

Lucy nodded her head, a flicker of a smile crossing her lips.

'I'll come with you. I wouldn't mind a breath of fresh air.'

'How long are you over for? Where are you staying?

'I'm staying in our hostel. It's only for the duration of the course.' Hannah suddenly realised she was becoming good at telling lies. 'You're in a bad way though, Katie. Something will have to be done.'

Katie lifted her scraggy shoulders and looked hopelessly at Hannah.

'This is his idea of how a wife should be treated. He doesn't know any better. If it wasn't for the elderly couple downstairs I think he'd have murdered me.' A look of desperate sadness swept over her face for a moment, then she busied herself again. 'We'll go to the park now, Lucy. Get your coat. Hannah, give me a hand with the pram. We'll get something nice for tea.'

'Sweeties.' A glimmer of a smile edged the corners of the little girl's mouth, her eyes almost swallowing Hannah up in their intense gaze. 'Daddy'll be home soon,' she said. 'Do you know my Daddy?'

Before Hannah had time to answer she heard the footsteps on the stairs and turned towards the door as it was flung open.

Patrick stood there taking in the scene.

'So we have a visitor, have we?' He crossed the room and confronted Hannah.

'You don't recognise me, Patrick. I'm Hannah.'

'You haven't changed much. How did you find us? No, let me guess. She wrote to you in desperation, complaining about the life of hell I was giving her. Right?'

'Wrong.' Hannah rose from her chair and confronted him.

He had changed. He stood tall and gaunt in blue overalls, streaked with oil. His dark flashing eyes had the same defensive look. His black hair was slicked back with Brylcreem.

'Why didn't you tell me you were expecting visitors, Kate? We could have killed the fatted calf, or the sacred cow, for such an important guest.' The look he threw Katie was aggressive.

'I didn't know.' Katie's hands trembled as she put the baby in the pram. Suddenly the air was tense with her fear. Lucy moved stealthily behind a chair, making herself invisible.

'We'll have to celebrate. I'll get in a few beers. What do you drink, Hannah?'

'I don't drink, thank you, Patrick.' That simple response seemed to propel them all into a menace-filled tension, with Patrick as its central focus.

'I'd better go.' Hannah glanced at Katie.

The room was charged with an almost tangible danger, the slow rhythmic sucking of the baby the only sound. Hannah stood up, every fibre of her being aching to be gone. All her physical effort went to make the appropriate gestures. 'I'll call again, Katie.' She felt foolish and angry at the absurdity of the scene and at her own inability to do anything about it.

Katie nodded as Hannah made for the door. Patrick opened it for her. Hannah could see why

Katie had taken such a complacent attitude. He'd killed her spirit. Why didn't someone do something? Katie had firmly closed herself off, as if she and her children were a social disease that would not go away. To see her reduced to that state of exhausted indifference and blatant defeat horrified Hannah and made her think that her own situation was not so terrible. What a change in Katie! Where was the strong, confident, lovely girl of their childhood? She was now reduced to being a helpless, hopeless woman.

The more she thought about Katie, the more Hannah was reminded of her mother. Now it dawned on her that her mother took refuge in her passivity, because there was no hope of deliverance from her oppressor. Had her father been deliberately cruel like Patrick Byrne? She never saw it like that as a child. He was so gentle with her. So kind and loving when he was there. Why had she not seen her mother's side of it? She would not have judged her so harshly all those years ago when she laid the blame for her father's leaving home squarely on her mother's shoulders.

Next day Katie said, 'Don't look at me like that, Hannah. What choice have I got? I might as well face it. Who wants me and two kids? My mother would die rather than have me back in the town with Patrick Byrne's brats.'

'That's not a good enough reason for staying with him. His behaviour is atrocious.'

'He's getting worse.' Katie lowered her dress to reveal marks on her throat. 'I'm not able to make a move on my own. I'm stuck in this mess. You can see that for yourself. Where would I go? What would we live on? Nobody wants a baby.' Her face had a marble quality as she spoke.

'I'll help you. I'll find a flat for both of us. We'll look after the children between us. I'll get a job.'

Katie looked at her, startled. 'How can you do that? You're not thinking of leaving the convent, are you?'

They were sitting in the park on a day of rare sunshine. Hannah bent over the pram and talked to the baby to distract Katie. The thought of having her own baby suddenly seemed like a wonderful prospect. Someone belonging to Stephen whom she could love unconditionally.

'I'm pregnant.' It was the first time she had said it out loud.

'You're what?' Katie stared at her stupidly, her mouth open.

Suddenly the inertia that made her look dull and heavy left her face and her cold indifference gave way to a roar of laughter. The old resilient Katie was back, broken loose by this piece of amazing news.

Hannah nodded mutely, eyes fixed firmly on Katie's face. The enormity of what she had said struck her with terrifying reality. She saw her new life unfold clearly before her eyes. A baby wailing and needing constant attention, while she struggled with a job to support them both. She looked at Katie.

'How did it happen? I mean, how did it happen to you? I thought you were safely locked away from all vices. Don't tell me you were raped.' She laughed and stopped abruptly when she saw the expression of sadness on Hannah's face. 'I'm sorry Hannah. I'm a thoughtless bitch. What happened?'

'I fell in love. Simple as that.'

'How on earth did you manage that in the convent?'

'He's a priest.'

'Oh, Christ.'

'No. Just an ordinary priest.'

They both laughed uneasily.

'I can't believe it. All the time you were masquerading as a saint, you were ...'

'I never claimed to be anything but human.'

'Oh, come off it, Hannah. You frowned on your mother and father. You never really forgave them for not being happy together. You suffered fools badly ...'

'Alright, so I got pregnant to prove I'm human. If you prick me I bleed. That sort of thing. Don't rub it in, Katie.'

'Sorry. I'm so shocked. Here you are, horrified at my situation, offering help to cover up your own problems. Typical.'

'If we threw in our lot we could bring up the children between us.'

Katie sighed. 'Sounds great in theory. It's not practical. You'd be landed with three children to support, and I'd have all the shit-shovelling. Not a man between us.'

'So what? It was men who got us into this plight in the first place.'

'How would I get rid of Patrick? If I threaten to leave, he threatens to kill me.'

'You could come home to Ireland after I've had the baby.'

'Holy Catholic Ireland. Don't make me laugh.'

'You could live in Dublin. Get a job when the children are in school. It would be easier to bring them up in Ireland.'

'Hannah, you're sweet and thoughtful. But you're in no position to think of anyone but yourself at the moment.'

'You'll have to leave him eventually. He'll kill you if you don't.'

'And he'll kill me if I do.'

'Listen, Katie. Your position is intolerable and the kids are suffering. Can't you see that?'

'I haven't the strength to fight him. I can't cope with even thinking of uprooting myself. If it wasn't for the kids I'd crawl into a corner and die.'

Hannah took her hand and held it in hers. 'Don't say that. I'll help you. We can leave quietly when he's at work. I'll get a good solicitor. I've some money saved.'

'No.' Katie sat bolt upright. 'I'm grateful, Hannah. Very grateful.' She smiled and the lines in her face disappeared. She looked young and vulnerable again. 'I can't leave him. Not now. Things are bad for him in the job. I can't desert him. Besides,' she looked shyly at Hannah, 'I still love him.'

'Oh, my God,' Hannah said.

'Let's talk about your problem. Tell me everything from the beginning.'

The weather broke. Hannah stood looking out of the windows, lashed by the steely rain. The sky was dark, making her bedsitter dull and sombre. The windows rattled. She dreaded going to bed because she found it difficult to sleep. She lay between the threadbare sheets thinking of Stephen. The way he made love to her. The loneliness drove her crazy. She felt her life ebbing slowly from her as the new life in her shaped itself into a tiny bump, a constant reminder of him. Would the convent send on her post, or was there a letter from him waiting for her return? Several times she was tempted to write to him, even going as far as buying notepaper and beginning with her new address at the top of the page. Something always stopped her.

Her qualifications secured her a position as a social worker, doing community work. There was no difficulty in persuading her new employers that she had taken a year's leave of absence from the convent. Her first job was to take care of the children of a rapist while his wife attended the court hearing. They sat calmly eating sandwiches Hannah made for them, in front of a blaring television, unaware that their daddy was about to be locked up in prison for a long time. It was not until their mother returned, eyes moist, face tortured, that they realised that there was something wrong.

'Don't tell them. Not yet. You're too upset.' Hannah sat her down with a cup of tea, and got the children to go out to play.

Later she dragged herself home in the evening, too tired to cook a meal. She was thin, except for the neat bump that protruded through the folds of her skirt.

Tired, feet aching, she walked home late every evening to her desolate room. One evening when she discovered she had no milk she went back out in the dark to get some. She did not see the oncoming car, just heard the screech of brakes, and felt the thud of her own body on the ground.

She cried out. In her drugged stupor she willed her disconnected arms and legs to move, but no matter how she tried she could not move them. She was floating away from herself. Terrified, she opened her mouth to scream. Only dribbled words leaked out. Estranged from everything and everyone around her, she thought she had floated up to heaven. She could smell the night air and in the silence she heard herself breathe, so she knew she was still alive. Everytime she tried to get down from the sky she felt herself being pressed back.

'It's alright. You're fine.' Distant words of reassurance made her lift her heavy eyelids.

Her mouth opened to speak but her tongue got stuck in its roof. She forced herself to open her eyes and look closer at the shadow which hung over her. It was Stephen. She knew he would come. She looked closer and saw the accumulative pain, relief and joy in his eyes. She tried to say his name.

'Don't try to talk.' His voice was strong and she clung on to it.

She did not open her eyes again because it was enough to know that he was there. The sound of rubber squeaking on floors and whispered voices comforted her. Hands gently lifted, arms enfolded her. When she felt safe she fell asleep. She was back in her cell and all the sisters were hovering around her. They were weeping in her dream and she wondered what all the fuss was about. They must have discovered she was pregnant. Ah well, she had postponed the inevitable long enough. She would make her decisions another time when she was fit to talk to them all. They would understand. Pain woke her. A heavy, crushing pain in her stomach that took the very breath out of her. Hands covered her, touched her face. She saw flashing lights and robed figures. How did she get back to the convent? Nowhere else was there that gentle quiet care that she had missed so much.

Suddenly a pain stabbed her. She pushed it out of herself. Pushed and pushed to rid herself of her pain forever. As it slid away she lay still while someone took her pain and gently stroked her forehead. Sharp needles pricked her arm and she fell into a floating sleep. Rest, so badly needed. The doctor had told her that only last week.

Hannah knew she was not alone although she still did not open her eyes. In her mind's eye she saw Stephen. Knew he was there. Watched his eyes shine shyly with wonder when he saw her without her veil. Remembered the devastation in his voice when he told her he was going back to Nigeria. He spoke her name. She opened her eyes slightly and saw his distant face.

'Wake up, Hannah. Wake up. It's me.' He shook her gently and then his arms encircled her and it wasn't Stephen anymore.

It was her father rocking her to and fro. The ghost of her childhood returned and she rose to meet him. 'Daddy, take me to your island to see the dragon spitting fire.'

He laughed and off they went to watch the sparks dance across the sky, lighting up the sea, swirling and rising in the wind under the stars. She tugged her father's hand, broke loose and raced towards the fire. 'Hannah, come back. Don't go there. Hannah, don't enter that convent. Hannah, don't go. I can't let you go. Hannah ...'

'I'm going because you're so cruel to Mammy. You left her. You let her lose her baby and caused her all that pain, without giving her a word of consolation. I'm going because you made her suffer. No man will make me suffer like that. I'm out of reach ... '

'Hannah ... Hannah ... Hannah ...'

Reluctantly she retraced her steps, disenchanted with the island, and lapsed into her own world of quietness. Hands refused to let her rest. They tugged her body, bathed her, lifted her. Still she refused to wake up. Why did they not understand her need for sleep?

'Reverend Mother, don't you know that I don't want to face the depression anymore? You always understood me. Now leave me alone.'

Pain and sounds stirred her back from her dreams. She drifted back and forth between past and present, an insistent voice calling her name. 'Hannah, look what I've brought you.'

It was Stephen's voice again and he held an ice-cream to her burning lips. 'Let's go for a walk along the cliffs.' The sharp tang of the sea assaulted her nostrils, the waves sucked at her feet, drawing her into the tide. He pulled her back, laughing, hugging her, then raced ahead. The sea mist swallowed him up. 'Stephen, Stephen.' Hannah could not find him anywhere. She thrashed around the bed.

'She's coming to. There's movement.'

'Good.' The voice was familiar.

She cut herself free of the tangled sheets and ran after Stephen, but it was the throb of the disco she heard and Sandra weaving her way towards her. Her cloying perfume filled Hannah's nostrils. She heard laughter and music and they all danced together. Girls swirling in wide dresses, Stephen holding her, kissing her, his golden hair carelessly tossed back, his face sheened in perspiration. Close, oh so close, his breath fanned her face. 'Take me back with you. Take me back. I can't live without you.' The music faded and she fell into an exhausted sleep.

'Hannah, Hannah.' She struggled to push the nuns away because she did not want them intruding on her time with Stephen. How had they found out? She fought the tears, the pain, the cramps in her stomach. Hands touched, probed, so that she lost all sense of Stephen again.

'She's coming to.'

A hand held hers and gradually she stopped the fight and let herself open her eyes.

'Daddy.' She felt the weight of her father's body as he held her. Saw the tears on his cheeks.

'You came back to us, my darling.'

'What happened?' she whispered.

'You had an accident. We thought we'd lost you.'

'What about the baby?'

He looked helplessly at her, the expression on his face telling her everything.

'I've made a mess of it all, haven't I? Her hands fluttered like trapped birds.

He caught them in his. 'No, you haven't. As long as you're alive and well. That's all that matters.'

The wind beat the rain against the window pane and silently they listened to it.

'Do you remember, when you were little, you didn't like the sound of the rain?'

'It hurt my head. I was frightened when you were out in it.'

'I told you stories when I came home. Remember you used to fall asleep on my lap.'

'Yes.'

Her father was thoughtful for a minute. 'Snow White was your favourite. You liked the bit where the prince kissed her awake.'

'That's what happened to me. If only I could go back to sleep.'

'Don't, sweetheart. You can't go back to sleep. You're young. You have work to do.'

'What use am I now? Who'll want me?'

'Hannah, stop. You could have been killed. You fractured your skull. The concussion was our greatest worry.'

'And I lost my baby.'

'Yes, my darling, you did. But you're getting better now. I'm taking you home as soon as you're well enough.'

The wind assaulted the windows. They shook and rattled in protest. Hannah howled in her father's arms for her lost baby, her thin body shaking out her misery.

'Do you think you can make it to the bathroom?'

The young Irish nurse gently pulled back the bedclothes and helped Hannah to her feet. 'You're doing fine. You'll be up and about in no time.' Her arms encircled Hannah's waist encouragingly.

'Yes, I think I can manage.' Hannah's voice was weak as she straightened herself up.

'You'll find yourself getting stronger every day. Now take your time.'

Katie sat in the uncomfortable hospital chair beside Hannah's bed. The wind moaned and sighed against the window, shaking the last of the leaves from the trees.

'You won't disturb our cosy routine now, Hannah.' She looked sad. 'Your father is taking you home.'

Hannah stared out of the window. 'It's real autumn weather, isn't it?' She turned to Katie. 'I feel dreadfully guilty about losing the baby.'

'It wasn't your fault.'

'I wasn't looking where I was going. I was miles away.'

'You couldn't carry the burden of it all alone, and I certainly wasn't much help to you.'

'I let myself fall in love with him. Kept it at bay for years, then let it happen. Wanted it to happen. I have no one to blame but myself.'

'He ruined your life.' Katie's voice rose, didactic and ranting.

'How dare you! You're a fine one to talk. I suppose Patrick's brutal beatings were good for you.'

'Patrick had a tough upbringing himself.'

'So that makes it right for him to brutalise you and the children. Men who have been battered by their parents in childhood are exempted. Cruelty breed,cruelty. Ignorance and poverty excuse him. I won't buy that, Katie.'

'Oh, shut your sanctimonious mouth. I'll be in touch.'

Katie flounced out of the room, more energetic than Hannah had seen her since her arrival in London.

She lay watching the traffic lights move slowly across the wall into the night. Thinking of Stephen, she wished she could return to her world of dreams. At the same time she realised that perhaps for the first time in her life, she, Hannah Dempsey, Sister Marie Claire, would have to face the future realistically.

'Probably for the best.' The surgeon's voice was official as he examined her. 'The damage the impact caused to your head was a worry. Apart from the concussion, you sustained fairly minor injuries. Nothing that won't mend.'

'I lost my baby,' Hannah said with passion.

'I know you did. But you're young and healthy. You'll have more children one day. No reason why you shouldn't.'

Chapter 16

The problem was removed. The sense of inevitability over. No waiting for fate to take its course anymore. Hannah found that the balance of her life shifted once again. Being 'in trouble' was equated with being isolated, in a strange country, a wasteland; now she would have only a memory of the hormones in her blood that had driven her to this wilderness. She spoke to her father while still recovering from the accident. They were sitting peacefully together in her bedsitter.

'I want to explain about the baby, Daddy.'

There was silence. He crossed the room to her bed and sat down beside her. 'There's no need, unless it makes you feel better.'

She shook her head. 'It must have been a terrible shock for you to find out the way you did that your daughter, the nun, was having a baby.'

He reached out for her hand. 'Hannah, don't talk about it.'

'I want to explain,' she insisted. 'I owe you that much at least.'

'You owe me nothing.' He lit a cigarette.

'He's a priest.'

Hannah watched the bright glow as he inhaled, then saw his features relax as he blew the smoke through his nostrils. She wanted to explain about Stephen, tell him how much she loved him. That she couldn't help what happened to her. The shame of what it would seem to him, and his obvious embarrassment, prevented her.

'Seeing you so sad upsets me,' was all he said as he tapped his cigarette against the ashtray.

'I was foolish. He was already promised to God. So was I. I'm so sorry, Daddy, to have let you down. I never intended it that way.'

'We all make mistakes. The trouble with you was that you never did anything wrong.' His voice was gentle.

'Of course I did.'

'No. Let me finish. When you were growing up I often warned you not to strive too hard for perfection. You wanted everything to be right. Life isn't like that. You couldn't accept situations that weren't right. Like the difficulties between your mother and me.'

'No,' she whispered.

'When I left home that time you found it hard to forgive me. You didn't say anything, but I knew.'

'It wasn't all your fault.'

He was tense. 'No. I suppose if your mother hadn't fallen for someone else. It meant more to her than she ever let on. If I didn't drink. We could go on all night with the ifs. The thing is, it happened. We were so glad you carried on normally through it all. Your mother made sure you did. She was competent, efficient. You were responsible. She accused me of retreating to the pub, not caring, not helping.'

'You always cared about David and me. We knew that.' Hannah gulped, glad he couldn't see her face in the darkness. 'It was awful after you left. I was afraid I'd never see you again. I missed you.'

He stared ahead. 'I'm sorry. At the time I thought I was doing you both a favour. I felt that if the rows stopped you'd be happier. Our lives together were in such a mess. The only way I could cope was to leave.'

'I understand.' Hannah reached for his hand but he stood up abruptly.

'There's no use going back over it all. What I want you to know is that I understand what happened to you. I could blame your mother. God knows I was bitter. She could blame me. We could blame ourselves forever. We got to grips with our blame long ago. I want you to come to terms with yours.'

'Daddy.' She caught his hand and held it.

'Hannah, get on with your life as best you can. I'm grateful that you're alive.' After a moment he said, 'We all hurt each other, Hannah. We all forgive each other. Life goes on.'

'I know. That's the part I dread. Facing back to it all. Can you imagine what they'll say to me in the convent?'

'They're only aware of the accident. That could happen to anyone. If you don't want to go back you don't have to. You've paid your dues. Do what you want with your life from now on.'

Hannah, thinking of the convent, surprised herself by a sudden feeling of rejection.

'They probably won't want me.'

'Nonsense. They think the world of you. When I explained about the accident they wanted you back immediately, to take care of you. I had to beg for time for you to recover at home with us. What I really wanted was time for you to think. It's more likely that you won't want that life anymore.'

'Don't tell Mammy about the baby. It would kill her.'

He squeezed her hand. 'I had no intention of telling her.'

When they got home her mother reached out for her, her face twisted in anguish. 'I'm so glad to see you. I was driven out of my mind with worry.'

'Don't make me feel worse than I already do.' Hannah hugged and held her.

Much later Mary said to her, 'I'm glad to see that you're wearing your habit. It did cross my mind that you might be thinking of leaving.'

'What ...' Hannah tried to look shocked.

'Nowadays anything can happen. You know yourself. Religious life isn't like it was in the old days. They're dropping out like flies.' Her mother scrutinised her. 'Everything is alright, isn't it, Hannah?'

'Everything is fine,' Hannah reassured her.

She wrote a progress report on her health to Reverend Mother and asked for her post to be sent on. There was no letter from Stephen. She had trouble sleeping. Sometimes whole nights went by without sleep. She'd watch the light seep into the room as the dawn broke. She dreaded the daylight, knowing there was no escaping the day.

She drew a certain comfort from talking to her mother.

'When Daddy left us that first time, were you glad?'

'No, though I pushed him out. You see I knew he wanted to leave. It was his way of dealing with the misery of our lives together at the time. He never forgave me for what happened between me and John.' Her voice went dead. 'When he lost his job, everything that had gone wrong between us reared up again. He couldn't cope. I understood and didn't argue.'

'It must have been very difficult for you.'

'I went hysterical. I cracked up, simple as that. You must remember. You took over, looking at me with those big sad eyes, begging an explanation. I couldn't give you one. Then you seemed to tumble to the solution yourself. I suppose I couldn't stand his toleration of me. He only stayed for you and David. He loved you more than he ever loved me. The rows were terrible. It got to the stage when I didn't care anymore. That was worse.'

'What kept you going?'

'You children, I suppose. My religion.' She gave a bitter laugh. 'Weren't we always taught tolerance? I tolerated everything until one day it dawned on me that I was actually happy with my lot. My tolerance had paid off. I missed your father. Make no mistake about that. I talked to the priest. His advice was wonderful. He said that man's love on earth is pitiful and flawed compared to the love God has for us. I concentrated on God's love and through him came the gift of acceptance. When your father came home I realised it was divine intervention. All the time I had been praying for it.'

'Tell me about your relationship with John.'

Her mother turned around quickly, surprised.

'I'd like to know. I remember John very well.'

Her mother looked confused. 'It wasn't planned. I didn't even know John was home from Australia. We knew each other years earlier, as children.' Her voice sounded childish, almost apologetic. 'It was after the baby's death. My world was falling apart. Your father didn't seem to understand. Wouldn't talk about it. The death of the baby left an emptiness, a void, in my life that I couldn't fill no matter how I tried. Nothing mattered. Your father wanted to forget about it, the way men do. John was so kind, concerned ...' Her voice trailed off.

'Did you fall in love with him?'

'Yes. I couldn't have had a casual fling. I'm not the type. I never intended to fall in love. It just happened.'

'You finished it for my sake?' Her mother saw her pain.

'Yes. I was so lost in my own sorrow that I forgot about your pain. John held me together, made me forget, loved me unconditionally.'

'You should have stayed with him.'

'Your father made sure I didn't. Oh, he didn't want me so much as he wanted you back, and me to take care of you. I know I wasn't a great mother. I shouted at you; sometimes I hit you. But I loved you more than John. That much I proved. I did all I was capable of.'

'Did you love Daddy?'

'It wasn't the same. He used John as a weapon against me. Oh, boy did he use him. I had to tread so carefully, let him do what he liked, drink when he liked, or he made life hell. He was hurt. I couldn't forgive him but I stuck it out, wanting to make the most of it. Saw no alternative. It cost me dearly to let John go.'

'Do you still love him?'

'Yes. Somewhere in the recesses of my mind I love him. I'm grateful to him for making me feel good about myself, at that low ebb in my life.'

'Where is he now?'

Her mother shrugged. 'I don't know. After he went back to Australia he wrote once to my mother's. He was ready for marriage so I suppose he married and settled down. I hope he found happiness.'

'Did you ever regret going back to Daddy?'

'No. How could I? I had you and then after David was born everything was alright for a while. Until he was made redundant.'

Hannah's throat felt dry. The emotion she evoked in her questions and the pain of her mother's responses made her sad.

'I shouldn't have asked such personal questions. I'm sorry.'

Her mother, now slumped in her chair, dismissed her apology. 'It's best to clear the air sometimes. If it makes us feel better.'

'I'm not sure that it does.' Hannah was thinking of Stephen and was tempted to tell her mother everything.

Something stopped her.

Hannah thought of God who at present was inexplicable and detached. So remote that she couldn't even pray. All the memories came together, tumbling through her mind, knocking one another over for attention. The damage she caused to a priest. Pain inflicted on them both. Harm to other people. The convent. Her sisters in Christ that she loved and lived with. She blamed herself, her weakness. Desires of the flesh. Lustful appetites. She couldn't even hold on to her baby. Here was a man who never really belonged to her, not even when they were making love. God was the obstacle between them. She always knew he would come to claim him and wasn't surprised when the time came.

Hannah imagined him, lying in the dark beside her, holding her. She felt the desperation to be with him again. To lie next to him, feel the texture of his skin, smell his smell. What was she doing hanging around her mother, living on the edge of life? A decision would have to be made. She phoned her doctor and made an appointment to see him.

After a thorough examination and many questions about her health he said, 'I think your problem is not a physical one. I suggest you see a psychiatrist.'

At the appointed time she arrived with a slight fear that quickened her pulse beat as she climbed the stairs, and took her place in the waiting-room. Doctor McKenna, beautifully dressed in a pin-striped suit, a red carnation in his buttonhole, gripped her outstretched hand. 'It's good to meet you, Sister,' he said, his eyes deep and smiling. 'Come and sit down.'

Without preamble he said casually, 'Are you home on holidays?' He smiled encouragingly, sat back and waited as if he had all the time in the world.

'Yes. No. I don't know why I'm here,' Hannah began. 'I'm staying with my mother. I needed a break. The work I do is fairly draining. Dealing with...' She was babbling.

He watched her with a patient smile. 'Tell me about yourself.'

She talked about her life in the convent, her career, her hopes and dreams for the people in her care. Her parents. Eventually she said, 'The reason I'm here, doctor, is to find out whether or not I should return to the convent. I thought you might be able to help me.' She looked at him, then shifted her gaze beyond his eyes to the bright sunshine outside.

He waited. There was no point in making any attempt to talk of trivial matters to evade the issue, to distract, like a game invented years ago when she was a child. Somewhere outside there was a thud, a woman's angry voice called out, and then silence again.

He let the silence grow.

Just as Hannah struggled to say something else he said, 'I can't make up your mind for you. I can only help you reach your decision.'

'I had a miscarriage.' She watched his face to see the shock register.

'I'm sorry.'

'Having the baby would have made all the difference.'

'Of course.'

'That baby would have set me free. Something salvaged from the wreckage of my life. Our lives. Something of its father I could keep. Something of my very own.'

'Is that how you see your life? A wreckage?'

Hannah was thoughtful. 'Yes,' she said bluntly. 'For the first time in my life I'm free to make a choice, and I can't even do that. I can solve other people's problems. I can put their lives back on course. Problems and conflict are my job.'

'Other people's,' he said. 'You buried your own feelings and emotions in other people's tempestuous relationships. By doing that you avoided any close relationships of your own. Then when it happened you couldn't handle it.'

'Any kind of intimacy is forbidden in our Rule, doctor.'

'I understand. Tell me about your parents. Your relationship with your mother.'

'I love my mother. My first painful memory associated with her is when she lost a baby. It changed everything in our lives at the time. It changed my mother. She had an affair and I hated her for it. It confused me. My father was furious and I blamed him for being so hard on her. He was always so gentle with me.' Hannah went on offering the details willingly without even an occasional prompt. 'I hated what it did to my father. I didn't understand.'

In the re-telling, the distance Hannah felt from her past fell away. Something unlocked itself and she began to cry.

Doctor McKenna sat watching her.

'I'm sorry ... I ...' she mumbled.

'Don't be. You feel something now that you weren't aware of then. For the first time in your life you're confronting what really happened and how it affected you. Now you can identify with your mother's pain.'

'I was judgmental. I blamed her, I suppose. Now that I've been through it myself I understand it better.'

'And the father of your child? How do you feel about him?'

'I love him.'

'Have you told him about the baby?'

'No.'

'Are you going to?'

'No.'

'Will you see him again?'

'I don't know. He's away. He's busy. I'm not sure if it's possible.'

'If you need to see him I think you could make it possible.'

'I have to sort myself out first.'

'Let's talk about the convent. Do you miss it?'

'Yes. That's the amazing thing. No matter what I'm doing, I miss it.'

'What do you miss most?'
'The constancy, the spirituality, the sisters ...'
'The dependency?'
'Yes.'

Her mother was waiting for her, her woollen cardigan thrown casually over her shoulders. 'I must have fallen asleep... I was worried ... upset ... you must be exhausted. Would you like a cup of tea? She gathered herself together, and straightened her dishevelled hair with her hands.

Hannah suddenly felt a surge of pity for her.

'I'd love one. I'll put the kettle on.' Then after a moment she went on, 'I'm sorry to worry you.' Her face crumpled. 'I must be a great disappointment to you. Not the child you reared at all.'

'Nonsense. You can hardly blame yourself for having an accident. When I think of how hard you were working. How run down you were. Not enough sleep. No regular meals. Then this happened. What did the doctor say?'

'Just to take things easy. Nothing to worry about.'

They sipped their tea silently.

'A wonderful nun doing wonderful work for God,' her mother said, almost to herself.

Hannah sighed. 'It's not like that at all, Mammy. I'm human. I've got faults.' Her own voice sounded childish to herself.

She stood up and crossed the room to the fire.

'There's an empty space in my life, that even my life as a nun hasn't managed to fill.'

'What are you saying, Hannah? That you're unhappy?'

Hannah's mind flashed suddenly through her life. She felt she was measuring everything against what it was like before Stephen, and the vast cavity his departure and the miscarriage left.

'Yes. Believe it or not even that peaceful life you keep talking about, in communion with God, has its difficulties.'

'Are you trying to tell me that you're thinking of leaving the convent, Hannah?' Her mother looked shocked.

'I don't know what I'm trying to say.'

Was she going crazy? Doctor McKenna seemed to draw an imaginary line between the times when her life seemed normal and happy, in school, in the convent, and that other time with Stephen. A wilderness he called it. A time when she actually lived life, using all her senses to the full. He forced her to look at her two lives and compare them.

'Do you think I'm going mad?' she asked him on her next visit.

'No. I don't think you're going mad. I think what you did was a symptom, a kind of craziness, to give vent to a suppressed anger. Anger you weren't aware of, couldn't name, that was growing inside, you while you enacted your role of perfection in your convent. Stephen was the cure to your unhappiness.'

Hannah was brought slowly to the conclusion that her actions were more complicated than she had ever imagined. Her miscarriage, her accident, although physical, were afflictions that forced her to look at the spiritual element of her life, and question it. Doctor McKenna showed her how during her years in the convent she had led her life through others, in an unrealistic way. Prayer and adherence to her vows gave her the strength to continue, even when obstacles seemed insurmountable.

'When a voice, at a deeper level, urged you to look more inside yourself, you ignored it. Your anger was suppressed, but was nevertheless built up, and the more you prayed for guidance, the more you realised that prayer alone was not enough. You needed to admit your problems to yourself, identify them and have courage to find a solution.'

Only she, Hannah, could decide that she wanted to be cured, of what she was not sure. She wanted the gift of acceptance. Acceptance of Stephen's love for her and his subsequent neglect. The gift of endurance so that she could cope with the dawning of her real self. Soon she would close a door on one or other of her lives, one or other of her selves. Which Hannah would emerge she was not sure.

She said to her father when they were alone, 'The only time I really lived was when I was with Stephen.'

Her father looked at her. 'That intensity of living isn't real, Hannah. Even if you had stayed together it wouldn't have lasted. You'd have settled down to a humdrum life eventually. Everyone does.' His voice held a thread of great gentleness and patience.

Alone, all the memories and their attendant pain came rushing back. The long dark hours of night brought out the blame, the self-recrimination. Hannah could see the anguished faces of the sisters as they waited for her decision. Reverend Mother's scolding face hidden in the shadow of her veil, waiting for Hannah's own explanation of the events leading up to her accident. The reason for her prolonged recovery. Her baby's unseen face, tiny unformed eyes looking accusingly at her for letting it die. Billy's sad face for deserting him when she promised she'd be there to help him rehabilitate. Sandra's despair when she came out of hospital.

Reverend Mother phoned her. 'When can we expect you home?' Her voice was soft and motherly.

Hannah's case was at the foot of her bed, half-unpacked.

'I don't know, Mother,' her voice faltered.

'Take all the time you need. There are big changes coming up in our next chapter, Sister.

You'll need all your strength to cope with them. I'm not sure where any of us will be this time next year.' There was anguish in her voice and Hannah knew she was worried about the growing expense of keeping an almost empty convent, the changes brought about by the lack of vocations.

'I'll phone you soon, Mother.' Hannah replaced the receiver without making any commitment.

In her mind's eye she could see Stephen. Handsome, lonely in his mud hut in the middle of Nigeria. She yearned for him. If only he had written as he promised, she might have replied and explained what happened. He might have come to her then. Remembering the expression of pure sorrow on his face as they struggled to come to terms with their lives, their vows, Hannah knew that Stephen could never face the renewed pain of another meeting, perhaps another parting.

When she returned to the convent she did not go immediately to see Reverend Mother. Instead she sought out the stillness of the chapel to pray and think about her life, in the place where she had emotionally developed.

She could see Stephen saying mass in front of the altar, young and graceful. She walked into the sacristy and stood in the vestry, remembering him robing for mass. Remembering the day her hands smoothed the vestments into place on his shoulders. He had caught them and held them for an instant. An innocuous gesture that led to a consuming love that had no place in their lives, that no self-denial, pain, discipline, or vows could quench until it was consummated. They confronted it and they did not change their lives because of it. She accepted his decision without challenge, because she truly loved him. She would always love him, while she too put her love of God before him.

Finally she made her way to Reverend Mother's office, knowing what she must do.

'It's so good to see you, Sister. Why didn't you come to me sooner?' Reverend Mother embraced her.

'I would have helped you, prayed with you.' Her voice was low.

'I had to make some decisions, Mother. I wanted to make them alone, without any outside influence. I had to be certain about what I was doing.'

'God called you, Sister. That much is certain. Whether you wish to remain one of his chosen ones is up to you. That's where the gift of free will comes in.'

'I wish to remain one of his chosen ones,' Hannah said softly. Reverend Mother reached out her gnarled hands and caught Hannah's in a warm grasp. 'You are a good nun. You acquitted yourself well, carrying out your duties and obligations without question or complaint. A nun's life is not an easy one. You don't need me to tell you that. As I said to you on the phone, there are a great many changes occurring in the Catholic Church. Attitudes have changed and we have to move with the times. Here we have to face the fact that the convent eventually may have to be closed down. We need young blood, enthusiastic ideas. We need a youthful Reverend Mother who can adapt the old values to suit the new attitudes. Who can modify the Church's teaching to suit life as it is today.'

'I realise the whole structure is changing, Mother. I see it all around me. I also realise that I'm changing with it. For the better, I hope.'

Hannah walked along the path by the lake, past the rhododendron, azaleas and rose bushes she had planted so long ago. She liked the quietness of the evening best. Nothing to disturb her thoughts, only the gentle lapping of the lake, and birds rustling among the heavy overhead branches.

Mother Francis strolled beside her, silent yet alert to Hannah's mood. This was the time when they discussed convent matters, if Hannah felt so inclined, or anything of an urgent nature.

'It went well,' Hannah finally turned to Mother Francis.

'It was a magnificent day. Went without a hitch. Praise the Lord.'

They were discussing the first professions of the their two novices. For the past two months the whole convent lived in an state of exhausting drama, while every emotion was played out in the rehearsals that led up to the big day. Nervousness, tears, regrets, happiness, desolation. Hannah had seen these emotions etched on the faces of the about-to-be-professed young nuns in varying degrees, and identified with them all. Her job was to encourage and repress where the need arose. To allay the fear among the community that the last-minute preparations might collapse. To build up the confidence of the novices, and not let the weight of their new responsibilities get them down. Hannah carried her responsibility for her nuns with subdued calm. The inner turmoil of seeing each day through, fearing what was to come, manifested itself only in the intensity in her eyes.

Next on her agenda was the sisters' holidays. A pleasant duty to perform, after a tough year. Those who had families would go to them. The old sisters, whose families were scattered, or who didn't want to leave the routine of convent life, would go to the sister house in Co. Clare, beside the sea. Tomorrow she would write up her holiday schedule and then decide what she herself would do with her fortnight.

At the end of the path they silently knelt to pray before the statue of Our lady. Hannah offered her thanks to God and said a prayer for her new sisters in Christ. She stood up then and said to Mother Francis, 'I think I'll walk alone for a while, Mother, if you don't mind.'

Mother Francis appreciated Hannah's well-known preference for solitude at certain times.

'Of course, Mother.'

Hannah walked to the edge of the lake and stood watching the paddle of ducks, remembering her Grannie's farm, and Danny and herself shouting and scattering the inoffensive creatures with their sticks. The murmuring of starlings stirred her memory to the times she lived in Wicklow and swam along the river bank in the holidays.

She took the letter from her pocket and unfolded it, looking at it for a long time. Slowly she slit open the envelope and studied the familiar handwriting.

Dear Hannah,

Thank you for your letter. You have been awarded the highest prize. The authority above them all. Congratulations and well deserved. Well fought for and won. Only I know that you made the ultimate sacrifice ...

The sadness I felt during the weeks leading up to your decision is easing now. I knew that if you decided to accept your promotion you would be lost to me forever ...

I realise we broke our vows, Hannah. It was a sacrilege. We didn't do it lightly. We were thrown together. I was a priest and wanted to remain one.

Yet I prayed for a reunion, and I plucked you out of your community at that time, in my desperation to see you again. I harmed you, there is no denying that. I was so emotionally involved with you for so long that I couldn't judge the situation clearly. What I found with you I never dreamed existed. I never wanted to leave you because I loved being with you, talking to you, sharing with you, making love to you. I miss you and will continue to do so for as long as I live ...

I have never been able to regret what happened between us. How can I regret loving? It was wholesome and perfect in as far as any human act can be ...

I suppose what I am trying to say is that life has never been the same since that precious time. I want to come to you but I know I can't without your permission. Our lives are not in our hands, and we are apart because it is meant to be that way. Please don't condemn me for loving you ...'

She folded the letter, replaced it in the envelope and with head bowed continued her lonely walk. She would pray, ask God to remove the pain in time, the loneliness. She had prayed since her return to the convent for guidance, for wisdom to do what was right. She would need to pray more. Pray for him. She had marshalled all her doubts, regrets, losses, fears and anxieties, and looked at them coldly. If she were to embrace her new position as Reverend Mother with its attendant responsibilities, she would have to turn away from him forever, and willingly face her role, with its ordeals, its dangers, its solitude. If the hierarchy saw fit to place her in such a responsible position then she was compelled to do her best and take pride in her high office. To have got this far in the Order did give her a sense of great pride and self worth. She remembered the struggle she had with herself to stay with the Order after Stephen first went on the missions. Then the struggle to return to it when he left the second time and she suffered the loss of her baby. Facing up to his silence when she needed him most. Her father's unbearable heartbreak when she told him she was returning to the convent. Her mother's delight, in spite of her understanding of Hannah's struggle.

Now she was back in the place where she had been moulded and shaped into what she now was, a Reverend Mother rewarded by her community for her dogged commitment to her chosen life. She could give back to her community the love and devotion that she had experienced from her sisters, along with her own love, her own reassurances, her own brand of living. She would happily return to her responsibilities.

Hannah couldn't see into the future, but she hoped that any ordeal sent to test her could be overcome. She was stronger now after her experiences in the world, and she could use her accomplishments to further God's work. Suddenly, and to her amazement, she realised that she was happy.

This evening she would write to Stephen and console him.

THE END

Glenallen

MARY RYAN

A powerful new novel of friendship, love and family feuds. Set in Ireland in the early 1930s.

Three young women become friends at boarding school and soon their lives become intertwined through their association with **GLENALLEN**, the mysterious and forbidding home of the Fitzallen family. The story moves between Ireland and England, under the shadow of war, tracing the lives of Cissie, Mary and Peg, caught in a web of strong emotions, family hatreds and the intangible presence of an ancient, chilling force.

Mary Ryan's best-selling first novel, *WHISPERS IN THE WIND*, was published by Attic Press in 1990. 'Its characters are real, vibrant people, who involve the reader in their pain, their triumphs, their personal growth. Marvellous.' *RTE Guide*

£4.99

Whispers In The Wind

MARY RYAN

A richly satisfying novel on the grand scale. **Whispers In the Wind** is a magnificent saga of love and intrigue set in Ireland during the turbulent years of the early 1920s.

Unwittingly swept up in the tragic upheaval of Ireland's War of Independence, Kitty Delaney is a woman of strength and passion caught between her loyalty to her husband, Leonard, and her deep love for the enigmatic and disturbing Paul Stratton.

Kitty, a young Dublin woman, marries widower Leonard Delaney and goes to live with him in County Roscommon in the west of Ireland. Kitty is many years younger than her husband and soon discovers that marriage is more a trap of intolerable loneliness than the paradise of love and blissful companionship she had hoped for. When the handsome Paul Stratton, 'squire' of the local great house, returns from London, Kitty falls passionately in love with him with disturbing consequences.

£4.99

Daisy Chain War

Joan O'Neill

Set in Dublin during the late thirties and forties, **Daisy Chain War** is an enchanting story about cousins, Irish Lizzie and English Vicky, growing up during the difficult years of 'The Emergency'. All the hopes and fears, the yearnings and achievements of teenage life are perfectly captured in this heartwarming novel of everyday life in wartime Ireland

£4.99

For a full list of Attic books
please write to us at:

4 Upr Mount Street
Dublin 2

Tel: (01) 616 128
Fax: (01 616 176